Praise for
TESSA BAILEY

"Tessa disarms you with a laugh, heats things up past boiling, and then puts a squeeze inside your heart. The tenderness, vulnerability, and heat I am always guaranteed with a Tessa Bailey book are the reasons she is one of my all-time favorite authors."

—Sally Thorne, bestselling author of
The Hating Game

"Her voice feels as fresh and contemporary as a Netflix rom-com...Bailey writes banter and rom-com scenarios with aplomb, but for those who like their romance on the spicier side, she's also the Michelangelo of dirty talk."

—*Entertainment Weekly*

"Bailey crafts an entertainingly spicy tale, with humor and palpable sexual tension." —*Publishers Weekly*

"Tessa Bailey writes pure magic!"

—Alexis Daria, bestselling author of
You Had Me at Hola

"When you read a book by Bailey, there are two things you can always count on: sexy, rapid-fire dialogue, and scorching love scenes..." —*BookPage*

"[A] singular talent for writing romantic chemistry that is both sparkling sweet and explosively sexy...one of the genre's very best."

—Kate Clayborn, author of *Love at First*

TOO WILD TO TAME

TESSA BAILEY

FOREVER

NEW·YORK BOSTON

Copyright © 2016 by Tessa Bailey
Excerpt from *Too Hard to Forget* copyright © 2016 by Tessa Bailey
Cover art and design by Caitlin Sacks. Cover copyright © 2022 by Hachette Book Group, Inc.

Forever
Hachette Book Group
1290 Avenue of the Americas
New York, NY 10104
read-forever.com
twitter.com/readforeverpub

Originally published by Forever in January 2017
First trade paperback edition: October 2022

Forever is an imprint of Grand Central Publishing.
The Forever name and logo are trademarks of Hachette Book Group, Inc.

The publisher is not responsible for websites (or their content) that are not owned by the publisher.

The Hachette Speakers Bureau provides a wide range of authors for speaking events. To find out more, go to hachettespeakersbureau.com or email HachetteSpeakers@hbgusa.com.

ISBNs: 978-1-4555-9414-6 (ebook), 978-1-4555-9415-3 (mass market),
        978-1-5387-4183-2 (trade paperback)

Printed in the United States of America

LSC-C

Printing 2, 2023

To Mackenzie
Love all, trust a few,
do wrong to none.

ACKNOWLEDGMENTS

I would like to thank the following people, because they were my lifelines while writing this book—and in some cases, every book. Authors very rarely accomplish anything alone and I'm definitely no exception. This is a team effort between me, my loved ones, my editors, coffee, the universe, luck, sleep deprivation, and Spotify. But mostly, these folks...

My husband, Patrick, and daughter, Mackenzie. I love you both with all my heart.

My editor, Madeleine Colavita, for pushing me just a little harder each time and encouraging me to write the best books possible.

My parents, Michael and Susan, for being a supportive, loving part of my life. You wouldn't let me watch MTV or *Friends*, so I read explicit romance books in my room instead. I win!

My friends Shannon, Jillian, Siri, Caroline, Nelle, Ashley, and Bernice, your encouragement and support mean everything to me. I'm sorry for being shit at returning e-mails/text messages.

My brother, Michael, who I recently found out has a romantic soul of his own and uses it to write beautiful music. I can't wait to hear what comes next!

My beta reader and pal, Eagle, who always manages to hint at things I missed without actually telling me outright and splitting me in half. That's an admirable trait and your thoughts are beautiful and invaluable.

My Facebook reader's group, Bailey's Babes, for keeping me positive, motivated, and inundated with pictures of JJ Watt, David Gandy, and #PMBs.

THANK YOU!

TOO WILD TO TAME

Miriam Clarkson, January 9

Alrighty. I suppose I've talked enough about Rita. When you bump hips with someone in a kitchen often enough, you learn their habits. The little things they say beneath their breath when they think no one is listening. The way they handle victories, or more importantly, defeats. So my daughter slash apprentice was the nut I decided to crack first, here within the blank whiteness of my Rite-Aid-purchased notebook. Oh, and just in case anyone skipped the first twenty pages, let me catch you up to speed. My name is Miriam Clarkson, and I'm probably dead.

Now that we're basting in the same sauce, I'd like to talk more about my children, also known as the four complicated mazes some lucky significant others will have the pleasure of winding through someday. It's not their fault they can't adequately express themselves. After all, look at their mother, hiding in a dark kitchen, finally putting her soul on paper like some ass-backward Martha Washington. But let me see what I can throw together.

In every recipe, there is an ingredient that brings the entire meal into focus. I call it the ringleader. Added via spoon or measuring cup, it filters through the scattered components, urging them to join the taste good club. It wants—it needs—those erstwhile ingredients to be successful. To be happy. And because I apply cooking logic to everything until it makes sense to me, I see my children as four groupings of haphazard ingredients. All their parts are vital and beautiful, but they each need someone or something to yank them into cohesion.

I might be older now. My boobs might be sagging beneath my apron. But I remember my ringleader. He was there once—he helped me pull my shit together—and then he was gone. I don't blame him for anything, mind you. I celebrate him. The words, actions, and shared experiences that became my fork in the road were necessary to change me from a girl pointing in seven directions, to a woman with one goal. To cook. To have a family.

Cooking came before family too often, but someday they'll find this notebook and understand, as adults, that all their parts are perfect. They just need to take their lids off and allow in a ringleader.

CHAPTER ONE

Welcome to hell," Aaron muttered, maneuvering the Suburban to avoid a patch of ice on the narrow road. In the passenger seat, Old Man lifted his white, furry head—and if dogs could grimace, Aaron's new, unexpected pet was nailing it. Their eyes met across the console, one fuzzy eyebrow twitching as if to say, *This is where you bring me, human?*

Aaron sighed and went back to scanning the street for the campsite. The term *man's best friend* was apparently up for interpretation. He'd hardly achieved grudging respect from Old Man between New Mexico and Iowa. Still, the bare minimum of mutual appreciation was more than he could garner from the other occupants of the Suburban, wasn't it? When it came to his siblings, he took what he could get. Although now that only three Clarksons remained, as opposed to the four they'd started the journey with, there was even *less* for Aaron to take.

A cross-country journey with no discernible purpose.

Unless you counted fulfilling your mother's dying wish as a purpose. In Aaron's opinion, they were simply indulging a whim that might have been entirely different if Miriam had eaten something else for breakfast or gotten distracted by a new cassoulet recipe.

Rita, his oldest sister, had shaken them in New Mexico, making for greener pastures...or rumpled bed sheets, depending on if you were a realist or a romantic. Aaron still considered himself the former, even if he'd definitely felt a minor blip of something gooey over the whole inconvenient business. With Rita shacked up in the desert with her boyfriend, only Aaron, Belmont, and Peggy Clarkson remained. Sage, too, although the wedding planner wasn't related by blood. *Some people are just naturally lucky.*

Aaron caught sight of the campsite turnoff up ahead and gave a loud cough to wake up the other travelers, before easing the rust bucket that passed for transportation to a stop outside a small redwood building marked Tall Timbers Rental Office.

Okay, it wasn't the Ritz-Carlton, but with a series of preelection events set to begin the following morning, every fleabag motel from there to Des Moines had been booked out. Fortunately, they were only a short drive from some of the event sites, where his fellow politicians would begin holding rallies for the hometown hero and rising star senator, starting bright and early tomorrow morning.

Or they *had* been his fellow politicians at one time—his equals—before he'd gone and fucked his rapidly growing career to hell. Now he'd come to Iowa to fight his way back in, by fair means or foul. Yes, for the first time in his life, Aaron was desperate. Desperate enough to share a cabin with his brother in the back woods of Iowa in a place with a half-lit *Vacancy* sign.

Jesus Christ, don't let this vacation in purgatory last forever.

"Are we there yet?" Peggy asked on a yawn, her stretching arms visible in the rearview mirror. "I'm starving. Is there a bathroom?"

"Yes. What's new? And probably," Aaron answered, pushing open the driver's side door to climb out of the Suburban, followed closely by Old Man, who trotted off, presumably to take a leak, maybe chase a squirrel or two. This was how their arrangement worked. Aaron chauffeured the dog around, fed him, and didn't meddle in his business. Old Man would show back up when he was good and ready.

Aaron stopped short when he saw that Belmont had somehow already beaten him out of the vehicle, all without making a sound. His brother stood still as a monument, hands tucked into his jean pockets, running cool eyes over the wooded campsite.

"Good enough for you?" Aaron asked, moving past his brother at a crisp pace, eager to drop off his luggage and hit the bricks. If he wanted to find a way into the first function tomorrow morning, his work began now. *Would* have started last week if Rita's boyfriend hadn't sabotaged their only ride out of New Mexico.

As expected, Belmont didn't answer him, but Aaron hardened himself against giving a shit. Ever since Belmont had knocked his tooth out and cost him four hours of dental surgery, their relationship had gone from dwindling to nonexistent. In a barely conscious gesture, Aaron prodded the sore tooth with his tongue, watching as Belmont turned and helped Sage from the Suburban, in the same fashion a reality television baker might transport a wedding cake. Even Aaron found it impossible not to watch his brother and Sage orbit each other, like two slow-moving planets. They were simultaneously a frustration and a fascination. Frustrating because they refused to just admit the attraction and bang—at least that Aaron knew about—and fascinating because Sage seemed to be the only person capable of getting reactions out of Belmont. Hell, Aaron had busted his brother's nose and barely gotten a middle finger for his trouble.

Moving on.

"Right." Aaron tugged at the starched collar of his shirt. "These cabins are shit cheap, but after the extra nights in the motel back in Hurley, not to mention the car part, I think we should limit it to two rentals. Sage and Peggy in one. Me and Bel in the other." He traded an uneasy look with his brother. "I don't plan to be here much, so you can brood in the dark and write sonnets—or whatever it is you do—until the cows come home. Just don't use my good aftershave."

Being the plan man felt good. This was his role in the Clarkson tribe. The asshole with the directions. The one whose lack of a functioning heart gave him the ability to make hard decisions on everyone's behalf. Aaron was more than fine with that job description. History didn't remember the nice guys; it remembered the sons of bitches who got things done.

"Do you need help?" Peggy asked, a little breathlessly, setting down her oversized suitcase. "You can bring me along to charm people. I'm *very* charming."

Beside Peggy, Sage nodded. "She can't help it."

Aaron wondered if Sage realized she was stunner herself—albeit on a far less flashy scale—but mentioning it would result in getting another tooth knocked out, courtesy of Belmont. And he didn't have time for another sojourn in the dentist chair while being subjected to smooth jazz. "I'll let you know if I need help," Aaron said, knowing he would always fly solo if given the choice. "Let's stick to the plan. Once I've secured a position with the senator, you three can keep driving to New York. I'll meet you there for New Year's." He picked up his leather duffel. "For now, let's go rent some cabins and hope they're livable. As if the last time we camped together in California wasn't traumatic enough."

As he'd known she would, Peggy laughed, following his wake toward the office. His younger sister was desperate to bond them all on this trip, and while it would never happen, sometimes Aaron had a hard time turning off his greatest talent. Telling people what they wanted to hear.

"Aaron sprained his ankle in a gopher hole, carrying me back to camp after I was stung by a jellyfish," Peggy explained to Sage. "Mom was too busy perfecting her s'mores technique to keep track of us. Rita staged a protest of the outdoors and wouldn't come out of the tent. Belmont, where were you?"

Refusing to look curious, Aaron nonetheless paused with his hand on the wooden handle of the office's front entrance. Belmont might have no qualms with ignoring everything out of Aaron's mouth, but when it came to their sensitive baby sister, feigning deafness wasn't an option. "I fell asleep on the beach." His voice sounded like a creaking boat hull, lifting on the water. "When I woke up, you'd all gone to the hospital."

Silence passed. "I don't remember that," Peggy said, a wrinkle appearing between her eyebrows. "How did you get hom—"

Belmont moved past them, pushing open the office door and ducking inside. Aaron stared after his brother a moment, weighing the impulse to tackle his hulking ass from behind and maybe divesting *him* of a tooth this time around, but managed to hold back. Instead, he nudged Peggy with his elbow. "It's your fault for surpassing your one question per day maximum."

This time, his sister's laughter was forced. "Silly me," she breathed, moving past him to join Belmont inside.

Aaron turned his head to find Sage looking like a deer caught in a pair of high beams. "What about you, *Ms.* Alexander. Are you the outdoorsy type?"

"I've planned some outdoor weddings," she answered softly, still not giving Aaron her full attention. Pretty unusual, considering she was a woman with a pulse, but he'd had eighteen hundred miles to stop taking it personally. Aaron started to ask if she was planning on standing there motionless all day, but she hit him with a look. "He doesn't mean it."

Aaron braced a hand on the doorjamb. "Who doesn't mean what?" he asked, even though he already knew the answer.

"Belmont. He doesn't mean to cause everyone frustration. This trip…being away from his boat…he's trying. Really, he is." From the way her breath caught, Aaron knew she'd locked eyes with the man in question, over Aaron's shoulder and through the glass windowpane. But Aaron zeroed in on the curious hint of the South in Sage's accent instead, which he's never caught before. Even after all this time in the same vehicle, the wedding planner remained a mystery to him. Maybe to all of them, even Peggy and Belmont. "While we're alone, I just wanted to say, thank you." She spoke in a rush now, which probably had something to do with the footsteps that grew louder, pounding toward the exit. "For complimenting my dress yesterday. It was really nice. But if you do it again—or flirt with me to make Belmont angry anymore—I'll break your nose."

Sage delivered the final word of her promise just as the door swung open, Belmont's shadow appearing on the staircase where Aaron stood with Sage, with what felt like a bemused expression on his face. *It's always the quiet ones.*

"Come inside," Belmont rumbled. "Please."

With a final nod in Aaron's direction, Sage pushed a handful of light brown hair over her shoulder and sailed past, somehow managing to keep a thin sliver of daylight between herself and Belmont as she moved through the doorway, joining him and Peggy inside the rental office.

Aaron dropped his head back, imploring the bright blue Iowa sky for patience, consoling himself with the fact that as soon as he got away from his complex family, there would be peace. Order. *Serenity now.* He would be back in a situation he could decipher and handle, rather than navigating the rocky terrain of Emotion Mountain, also known as the Clarkson clan.

A prickle at the back of his neck had Aaron pausing once again, one foot inside the door as he looked toward the woods, but he shrugged it off and continued into the office, holding up his credit card in a signal for his party to make way.

All hail the plan man.

* * *

What brought Aaron to the edge of the forest in the middle of the night? Not a damn clue. His excuse for pulling on rumpled dress pants—not his usual look—and crunching through the woods was to look for Old Man, but when the dog had found him first, their pity party, table of two, had kept on going. Now the mutt walked alongside him, throwing him an occasional *what the fuck* glance.

"You're free to go back, you know. I don't remember issuing an invitation."

Sniff. Sniff sniff.

"What is that? Morse code?"

Okay, Aaron had *some* idea what had sent him on Nature Quest. He just had zero notion of what he hoped to achieve by walking to the site of tomorrow morning's "Breakfast and Politics," a nationally televised, invite-only event to which he was most definitely *not* on the guest list. Oh no, he was only on *one* list, and the word NAUGHTY was in permanent ink at the top. Presidential hopeful and Iowa Senator Glen Pendleton however, would be in attendance, and Aaron needed to get the man's ear.

Before Aaron had flushed his career down the toilet back in California with one bad decision, his boss had confided that Aaron was in the narrowed-down running for an adviser position with Pendleton himself. A big-ass deal when the man already had one foot in the White House. What he'd needed was the youth vote—and that's where Aaron would have come in, if he hadn't neatly erased his chances, simply by behaving true to character. So little consequence went into being immoral in his world, he'd never stopped to consider he was doing something wrong. Or irredeemable. And that had been the final confirmation of something he and others had always suspected.

Aaron didn't have an ounce of good inside him.

Regardless of that nifty facet of his personality, he needed face time with Pendleton tomorrow. The question was *how*.

As Aaron and Old Man reached the perimeter of the forest, a series of connected buildings came into view. The local high school, which would serve as the site of Breakfast and Politics come morning, packing the big cafeteria in the center with egos instead of students. Already, news vans were parked outside. Police vehicles. What the hell was his goal here? To get arrested for trespassing? Hey, at the very least it would save him from the awkward morning tango around the coffeepot with Belmont.

Old Man seemed to be asking the same question with a silent look, so Aaron moved in the opposite direction of the congregated vans and prepared to head back toward the cabin and get some much-needed sleep. The kind that would allow him to bring his A-game in the morning. As if he ever brought anything else.

Just as he turned, Old Man stopped, ears pricked, nose twitching. A noise behind them. Aaron heard it, too. The long creak of a window sliding open. Better than the sound of a gun being cocked, but definitely not what he expected to hear in the pitch-black woods at midnight. Aaron stepped back behind a tree, giving himself a good view of the school's closest building. He watched as a leg dropped over the southernmost windowsill, dangling a moment, before a head ducked under the frame. The figure jumped to the leaf-padded ground without a single crunch, arms stretching out at the sides for balance.

Girl. There was no question. In the dappled moonlight, he could make out curves beneath fitted clothing. Slight ones, but...*nice* ones. And even if his attention hadn't been magnetized by the tight jut of her ass—*fuck*, he'd been a while without having a woman's cheeks in his hands—the hair would have tipped him off. It was *everywhere.* Even the muted darkness couldn't hide the wild, colorful nature of it. The mass of it fell to mid-back, interrupted every inch or so with a corkscrew curl or a braid or a ribbon. Her hair was schizophrenic. Looked like it hadn't been brushed in a while, but maybe the lack of diligence had been on purpose.

Old Man chose that moment to make a *sloff* sound, which jolted the girl, sending her careening back against the building. She slid to the ground into the shadows before Aaron could get a good look at her face, and for some reason the delay made him anxious. What kind of a face went with hair like that?

"Hello?" she called, just above a whisper. "Please don't be a bear. Again."

Again? Aaron didn't grab Old Man's collar in time, the furry bastard slinking toward the girl, evading Aaron like some kind of stealthy ninja canine. He lay down a few feet from the shadows where the girl was hiding, laying his face on two paws. *Showing her he isn't a threat?*

Just when you think you know a dog.

The girl entered the moonlight again, this time on her knees, hands reaching out—palms up—to Old Man. And so the first time Aaron saw her face, it was washed over with pleasure. "Hi," she breathed. "Hi, pretty...boy? Boy, I think. Thank you for not being a bear. Again."

Aaron felt a twinge in his fingers and realized he'd been gripping the bark of the tree too hard. That *voice*. He immediately wanted to hear it up against his ear. But no. Because then, he wouldn't be able to see her face. Even in the lack of light, he knew that would be an inexcusable shame. Her expression never stopped shifting. Surprise, happiness, curiosity. Hiding nothing. Unlike him, who had nothing on the inside *to* hide. *This is why I came into the woods. She's why.*

"That's ridiculous," he muttered, raking the sore hand down the side of his trousers. He was prowling around in the middle of the night on some misguided mission to get the lay of the land for tomorrow. Not to accidentally run into a girl with freak show hair and an unrealistic fear of Smokey.

"Are you alone?" she asked Old Man under her breath.

Aaron made a sound of disgust as the pooch turned his head, tongue lolling to the side like a drooling fool. He had no choice but to step out from behind the tree, but felt the need to put his hands up. So she would know he wasn't a bear, for the love of God. "It's just a human. You're safe."

The girl shot to her feet, her back coming up hard against the stucco building again. Her eyes were as turbulent as her braided mane of hair, but they seemed to calm when he halted his progress. Nothing inside him was calm whatsoever, though. Some whisper in the back of his mind tempted him to go forward, settle her down by coasting palms down her thighs, across her belly. *What is wrong with me?* "Humans are most dangerous of all," she finally said. "Why aren't you wearing a jacket?"

O-kay. He had to be back in his cabin dreaming, right? "Excuse me?"

"It's freezing and you're wearing a T-shirt."

Aaron looked down, as if he wasn't fully aware of his attire. Come to think of it, he *was* pretty goddamn cold, but he'd been too distracted to notice. "I'm from California. We have T-shirts and ski jackets. Nothing in between."

She nodded gravely. "Are there bears in California?"

"We have a brown one on our state flag." He chanced a couple steps closer, but Old Man actually growled at him, cutting off his progress. *"Really?"*

"Your dog doesn't seem to like you very much," the girl remarked.

"His name is Old Man. And yeah, thanks for noticing. The feeling is mutual." Aaron tilted his head, irrationally vexed that her face was half shaded by shadows again. "Hey, do you mind coming out here into the light?"

A beat passed. "Yes, I think I mind."

Not what he'd been expecting, at all. Had he completely lost his touch with women? "Are you just trying to be mysterious or is there another reason?"

"You saw me climbing out of the window." He could hear her swallow across the distance separating them. "I didn't do anything *wrong*—not really—but if someone were to disagree and claim I *did* do something wrong, you could identify me."

Aaron snorted. "I could pick your hair out of a thousand-person lineup."

"Thank you," she murmured, her hand reaching out of the darkness to scratch behind Old Man's ears. "Yours is nice, too."

"Are you talking to me or the dog?"

She laughed and the sound twisted in the wind, as if she were one with nature. Something sprung up from the earth. His desperation to catalog her features shot into the stratosphere. They would provide some type of answer to the riddle of a carefree cat burglar...and honestly, why was he even confused? Even his confusion was confusing.

"What were you doing inside the school?" The question came out harsher than intended, and he watched as her hand stilled on Old Man's head. A movement that increased his suspicion, even though he kind of wanted to go on ignoring the elephant in the forest.

"What do you *think* I was doing?"

Her throaty answer caught him below the belt, thickening the flesh inside his briefs. Ten seconds earlier, they were just two people crossing paths in the woods, but with the issuance of those two questions, they were challengers. It didn't help that the girl was still on her knees, while Aaron stood at full height. The symbolic positions caused even more awareness to infiltrate. "You're not a student inside that school, are you?" he asked, because it seemed relevant now that his cock had exhibited a hearty appreciation for her voice, her...presence. "You're not a high school student."

"No, I went to private school." A pause. "And I graduated."

Aaron cleared the relief from his throat. "In my experience, students sneak into their own high school at night to vandalize it, set up a senior prank, or make out." *She better not have been making out.* The thought sped past out of nowhere. "So if you're not a student, we can rule those out." He waited for her slow nod and another punch of relief to pass. Then he held up his fingers and begun ticking them off. "Are you a journalist? Maybe setting up a hidden camera to catch politicians in some secret ritual where they drink the blood of middle-class Americans?"

"Yes. That's what I was doing."

"Ah," Aaron said, shaking his head. "See, your agreement was too quick."

A long sigh came from the shadows. "Are you a lawyer?"

Aaron reached for the knot of his tie to adjust it, before remembering he only wore a T-shirt. "I went to law school—"

"Politician?"

"Of a sort," Aaron hedged. "But you're changing the subject."

"If you're a politician, you must know all about that."

Old Man growled at Aaron again, but the girl reached over and placed a hand on the dog's head, quieting him. Aaron curled his lip at his pet, wondering when the hell his famous loyalty was supposed to kick in. "Listen, I really don't want to report you."

"But you will?"

Would he? The high school cafeteria would be filled with politicians, voters, and media tomorrow. Despite his gut feeling to the contrary, she could very well have an agenda that included locking everyone inside, setting the place on fire, and dancing among the ashes. Stranger things had happened than someone using a political event to make a statement for their cause. Still, he couldn't connect that particular psychopathic dot to *this* girl. Even without having gotten a decent look at her face. "I don't know."

She was silent for long moments. "Really?" Her tone was laced with surprise. "When was the last time you said those words?"

"I don't know?" He searched his brain. "I don't know."

Her laughter almost pulled him headfirst into the darkness. No reservations, just pure joy. Where had she been existing until now? Not the same world as him, that much was for certain. "I can..." Now she sounded almost shy. How often were they going to switch gears here? "I can owe you a favor. If you just pretend we didn't meet."

Fuck that. The words very nearly left his mouth on a shout. He couldn't make sense of the silent denial, but he really didn't feel like pretending this encounter hadn't happened. It was the epitome of *happening*. Another hour or so in the forest and he would have the frostbite to prove it. Maybe he'd already succumbed to the initial stages of delirium because he was placing way too much importance on this interaction.

If he were a different man, he might have enjoyed this loss of equilibrium. At a young age, however, he'd learned to shut off pain to combat losing his brother's friendship. Hell, losing him altogether and being found unworthy, it seemed. Unfortunately, other vital parts of his humanity had bailed, too, along with pain. Compassion, happiness. Almost like he'd made a deal with the devil to prevent feeling hurt, and the fucker had taken the full deck. His father, different from Belmont's, had been proud of Aaron's ability to steel himself against the melancholy typical of youth. Encouraged the cynical nature that had grown in the place of his sadness. The nature that visibly made his mother, his siblings, nervous. *What does someone like you need feelings for? You've got the three B's. Brains, balls, and blinders.*

Someone like you.

He needed to get out of there and gear up for tomorrow. Tomorrow was what mattered. "Look, forget it." He signaled to Old Man, as if that was going to work. "There's nothing you can offer that would help me. Just..." Discomfort invaded his throat. "This never happened."

Walking away felt distinctly shitty, but what else could he do? Stand in the freezing cold woods in a T-shirt with a spiteful dog and a probable anarchist for another hour?

"Wait."

Aaron turned at the sound of footsteps jogging up behind him. And then he just stared. Her face fully exposed now in the moonlight, the girl blinked up at him with vivid green eyes, that wild hair blowing around her shoulders. A mouth that couldn't be re-created by the world's most talented artist. His stomach dipped like a ladle into a pot of boiling soup and hung there, the forest feeling stiller than death around him. Anything would feel still so close to so much...life. So much *purity.* And goddammit, the corrupt piece of shit inside him wanted to drag a finger right through that goodness, because he didn't understand it. Resented being left out in the cold when it came to something...someone...so warm and inviting and the opposite of him in every way.

He wanted to climb on top of this girl and absorb the light seeping from her. *Go back to the cabin. Or wake up from this bizarre dream. Just do something before you go completely insane.* "What am I waiting for?"

"Me," she whispered, before squeezing her eyes shut

and shaking her head. "I mean, I asked you to wait. I can help you."

"How do you know I need help?" The question was reminiscent of teeth rattling.

She looked almost perplexed. "We all need help."

Why couldn't he get his stomach to stop twisting and diving? "Not me."

"No?" She broke his stare to gaze out at their surroundings. "You were out here for a reason, too. What was it?"

"I don't know anymore," he murmured, ready to give in and try to kiss her. Just melt forward and take everything this beautiful product of the earth had to offer. But what did he have to offer back? An empty vessel. *Someone like you.*

"That's the fourth time you've said *I don't know* now." Her smile revealed her teeth, two overlapping ones up top. "Isn't it wonderful?"

Jesus, he almost said *I don't know* a fifth time. Maybe she was a witch. "I need to get into that breakfast event tomorrow morning. I doubt you can help me with that, so—"

"I *can*, actually," she said, arching a cocky eyebrow.

"Really." He doused the flicker of hope, but it was mostly at the prospect of seeing her again. "Through a window, I assume?"

When she shook her head, braids and curls and ribbons rioted everywhere. "I'll walk you right past security through the back door."

"Not the front one?"

Another flash of those imperfect teeth. "Beggars can't be choosers."

That husky tone of voice was back and it flexed his

abdomen muscles, compelling him forward a step so he could peer down into her uniquely pretty face, blown away by the soft look of her mouth, the dark fan of her eyelashes. "My name is Aaron." *Take the warning. Please take it.* "And I never beg."

"My name is Grace." A deep breath, a step back. Away from him. "And I know better than to say never."

Aaron stood at the edge of the woods, watching as Grace slipped around the building outcropping and into the darkness, still convinced he was dreaming. But dream or not, his calf muscles burned in their desire to sprint after her, make her repeat seventy-seven times they would see each other tomorrow.

The temptation was momentarily culled when he felt a warm, liquid sensation on his right foot, and found Old Man pissing on his favorite pair of loafers.

"Really?" With one more pitiful glance the way she'd gone, Aaron removed his foot from the line of fire and shook it. "We're literally surrounded by trees, mongrel."

Finally, with a concentrated effort, Aaron convinced himself that darkness and a lack of sleep had caused his senses to play tricks on him. Tomorrow, he would see her again and experience the same detached attraction he usually got for women. Easy to ignore or pursue if he chose, but never...consuming. Or spellbinding. Never that.

Although as he walked back to the cabin, some premonition warned him that tomorrow wouldn't be any less confusing than tonight.

Chapter Two

With a piece of licorice dangling from her mouth, Grace Pendleton watched from a copse of trees as Aaron paced back and forth a few times, then came to a stop at the center of their meeting spot from the night before. She couldn't leave him standing there for long, considering— unlike last night—the school was crawling with security, bomb-sniffing dogs, and journalists. They would wonder why someone *not* on the security list was cooling their heels in a secure area, so she would have to collect him soon. But she needed one more minute.

Maybe two.

Whether Aaron wore a T-shirt or a tailored suit, he didn't belong in the scenic nature landscape spread out between them. Much as she wanted to, though, she couldn't really place him rubbing elbows with a room full of state officials, either. His eyes weren't... flat. He'd looked right at her last night. Looked and looked like he'd wanted to *see*. Instead of already having the notion that she was troubled or damaged. For the first time in a long time, she'd met someone and handed them a fresh slate.

She'd been a little disappointed when he hadn't appeared to write anything on that invisible chalkboard. Or hadn't *wanted* to do so, more like. Blocked himself off from it. But for the first time, she'd gotten the impression that another person had the ability to listen to her. To make out more than just the surface of her words. Just maybe.

Sighing, Grace fed the length of licorice into her mouth, chewing the candy with great relish. After gulping down the final bite, she stowed the blue and white striped box beneath a pile of pine needles, where she could come back and find it later tonight. Then she stood, brushed the dirt off her pants, and moved slowly in Aaron's direction. The way a hunter might stalk a deer. Only in reverse.

When she stepped on a patch of leaves, Aaron's head whipped around, his eyes locking in—and she froze. Not because she was scared. Oh no. She knew very well when a situation called for fear. No, Grace halted in her tracks because her instincts called for her to walk over and study him. Touch him. Check for shaving accidents on his jaw, find out the exact color of his eyes, since it had been too dark the night before. Trace the lump of his Adam's apple with her pinky finger. Even the idea of touching him above the neck caused a disturbance in Grace far lower. A slow, wicked twist. Especially when she considered what his reaction would be. What if...what if this incredible, physically faultless man closed his eyes and moaned?

She fanned herself, then stopped, remembering it was December.

Boundaries, Grace. She'd spent so much time living

without them that relearning had been necessary. *Don't comment on someone's appearance. Don't touch people.* She'd almost broken the rules last night when he'd leaned down over her face and spoken with such masculinity. The kind she'd never had so close. *That* close. Maybe he'd wanted to kiss her. But if he hadn't, she would have embarrassed herself, right? Embarrassment. Another thing she'd supposedly relearned, although she couldn't remember the last time she'd felt it.

"Hi, Aaron, who never begs."

He performed that eye-crinkling smirk she remembered from last night. Really, the man was so incredibly handsome, he must feel wonderful every second of the day. Just walking around, catching eyes and pretending not to notice, like an A-list movie star. "Hey, hippie, who never says never."

Pleasure caught her unprepared. A nickname. Even if she didn't understand the meaning behind it, she liked that he'd thought of one, used it. "Oh, um. You remember that, huh?"

His teeth slid along the inside of his bottom lip. "It was only eight hours ago." He frowned down at her attire. "Are you going in dressed like that?"

She looked down at her chapped brown leather pants and denim shirt. "I'm only going far enough to prove I can help you."

His arms crossed over his chest. "Why do you need to prove that?"

"Because you were so sure I couldn't." Grace scanned the area behind Aaron, tilted her head in either direction. "Where is Old Man?"

"With my sister." His smile was devilish. "Getting a bath."

A smile passed over Grace's lips, but she let it slide away. He was probably in a hurry, wondering how long he needed to feign interest in a girl he'd never see again. "This way, if you please," she said, gesturing for him to follow her around the back of the school building. They were a good five-minute walk from where the action was taking place in the cafeteria. "I didn't realize you were here with family."

Aaron's purposeful strides had him catching up beside her in seconds. "It's a long story full of dysfunctional people and uncomfortable crying. I won't bore you with it."

"Don't you know politicians never turn down a chance to talk?"

A corner of his mouth lifted. "How do you know so much about politicians?" He scrutinized her. "Matter of fact, what is your purpose for being in Iowa? I'm going on a lot of faith here, considering I know nothing about you, apart from your fear of bears."

Grace separated from Aaron's side briefly, so they could circumvent a tree stump. "Does that mean you're desperate, Aaron?"

She wished she could tug back the question, but it was already out, too personal and too inappropriate. In keeping with her usual behavior, if you asked her mother, father, or any one of the myriad therapists she'd been shuffled in front of over the last six years. She started to say, *Forget I asked*, but Aaron surprised her by answering, "I guess you could say I'm a touch anxious. But I won't be for long."

"I believe you," Grace responded honestly.

Aaron's body heat warmed her side and the sensation was so nice, Grace moved a little closer. Judging from their progress along the back of the school, they had only another minute or so. It wouldn't hurt to savor his company just a little, would it? From Aaron's narrow-eyed glance at the marginal distance between them, he noticed she'd edged nearer, but when he spoke, it wasn't to reprimand her. Or explain that he had a girlfriend. Or whatever men did when a woman approached without encouragement. "We're driving to New York. Me, my brother, sister, and her best friend." He blew a sigh into the forest. "My mother passed away last year and we're jumping into the Atlantic on New Year's Day to fulfill her final wish."

Grace halted, her mouth falling open. "Wow. Really? Wow." It might have been the most glorious thing she'd ever heard. And definitely the last thing she'd expected from a man who seemed the farthest thing from whimsical. Or the type to indulge whimsy in the slightest. "Why?"

"Good question." Aaron kept walking, so Grace did, too. "My mother had a weird sense of humor. I guess we'll find out when we get there."

Can I go? The pleading question was right there on the tip of her tongue, but she just managed to wrangle it back down her throat. "I hope you buy a jacket before then. You're going to need it when you get out of the water."

Aaron shook his head on a perplexed laugh, opened his mouth as if he wanted to say something in response, but closed it, his golden brown eyes shuttering. *Closed for business.*

She shouldn't feel such disappointment over the very pointed end to their short association, should she? But it simply didn't *feel* final yet. How would she find out *why* Aaron's mother had sent him on such a crazy mission? And more important, she'd never find out what Aaron might have written on her clean slate. Or what she could have written on his, if he ever decided to hand his over. Her thoughts were so loud, she worried Aaron might hear them, so Grace put some breathing room between them and sighed over the loss of such delicious body heat. "When we get to the back door, try to look about ninety percent irritated and ten percent worried."

His eyebrows shot up. "Worried about what?"

"Me."

The security guard at the rear entrance came into view, his familiar hawk eyes zeroing in on Grace. Then Aaron. Exasperation moved over the guard's features before he hid it by adjusting his earpiece. Activity swarmed on the front side of the building, the media, the shouted questions, the general scrape and hum of movement audible, even where they walked along the backside of the school.

Knowing once they were inside, she wouldn't see Aaron again, Grace smiled up at him, noticing he didn't look quite as confident as he had a moment before. "It was nice meeting you," she whispered. "Thanks for not ratting me out."

"I..." He smoothed a hand down the front of his ruby-colored tie. "I won't see you...around again?"

Grace's hands itched with the urge to burrow into her hair, latch on to the braids she'd completed this morning while waiting for Aaron to show. "Probably not. Why would you?"

Why was he frowning at her? She couldn't ask him why, since they were within earshot of the guard and the walk had ended way too soon. With a final memorization of his furrowed brow, she transferred her focus. "Hey, Marcus."

"Grace." Marcus dipped his chin at Aaron. "Who's this?"

Her neck grew stiff. "This is my handler for today. He's new."

Marcus split a look between her and Aaron, before consulting his clipboard. "No one ran a change in staff by me."

Grace could feel Aaron's sharp scrutiny and ignored it, attempting to breeze past Marcus with a casual smile. "I understand. I'll just go grab my dad, so he can clear it up—"

"No. That's okay." As predicted, a harried Marcus blocked her path. "Your father is busy. Just…" He gave Aaron another once-over, lowering his voice to a conspiratorial whisper between men, as if Grace couldn't hear every word. "You know the approved areas? Be sure to keep her within them."

"Yes." She was impressed when Aaron gave a brisk nod. "Will do."

Aaron took her elbow and moved them into the back hallway, past the kitchen, where the local Boy Scouts were rushing to mix pancakes and pour them on the oversized, industrial griddle. Once they turned a corner and Marcus was no longer in view, Grace reluctantly tugged her elbow out of Aaron's grip, rubbing the spot to keep the warmth alive awhile longer. "This is where we part ways."

Aaron's way too handsome face was the picture of bafflement. "Who are you, hippie?" The low, intense vibration of his voice made her shiver. "Why do you need a handler?"

She reached back and curled her fingers around the metal staircase handle. The one she knew was there—and where it led—thanks to last night's expedition. Her intent was to slip away without answering, but after ignoring so many compulsions that morning already, she couldn't deny the final one.

With a thready apology, Grace shot forward and up, locking her mouth with Aaron's, memorizing the way his stiffness melted in one big deluge. The way he gave a rough exhale through his nose. That gruff sound that drummed from his throat, a split second before his lips opened, tongue teasing in to taste hers. Just some. The most perfect, slick greeting. The two of them hung there, mouths open, lips wet and fitted together, breath racing, kitchen clamoring behind them.

Two ends of a silk rope pulled taut beneath her belly button, a tempting lick of his tongue clenching muscles she'd never acquainted herself with, nor could she point them out on a diagram. *Whoa Nelly.* And with her heart slamming against her ribs like a wrecking ball, Grace cut out that snippet of time—so shimmering and unmarred— tucked it into her pocket, and stole down the staircase, wondering how long the memory of Aaron's kiss would stay with her. Praying the answer was forever.

* * *

What the hell just happened?

Too many things. All sorts of…things. And he'd never—not a goddamn day in his life—had a problem articulating. He articulated and gesticulated and stipulated for a living. Truly, it was his gift. Yet when he attempted to weed through the last twelve hours, he came up empty. She'd kissed him. Okay, there was nothing out of the ordinary about that. Women kissed him all the time—the last heinous week of road trip hell notwithstanding. But the prospect of not seeing any of *those* kissers again didn't make him want to slam a fist into the wall and shout *why?*

And there were a great number of reasons why he and Grace couldn't share oxygen anymore. For one thing, he kind of wanted to bury his fists in that epic mess of hair and use it to pin her against a wall. So he could give her mouth hell for issuing that breathy, too-quick tease and having the nerve to walk away without a polite glance over her shoulder. But at the same time, applaud her for blowing him off after one kiss.

Aaron chose women based on their level of unavailability. The *less* they wanted a relationship, or even dinner and drinks, the better. If they were only interested in one thing—sex—they couldn't peel back his surface and see nothing. A man who would rather walk across a bed of thorns than hold a woman while she cried or share a tub of popcorn at a rom com.

Getting close to another person was suicide, as far as he was concerned. People eventually walked away, although he wasn't sure if that was a universal rule, or one that pertained only to him. His father had replaced Belmont as the male rock in his life, built him up, and then he'd gone and fucked off, too, hadn't he? Left him bitter and self-sufficient. He was grateful for seeing human nature for what it was, deep down. The women he took to bed didn't seem to mind, either.

Grace—*whoever she was*—didn't have a place beneath him, being pressed down roughly into twisted sheets. He might have only made her acquaintance last night, but no way could she remain faceless, like the other women. Bed partners he respected, but didn't feel the need to call again. Something told him he would never forget Grace's face as long as he lived—and he didn't like the rise of hot matter filling his chest at that realization. Or the prospect of how he could mar that sweetness with one mistake.

God, he didn't even know if the way he felt about Grace was appropriate. How old was she? Early twenties, probably, but he hadn't confirmed. Furthermore, there was a delicate quality to her that—when combined with the fact that she had a *handler*—brought on a healthy dose of self-disgust. Was she...sick in some way?

And why did that just make him want to see her more? Demand she explain and let him...plan a *solution* for her? Instead of running high speed in the opposite direction, as would be wise?

Didn't matter. She was gone. Gone. And rather than slipping into the pancake breakfast like a phoenix from the ashes, he was standing there, actually considering going down the staircase after the girl. She would be surprised, too. For some strange reason, there was no doubt in his head about that. She wouldn't expect him to come after her—and that kind of pissed him off. Made him want to go after her *more*. Grab her by the shoulders and tell her he hadn't gotten hot from a single kiss since middle school and ask her to let his tongue in one more time...while he palmed her tits and listened to her whimper.

A loud crash in the kitchen tore the fabric of Aaron's inner mayhem down the middle, jolting him backward and away from the stairway. Jesus Christ, had he actually succumbed to frostbite last night in the woods, and this whole morning was one big-ass delirious imagining? *Look around you, man. You're in.* This was his shot. Some girl sure as shit wasn't going to throw a mental roadblock into his path, not when his game needed to be flawless.

Aaron ran his right hand down the front of his tie, making sure the top button on his starched collar was buttoned. Ignoring the burning urge to throw one final look down the stairs, he sailed down the rest of the hallway, bypassed a series of utility closets, and entered the cafeteria. After giving his eyes a moment to adjust to the bright television lights, in addition to the buzzing halogens hanging from the ceiling, Aaron noticed he'd entered the giant space behind a row of photographers. One of them turned in the process of shoving a cigarette behind his ear, giving Aaron a nod.

"Bathroom's the other way," he said in a gravelly voice, but halfway through the sentence, he did a double take and snapped his fingers. "Wait a minute. Golden Boy, right? Million Dollar Smile…"

While scanning the room for Glen Pendleton, Aaron gave a brisk nod. "That would be me."

The cameraman dug in his black canvas bag and produced a state-of-the-art Nikon, which was immediately put to use snapping pictures of Aaron. "Is it true you were fired from Senator Boggs's office for—"

"No." *Stupid.* Stupid to feel like the wind had been knocked out of him. He'd known his misdeeds would be put under a magnifying glass at some point, if he decided to remain in the political arena. Today was that day apparently. There was a twitch between his shoulder blades, however, that he hadn't expected. A need to turn around, check to make sure Grace hadn't followed him and overheard. Ridiculous. There was nothing behind him but a closed door leading to the hallway. "No, it's not true.

Would I be here this morning, looking so damn good, if it was?"

One final camera snap, before the Nikon was deposited back into the bag. "Guess not."

Aaron spotted Pendleton across the cafeteria, his ex-military bearing fiercely rigid as he moved through a sea of admirers, reporters, and constituents—some of whom were offering up babies—toward his pancake-laden table. The Iowa senator had announced his candidacy for president a year prior and had been leading in the polls ever since. His military background, combined with his sharp sense of humor, had made him an immediate favorite with the press and voters alike. Unfortunately, his competitor was running a very effective campaign, creating doubt about Pendleton's ability to win the nomination. This week in Iowa was intended to remind voters of Pendleton's success as a senator and remind them how much his constituents loved him, by parading that affection across all forms of media. When this week was over, however, the senator would be getting back on the campaign trail. Every move, every statement and neck tie color, would be important, and Aaron intended to be a part of it.

"Excuse me," Aaron said quietly, moving past the row of photographers.

He hung back during the meal, knowing he'd have to pick his moment. And that moment was *not* while Pendleton was mid-chew, his image being captured by a hundred news outlets. To the senator's right sat his wife and daughter, both of them attractive in a quiet, polished way. Tasteful brown hair, pulled back in low buns, modest clothing, indulgent smiles.

Nothing like Grace, with her—

Goddammit. Stop thinking about her.

Except...he hadn't said thank you. Had he? No. Had it been required? He'd done Grace a solid by not sounding the alarm that she'd been trespassing. In return, she'd snuck him into the event. A favor for a favor. So why did he feel like a prick?

Aaron realized he was licking his lower lip side to side, attempting to capture her taste, and groaned inwardly when he succeeded. Candy.

Pendleton pushed back from the cafeteria table, followed by his wife and daughter, although Aaron noticed they'd taken a grand total of one bite between them. "Don't tell my wife," Pendleton said with a sly wink. "But these might be the best pancakes I've ever had. We'll see about sneaking the recipe into her cookbook."

Everyone laughed on cue, then directed their applause toward the Boy Scouts who were hovering in various locations around the room, sweat dotting their brows, looking shell-shocked, but proud. After that, everyone moved at once. The pictures had been taken, sound bites captured, and now the herd moved to the next locale. Aaron knew the procedure well and his blood pumped, being so close to the action once again. *Finally, back where I belong.*

The senator moved through the press line and Aaron sidled left, through the gathering of supporters, who were beginning to dissipate, having gotten their prized shot for Instagram. When Aaron and the senator drew even, Aaron could see from the man's lack of surprise that he'd been aware of Aaron throughout the whole breakfast.

Pendleton's handshake was firm, but there was speculation in his intelligent gaze. "Thought we'd seen the last of you, Clarkson." His smile didn't waver. "My short list of potential advisers definitely has."

Aaron only smiled wider. "I'm here to change your mind about that."

"You've got under a minute to explain how." Pendleton sent a wave to someone beyond Aaron's shoulder. "Considering the transgression you committed, it better be good. Hell, even if it dazzles me, your character will always be in question."

His stomach pitched, but he didn't let it show on his face. "If we took the time to hold everyone in this race accountable for their mistakes, we'd never get anything done. And we're here to win an election." Aaron waited until the senator stopped waving and returned his attention once again. "You were considering me once to help garner the youth vote. Whoever you chose in my stead isn't getting it done or you wouldn't be giving me the time of day right now."

Pendleton laughed under his breath, shaking out his stance. "Let's say that were true. What would you do differently?"

"If I weren't up against my misdeeds, I would tell you to hire me and find out, but that's not the case." Aaron could see the man appreciated his honesty. Could see that he'd read Pendleton correctly. "Your social media presence is huge—bigger than your competitor's—but you're telling the eighteen to twenty-five demo what they should be outraged over. That's not how it works." The words were like honey rolling off his tongue. "Downplay your brand. Make them think they're discovering you on their own. And then urge them to vote. Just *vote*. Young people smell desperation like sharks in the water. Whoever is working for you is going to lose you the leg you have dangling in the ocean right now."

Aaron had statistics and ideas with which to hit the senator, but in the interest of practicing what he'd preached, he forced himself to ease off.

"Did you know your competitor is holding a Facebook rally this afternoon? Already has a million attendees logging in." Aaron threw a look around the rapidly emptying cafeteria. "This is a clip on CNN later tonight and no under-forty is watching. This won't make *The Daily Show*. Kimmel might make a joke about the way you hold a fork, if you're lucky." He gave the senator a final nod and stepped back. "If you're interested in getting in front of the right eyes, interested in getting clicks, I can do that for you. You'll have your own app by Friday."

The senator's wife moved up—in an act of the world's worst timing—slipping her arm through her husband's. "Everything all right?"

Aaron gave the woman a polite nod as the senator answered with a low affirmative, but Aaron didn't miss the subtle way the senator blocked his wife from view with the use of his body. It almost forced Aaron to lose the coffee he'd consumed that morning. When the senator put his hand out for another shake, Aaron hid his surprise. "We need to talk more." Pendleton hesitated for a few seconds. "Are you free for dinner tonight around six? It's just a casual family dinner at our house. Come early and we can speak beforehand."

Son of a bitch. Aaron managed to reel back the fist pump before it could happen. His throat ached as the senator was swept away by staffers. Ached because he'd just pulled off a monumental feat, and there was no one to tell. Not a single damn person. Peggy would be happy for him, but she would be more interested in what he'd wear to dinner. Belmont wouldn't give a flying shit. No one in his family ever had. Isolated celebration was nothing new. Hell, it was old hat at this point. His victories were his own, acknowledged with a drink in his monotone apartment before he began planning for the next one.

He didn't want to do that this time. No. Because he hadn't worked alone.

An image of curls wrapped around ribbons interspersed with braids flashed across his consciousness, and no matter how hard Aaron tried to shake the vision, it wouldn't go away. Nor would the texture of her mouth, the way her breath had coasted over his lips and seemingly straight down to his cock. He'd had a fucking semi since she'd left him standing at the top of the staircase. Yeah, there was no denying when he walked out of the cafeteria—through the front entrance this time—exactly whom he hoped to see.

A commotion to Aaron's right brought him up short. The senator had been pulled to the side by a harried-looking gentleman in a suit. Clearly an aide. One hand was pressed over his earpiece keeping it in place as he listened, then reported back to Pendleton. "How much was taken?" the senator demanded, not totally succeeding in keeping his voice down.

"All of it," the aide reported back grimly. "With the turnout, we were expecting five figures. The donation stands...someone cut out the bottoms with a damn soldering iron. Took the money after it was collected, had to be during the breakfast." He raked a hand through his thinning hair. "The bottoms must have been cut last night after the stations were set up, because they were *intact*..." The aide listened to his earpiece a moment. "They're checking surveillance tapes now from inside the building, but the custodian says they only run on the weekends..."

With a sinking sensation in his stomach, Aaron turned on a heel and began to weave through the crowd, trying not to show a reaction—which felt decidedly like fear— to the flashing blue and white lights rolling to a stop in the school's front quad. "Grace," Aaron growled under his breath.

CHAPTER THREE

The crying woman was the most beautiful person Grace had ever seen. Sitting on the forest floor, arms gathered on a tree stump, the blonde with loose, enviable curls sobbed up the sky, her face dappled with sunlight. Grace needed to move, but her legs wouldn't take her away from the sight. It looked like a painting. One that could be re-created into millions of duplicated posters and hung up in the bedrooms of aspiring poet teenagers. Grace had gone through that phase, hadn't she? Before she'd been sent to the camp.

Discomfort boiled below Grace's breastbone, but she took a deep breath and embraced it. Maybe it even passed quicker than usual because another human being was so miserable in her vicinity. She couldn't even remember the last time—or if ever—that had happened. When her mother made the decision to send her to YouthAspire the summer she turned sixteen—a leadership program that was a glorified summer camp for the children of affluent families—that almost comical sense of mutual suffering had been present in the beginning. Some of the campers had even bonded over being sent packing so their parents could go on a real vacation, but there had been no opening up. Or sharing of pain.

That had come later.

But it hadn't been in the form of sadness. It had been anger. Frustration. Unlike the sorrow pouring off this beautiful forest-weeper in waves, so heavy and frothy, Grace could feel it lapping at her ankles like ocean surf.

Sunlight bounced off the crying woman's necklace, and forgetting everything she'd been taught, Grace spoke. "Are those rings around your neck?"

"*Ah!*" The blonde even looked pretty when she was frightened, falling back onto her butt in a *whoosh* of leaves. "Who said that?"

Grace tipped only her upper body sideways, making it visible from behind the tree. Like an old-fashioned jack-o'-lantern, she imagined. "I really don't have time to introduce myself, but I'm Grace. What's your name?"

A beat of windy silence. "Peggy."

Grace would have thought Winifred or Guinevere. If they were in Camelot, knights would have jousted to win her hand. But somehow the name *Peggy* suited her, too. A bubble-gum-snapping waitress at a fifties soda fountain. "Can you point me toward the road, Peggy?"

"Um…yeah." Peggy came to her feet, her puffy eyes dropping to the dirt caking Grace's hands. "I have to get back anyway. I'll walk you."

"Oh. Thanks."

Despite her offer, Peggy didn't move right away. "Hot

damn. That is one wicked awesome hairstyle." Grace knew from experience what it looked like when a person had the urge to touch something, but held back. So she grabbed Peggy's hand and shoved it into the tangled locks she hadn't taken the time to brush this morning, pleased when the sadness in Peggy's eyes seemed to dissipate, her fingers moving with a fluidity that Grace somehow already associated with her. "Do you wear it like this for a reason?"

No one had ever asked quite like that. Out of pure, nonjudgmental curiosity. "When it reaches my waist, I'm going to cut it. They'll make wigs—"

"And gift them to cancer patients?" Peggy nodded, smoothing her fingers down a red ribbon. "I've heard of that."

Grace wanted to close her eyes and enjoy the sensation of someone other than herself touching her hair, but she managed to keep her lids up. "I guess I'm just giving it an adventure before cutting it loose."

Peggy snorted a laugh, Grace smiling as they fell into step together. Twice in one day she'd walked side by side with someone who wasn't doing so because it was their job. Never mind that Aaron had been *pretending* it was his duty. A tiny stab of regret made itself known in her side, thinking about Aaron. The kiss. The way he still hadn't moved when she backed down the stairs. She *liked* that he hadn't moved. "Why do you have rings around your neck?" Grace asked Peggy, hoping for a distraction. As if the cash she'd stolen wouldn't suffice.

"It started that…" The blonde swiped at her eyes with an impatient noise. "It started as a way to take responsibility for hurting the four men who gave them to me and asked me to be their wife. Or maybe a warning for anyone who gets a similar idea." She wet her lips. "But right now, knowing where we're headed next, I know I'm just wearing them to be selfish. I want him to see."

"Who's he?"

Peggy's laugh was watery as she threw a sidelong glance at Grace. "You're pretty nosy for someone who doesn't want to talk about why her hands look like they've been dipped in mud."

Grace observed her palms. "How do you know I don't want to talk about it?"

"Every time I look down at them, you shake your head."

Grace's answering smile was so heavy, she had to stop walking. "I wish I didn't have to go—" A crunch of leaves cut off Grace's statement, her body tensing. But when she saw the white dog approaching from the direction of the cabins, she deflated on a relieved exhale. "It's just Old Man."

Peggy paused in the act of petting the panting newcomer. "Wait. How do you know Old Man?"

"We met last night." Grace scrubbed her finger pads behind the dog's ears. "You weren't a bear, were you? No, you *weren't*. Just a handsome doggie. Yes, you *were*."

"Was Old Man with my brother?" Peggy asked with a raised brow.

Gravity thinned in her stomach just thinking about the dog's owner. Remembering how closely he'd watched her in the darkness. How he'd looked at her mouth as if he were angry with it. That final lick of his tongue this morning and the sense he hadn't been able to resist one last taste. How she'd felt that wet slide between her legs, as if he'd kissed her from his knees instead. "If Aaron is your brother, then yes," she breathed, sounding like she'd just swallowed a billow of smoke.

The sound of sirens in the distance propelled Grace forward, in the direction Peggy had already been leading her. "This way, right? It was nice talking to you. For what it's worth, I don't think you're selfish."

"Wait." Peggy straightened from her crouch, Old Man walking in a circle around her jean-clad legs. "Are, uh...are those sirens for you?"

Grace only hesitated a second, before nodding. "I can see that you're thinking of helping me, which is really...I mean, wow. That's nice." She rubbed her filthy palm down the side of her leather pant leg. "But I can't let you do that. I don't want to get Aaron's sister into trouble."

Peggy sniffed and pursed her lips, giving Grace a non-judgmental once-over that wasn't completely devoid of speculation. "I'm helping you. Move your ass."

A fair amount of Grace's life was dictated by other people. She was brought along to various places with her family so they wouldn't have to worry about what she'd do in their absence. They deposited her onto couches in stuffy offices and begged her to talk, to loosen the resentment they claimed she stored deep inside. As a result, she greatly disliked being told what to do. Her mind was sound, and she could choose her own path. But she'd never been made to feel like a coconspirator, the way she did as Peggy hooked their elbows together, hastening them through the woods. No, it was more camaraderie than someone knowing what was best for her. So with a smile flirting around the edges of her mouth, she ran alongside the crying woman with rings bouncing off her neckline.

"I really won't stay long," Grace breathed as they reached a grouping of cabins, the last of which Peggy led her up the creaking porch. "I just need somewhere to clean up and—"

"Yeah, yeah." Peggy dug a key from her pocket and opened the door, nudging Grace inside and gesturing to yet another pretty woman who sat in a yoga pose on the floor. "Sage, Grace. Grace, Sage. Tell me how you know Aaron."

Without opening her eyes, Sage waved in their general direction. "Hello. Be with you in a moment."

With a nod, Grace followed Peggy into the bathroom, where she had the tap running, steam already rising to fog the oversized mirror. "I helped him get into the pancake breakfast this morning."

"Really." A crease forming between her brows, Peggy squirted hand soap between Grace's wet hands. "Why did you do that?"

Grace lathered her hands, lifting them to her nose to catch the scent of magnolias. "Because he didn't think I could."

Peggy slouched to the side, catching herself with a hip on the sink. "I think you were a victim of a little reverse psychology. Aaron is kind of famous for that."

"Oh no." Grace couldn't help the smile from tilting one end of her mouth as she accepted a towel from Peggy and dried her hands. "I know reverse psychology when I hear it. He was just plain skeptical."

"Yeah, he's famous for that, too," Peggy murmured, watching her carefully. "Who should I expect at the door?"

Grace's stomach sank down to her toes at the idea of

getting her new friend into trouble. "Maybe the police. Or security personnel." She folded the towel neatly and laid it on the sink. "But don't worry, they'll just take me home. No matter what I do, they just take me back—"

A loud knock on the door cracked the air in half. Grace and Peggy exchanged a brisk, wordless look, before Peggy hustled her into the bedroom and straight into the closet, closing the door. Ensconced in darkness, Grace watched through the wooden slats as Peggy bent forward at the waist and snapped her hair back so it fell in waves around her shoulders. Then she strutted forward like a beauty queen during the swimsuit competition. When Peggy opened the door, Grace expected to see a member of her father's security team standing on the other side. But she didn't.

Instead, Aaron blew in like the north wind and Grace's heart lifted.

* * *

"Hey, Aaron—"

"I need a drink." He bypassed his sister, loosening his tie as he entered the tiny cabin. With a muttered hello in Sage's direction, Aaron jerked the silk from around his neck and tossed it onto the bed, followed by his jacket. He wanted everything off—*everything*—which wouldn't be happening in his sister's cabin, but every bit of fabric touching his skin was offensive. It itched with irritation, and he wasn't even sure why. Information. He was lacking in information and that was flat-out unacceptable.

The last half hour had been spent searching the forest for Grace, and the longer he'd gone without a glimpse of her haphazard mane of hair and earnest expression, the more his anxiety had mounted. Because he wanted to question her about the missing money. Right. That was *it*. He didn't give a shit why she needed it. Or if she would get into trouble. Or what would happen to her. Or if he would ever taste of her again. Do *more*.

"*Fuck*," he growled, slamming a fist down on the small corner table, screwing up a half-finished game of solitaire.

"Eh." Peggy removed a jug of vodka from the room's small refrigerator and poured the clear liquid into a paper cup, handing it over. "Bad morning?"

"That's not how it started." His anger went on an upswing, catching him around the nape of his neck. Although truthfully, he couldn't be sure if it was directed at Grace or himself, for putting his faith in a stranger. A stranger who sure as hell didn't *feel* like one. Not a typical reaction for someone who coveted his lone wolf status. Keeping people at a professional distance meant he wouldn't have to see that glint of discomfort in their eyes when he proved their initial judgment of him correct. Nothing below the surface but more calculation. It was better than opening up to someone or trying to be a good son and brother and only getting their retreating backs for his trouble.

"The morning started perfect, actually. I got an audience with the man I needed to see. He listened. I hooked him. He asked me to meet him later for dinner." He took a swig of the vodka, laughing bitterly into the half-empty cup. "Then this…this *crazy* girl jeopardizes the whole thing for me. I'm fairly certain she just stole a heap of cash and didn't think to mention it to me before we were seen together. *Dammit*."

Dimly, Aaron registered Peggy's face looking paler than usual. "Aaron—"

"I should have known." He drained the cup and set it down, pressing the heels of his hands into his eye sockets, trying to banish the image of Grace. And failing. Which only spurred his frustration. "The way she looked and talked and behaved weren't...*normal*. I should have known."

It took Aaron a moment to realize Peggy had backed across the room, her side pressed up against the closet door. Sage rose to her feet at his right, tidying the cabin with unnatural movements, even though it required no cleaning.

"What's going on?" Aaron asked, experiencing sudden numbness in his lips. "What..."

Of the four Clarkson siblings, he and Peggy's relationship had always come the closest to friendship. They'd been lumped together as the troublemakers of the bunch, so when they'd been separated on opposite sides of the room as kids, they'd learned to communicate without words. When she gave a subtle nod at the closet, Aaron knew. Knew Grace was inside, knew she'd heard everything he'd said since entering the cabin. And with a fist turning in his throat, he ran back the whole shitty monologue and ice cropped up along his spine. Inward. Freezing him right down to the middle of his stomach.

"She's..."

Peggy blinked.

Jesus. Funny, how—out of every unethical move he'd made in his life—this was when shame chose to make an appearance. It slunk in from all sides, crowding him like drunk people on a dance floor, erecting his defenses

into giant castle walls. Hating the mixture of sympathy
and censure being projected not only by his sister, but by
Sage, too, Aaron stormed toward the closet, ripping the
door open as soon as Peggy unblocked his path.

Grace sat on the floor, her knees pulled up against her
chest. All that hair, it draped around her body like a protective cloud. The lamplight filtered in from the bedroom
to highlight her face, and Aaron could see she watched
him, but nothing about her spoke of being offended or embarrassed. No, it was far worse. She looked at him as if
their encounter in the forest last night had never even happened. As if they'd never walked together or kissed inside
a noisy kitchen. Having those moments taken away from
him—in her eyes—shouldn't have been so god-awful, but
it was. It was like being burned.

"You have a lot of nerve looking at me like that," Aaron
heard himself say, even though it didn't really sound like
his voice, but some choked, gravelly version of the way
he usually spoke. When she didn't move or respond, the
castle walls that had constructed themselves in his chest
bolstered themselves with even more brick and mortar.
"You could have warned me, Grace. I would have found a
way in that didn't implicate me in a crime."

She shook her head, as if he'd spoken in Russian. "I
don't know what you're talking about."

His laugh was rife was disbelief. "Where is the money?
Who *are* you?"

Peggy ducked past Aaron, blocking his view of Grace
where she finally gained her feet in the closet. "Hey. Why
don't you back off?" His sister stared at him hard. "What
is *wrong* with you?"

I don't know. Saying those three words in his head

started a dull ache behind both eyes. How many times had he asked himself that same question? Come up with the same answer? In a family full of people who couldn't manage their goddamn emotions, couldn't help but *act* on those emotions—whether it be burning down a restaurant or leaving four pathetic suckers at the altar—he was the one who saw everything through cut-and-dried analysis. His mind made his decisions, probably because he didn't have a heart big enough to perform the job. It had worked for Aaron, kept everyone from trying to peel back layers and be disappointed by what they found.

"Apologize to her," Peggy whispered furiously, bringing him back to the moment with the force of a catapult. "For what you said. Apologize."

He hesitated. Aaron hesitated because he knew. If he looked into Grace's newly distant green eyes and said *I'm sorry*, he might mean it. He'd have to face hurting her feelings—head on—and take responsibility for that damage. God, nails were already digging into his kidneys at the very idea. Being responsible for someone else's feelings? *Jesus Christ.* No. He couldn't do it. He couldn't acknowledge how bad he'd fucked up, because that would mean she meant something to him.

Admitting to a mistake or a weakness meant an exchange of power. It opened the door for people to find his other faults, which was why he used a reinforced steel padlock to keep the entrance shut. His focus needed to be on tonight's dinner, not worrying about making someone *sad*, for the love of God.

Hardening himself, Aaron turned from the closet and retrieved the vodka, pouring a second dose into his paper cup. "Look, we don't have time for this. I only have the afternoon to prepare for my meeting." His neck prickled when Peggy and Grace walked out of the closet behind him. "We might be harboring a fugitive. A fugitive with a high level of security clearance. I'd kind of like to find out why, so why don't we stop worrying about how everyone feels?"

"Who said we're worried about how everyone feels?" Peggy murmured for his ears alone. "Maybe that's just your conscience talking."

The vodka burned in his stomach. "I never claimed to have one."

"Yeah? The lack is showing," said Peggy, sitting down on the bed and patting the spot beside her. Not for him, but for the girl still standing by the closet. In anticipation of Grace entering his line of sight, Aaron held his breath, but the floorboards creaked near the door instead, tying knots in his muscles.

"Where are you going?" Aaron rasped, feeling her imminent departure like a blow to the midsection.

She settled a hand on the doorknob, hair shielding her face until she tossed the wealth of it back, giving his eyes access to the smooth angle of her chin, the round tip of her nose. Vivid green eyes that he somehow knew would get darker, turn a mossy color, while he moved inside her, angling his hips to get her off hard. "If you feel the need to report your side of things, you should do it. I would never ask anyone to lie for me. Ever." There was finally a flicker of recognition when she looked at Aaron, but it died almost immediately. "I thought there was something a little magic about meeting someone in the forest at night. Meeting...you." She shifted side to side. "If wondering about things like magic makes me not normal, I think I'm okay with that. But I don't have to wonder about you any-more."

The pressure in his sternum ratcheted up, like a giant bolt being turned. Her name wanted to be called, he could feel the weight of it on his tongue, so he bit down hard. And when the door opened to reveal Belmont, Aaron tasted blood. Grace's head was still turned in his direction, so she attempted to walk through the door without looking—and ran smack into Belmont, bouncing off his immovable frame like a bird hitting a sliding glass door.

With a ripped expletive, Aaron dropped his cup of liquor and dove forward, just managing to insert himself between Grace and the floor before they could meet, catching her in his lap. The firm curve of her ass felt like it was locking home against his groin, right where it was meant to be. Clearly stunned, Grace looked up at Aaron, wind-reddened lips parted...and the room started to spin with his regret, his arousal, the betrayal that radiated from her. Clean, churned earth scent crept up and wrapped around his neck, and he couldn't stop himself. Couldn't prevent his fingers from winding through her hair, his palm from conforming to the side of her face.

"I didn't mean it, hippie." He fisted the locks of hair, watched awareness color her cheeks. "I didn't mean it."

Grace stared back at him for a moment that simultaneously stretched forever and ended all too quickly. He caught just the beginning of a moving sheen in her eyes, gutting him. Then she was gone, her tangled strands freeing themselves from his hands, her body sliding off his lap, before she rushed to her feet and vanished through the doorway.

The shocked scrutiny surrounding Aaron rushed in,

making him all too aware of his slumped position on the floor, the way he stared out into the midmorning light, wishing he knew where the fuck Grace had gone. Hating that he'd forfeited his right to ask. That could very well be it. He would probably never see her again. Fighting through a wave of nausea, Aaron surged to a standing position and straightened his collar.

"Can I use the Suburban tonight?" He leveled the question at Belmont. "Or were you planning some brooding drive through the countryside."

Without answering, Belmont slid the thick silver key—attached to a rabbit's foot keychain—from his pocket and tossed it to Aaron, who caught it midair. His brother was watching him with both eyebrows drawn like he gave a shit, and Aaron couldn't even remember the last time they'd made eye contact. Oh, *this* was the moment his brother chose to change up their dynamic? When he was already swimming laps in some unfamiliar emotional deep end? Well, he didn't have room just then to wonder what the fuck Belmont was thinking. Or what his brother wanted to see in him instead. Whatever it was, it wouldn't be there.

"What is it, Bel? Huh?" Aaron snatched his jacket and tie off the bed. "Did you find something about that entertaining? I guess you're not the only one who can make an ass out of himself over a girl, right?" *God*, he hated himself in that moment, but the roiling self-disgust only made him want to seal the deal. Finally make himself irredeemable with the Clarksons. Yes, with Belmont, the one who'd ended their association like a slammed door, decades ago. But the rest of them, too, because they'd followed suit. He could still recall the way they'd watched him at their mother's funeral with varying degrees of astonishment, possibly even disgust. He'd been the only one who could function that day. Shaking hands, smiling, performing his role. Or that's what he'd thought until he'd seen Rita and Peggy watching from the front pew, staring as though he were some kind of exotic reptile at the zoo.

Maybe I am, he'd thought. *If I can still operate as though I feel nothing, maybe I don't. Maybe I don't need to.* Maybe that's what his father and Belmont—and yes, even Miriam to a degree—had seen in him all along. *Someone like you.*

Aaron swallowed hard. Just then, he needed the attention on him placed elsewhere. Preferably on his brother, who apparently only gave him the time of day when disappointed. So much of Aaron's focus during the trip had been keeping attention *off* Belmont. Finding motels off the beaten path, smaller populated towns to stop in for food. Concessions the family had always made without a formal discussion ever since the day Belmont had been pulled from an abandoned well, after being missing for four days. Well, Aaron was flat out of concessions at the moment. He wanted banishment. How else would he stop imagining the feel of Grace on his lap? Stop hearing her condemnation, gentle in its delivery, but damning nonetheless.

"Looks like I'm rid of my girl, Bel. But what about yours? You going to make a move on Sage? Or wait for a *better* opportunity than this endless goddamn road trip?"

Belmont's eyes burned like two coals, the hands Aaron knew to be veritable weapons fisting at his sides—but it wasn't Aaron's brother that snapped him out of his rage. Sage's hand cracked across his face, which had the effect of cables being cut on an elevator. His anger plummeted and smashed to pieces, leaving nothing behind. Just nothing. He was empty of all things, unless a continuous image of Grace tucked into herself on the closet floor counted.

It did. It counted.

Aaron watched as Belmont came up behind Sage, taking hold of her wrist like it was an alien object, and leading it back to rest on his shoulder. Watching it sit there through steady eyes, as if it were the most fascinating appendage he'd ever seen. Sage went from bristling to breathless in a split second and Aaron couldn't— *couldn't*—witness any more of the naked emotion. Couldn't take another reminder of what he very obviously lacked.

"We could sell tickets to this fucking freak show," Aaron quipped on his way to the door, but his accompanying laugh cut off as soon as the door closed behind him. And he walked to the other cabin wrapped in the loudest silence he'd ever heard.

CHAPTER FOUR

Grace trudged up the driveway to her family's estate, well aware that they'd probably already clocked her presence through one of its many bay windows. This wasn't her first walk of shame—although it usually felt more like a walk of pride. Today was...different. Her spine refused to straighten, her chin wouldn't lift as high. She didn't have the usual head of steam that came as a result of executing one of her plans.

She'd been called crazy before. Even while attending art school. And that wasn't easy, considering crazy had been rewarded at the Art Institute of Austin, which she'd attended for three years. After the fallout with Youth-Aspire when she was sixteen and the subsequent therapy she'd undergone in the name of healing and recovery, college had represented freedom. People who didn't know her face or her story. A chance to reinvent herself, while exploring her urge to create.

Her parents had been optimistic that she would find like-minded people at art school and urged her to pick a focus. Painting, graphic design, sculpting. But none of those mediums had captured her attention. With the door to independence open, ideas had flowed in, but not in a way her professors could grade. Hanging hundreds of mirrors throughout one Austin city block overnight, leaving the city baffled over the culprit's identity, had earned her a written report sent home from the university, calling her impulsive and directionless. Mostly because she'd found it difficult to put the reasons behind her first project into words, only knowing she'd hoped to reflect the world back on itself. Force people to *look*. At themselves... what was around them.

Instead of attempting to understand, Grace's parents flew to Austin to secure a new therapist. They'd taken her actions as a sign that she hadn't fully recovered from what happened at the camp. She'd made an effort with the new therapist, because it troubled Grace to see her parents worried. After sessions, she'd even felt unburdened. Healthier. One day, however, the woman had begun posing questions to Grace that sounded too familiar. Sounded like they were coming directly from her father. And she'd just known. The therapist was reporting back to her parents and pushing their agenda onto her through a third party. If she hadn't known deep down they meant well— and hadn't intended to replicate the type of brainwashing she'd experienced at camp—Grace would have followed her inclination to disengage from the Pendleton family.

Instead, she'd begun using art as her therapy. Her fellow students had backed off as rumors about her past made their way to Austin. Thankfully, she'd already lost herself in creating, engaging with the people of Austin, even if they didn't know her identity.

When her father decided to run for president, her mother had flown to Austin and begged her to come home. Where they could keep an eye on her, make sure she didn't do anything to injure his chances at the White House. Grace had been so thankful for the honesty, that her mother hadn't tried to sugarcoat the truth for once, she'd agreed to remain with them through the election. So far, she hadn't done anything to blacken the family name. But that didn't mean she'd stopped creating in her own way. No, she'd merely amended her focus. In a way that wasn't always well received.

Okay, never.

Grace came to a stop at the porch, letting the toes of her boots bump against the red brick. At least the trouble she'd courted today would distract her from the knife handle sticking out of her chest. *Silly.* How silly she'd been. She'd had what could only be described as a crush on Aaron—the world's shortest crush, probably. That must have been why she'd read him wrong. Must be why his calling her crazy—a word to which she'd thought herself desensitized—had found the *sensitized* target she usually kept guarded.

One half of the oak double doors opened, finally forcing Grace to lift her chin. Her father stood outlined in the entrance, his forehead wrinkled, Grace's mother standing at his elbow. She spoke in a hushed tone, probably begging him to go easy with whatever he considered a suitable punishment for stealing upward of thirty thousand dollars. Grace felt a punch of sadness—not over the money—but for her mother constantly having to come to her defense. It was out of guilt, Grace knew. For sending Grace away during her sixteenth summer. Being the one to drop her off at the gate. Would her mother ever stop blaming herself?

"Come inside, Grace," her father ordered, his military background threading through his tone. "I don't wish to discuss something so embarrassing outdoors."

Discomfort spread down Grace's arms, making her fingers curl into the sleeves of her denim shirt, but she commanded her legs to climb the stairs. "I'm sorry if you find what I did embarrassing. That was never my intention." Having finally reached the doorway, she swallowed hard and met her father's eyes. "That donation would have only bought you thirty seconds of airtime. But it can be put to such better use elsewhere. I—"

"It's not up to you to decide how the campaign spends money," her father snapped. "Those people donated in the hopes of seeing me succeed, and your actions could do the opposite. You might as well be working for the competition."

Leaving those words hanging in the air, Grace accepted a half hug from her mother and followed them into the house, toeing off her boots in the entryway with two *thunks*. She found her father pacing in his den, went inside, and closed the door. Knowing better than to speak first, Grace leaned back against the wall and waited.

"Marcus said there was another person with you—someone without a badge. Have you recruited *help* now to sabotage me?"

"No." Grace kept her voice even through the spike in her pulse. "No, the guy was just lost and…you know I joke around with Marcus."

Her father pinned her with hawk eyes, a too long beat passing. "He could have been a security risk, Grace. Don't take it upon yourself to bring people into a secure event again."

"Understood," she breathed, silently praying her father would move on and stop asking questions about Aaron. He might have incorrectly referred to her as a crazy girl, but he'd been right about something else. Aaron wouldn't have gotten off with a lecture if he'd been implicated in her crime. No, her father's security team would have loved a chance to recoup the thirty grand by accusing someone other than Pendleton's daughter.

"I wasn't trying to sabotage you," Grace continued. "You know I want you to win, just as much as anyone else. But you have me stuffed in the guesthouse. I can't attend events like Mom and Emily. You keep me hidden and I understand why, but..." Tears clogged her throat, but she squared her shoulders and forced them back. If she cried in front of her father, the discussion would be over. "You're running for office to make a difference. I feel the same need. My methods are just different."

"They're *illegal*." The vein in his neck stood out. "I don't know what else to do for you, Grace. Honestly, I don't. You hate us for what happened and now we're being punished, is that right?"

"No," she whispered. "Not at all. I—"

"I'm keeping you out of the limelight for your own good. Everything we do is for your *own good*." He propped his right arm on the fireplace mantel and rubbed the bridge of his nose with two fingers. "I've tried giving you space, didn't want to keep you confined, but now I'm wondering if this campaign depends on it."

Grace felt the color drain from her face. "What does that mean?"

"It means, starting tomorrow, you'll have heavier security. No more running off into the woods or disappearing for long stretches." He wouldn't look at her. "It's obvious you can't be trusted."

His words were like tiny explosions, detonating in the air next to her ears. "You know I can't be...kept in one place too long," she said, trying to keep her voice even and failing. "You know I'll go—"

She *actually* almost said the word *crazy*, but stopped herself. Or maybe the stone lodged in her throat did the work for her. Either way, she couldn't breathe around the restriction as her father walked to the door. "We can have another discussion if you return the money, but judging from the way you continue to stubbornly defy what this family stands for, I don't see that happening. Nor would I know how to explain the sudden reappearance, courtesy of my own daughter." He continued on his way, pausing before he reached the hallway. "We have a visitor for dinner tonight. Will you be joining us or should I have your meal sent out to the guest house?"

She *should* do the right thing. Smile and make the right comments at the perfect moments, just like her sister. But the prospect of potentially disappointing her father again, right on the heels of taking the money, made the air around her feeling cloying. "Guest house, please."

A long pause. "You have to believe I didn't want it to be like this, Grace."

"I know," she managed, jolting when the door clicked shut.

* * *

Aaron buffed the front of the wine bottle with his jacket sleeve before ringing the doorbell. Honestly, ringing the bell was a mere formality considering he'd gone through a frisking at the gate that would impress the TSA and had his name checked against a list. He'd needed that extra time to pull his head out of his ass. One would think an entire afternoon spent poring over Pendleton's policy and voting records meant Aaron had his shit together, but he couldn't shake the tightness between his shoulder blades, the pinecone rattling around his rib cage.

How many times today had he stopped himself from searching the woods for Grace? Twice he'd gotten as far as the forest's edge, using the excuse of taking Old Man out for a piss. He just wanted to ask her a few questions. That was all. First and foremost, from which mystical land of wild-haired thieves had she been teleported? And what did she need the money for? Was she in trouble?

None of your business. Just like you are none of hers.

The door opened to reveal Pendleton's wife, dressed much the same as she had been that afternoon, a welcoming smile blooming on her face. Shaking off thoughts that shouldn't have been so troubling, Aaron held out the wine bottle, careful to keep a polite distance between himself and the senator's wife.

"Mrs. Pendleton, thank you for having me on short notice," Aaron said, waiting for her to step back so he could cross the threshold, which he did. "I've been on the road, so I can barely remember what a home-cooked meal tastes like."

"Please, call me Beverley." She closed the door. "And we'll have to remedy that, won't we?"

Aaron was relieved when the senator showed almost

immediately, wrapping one arm around his wife's waist, shaking Aaron's hand with the other, all while checking the vintage of the gifted wine.

"Very nice." Pendleton took the bottle from his wife and tapped a finger against the glass. "We'll get this breathing so we can have it with dinner. How long, honey?"

"Ten minutes." She floated off, presumably toward the kitchen. "Give or take."

"She knows I hate approximations," Pendleton sighed. "But she puts up with my bullshit, so I guess we're even. I hope security didn't give you a hard time."

Aaron fell into step beside Pendleton. "Oh, something tells me you wouldn't be too upset if they did."

The senator chuckled, casting Aaron a scrutinizing glance. "I don't want to like you, but you're making it difficult." They entered the dining room and Aaron counted five table settings—one extra?—but didn't have a chance to inquire about an additional guest before the senator continued, "Give me one word, Clarkson. *Change.* Arguably, that single word won a man an election. So what's mine? What's going to turn the tide on my campaign?"

"Respect."

Pendleton set the wine bottle down on the table, rattling carefully placed silverware. "Respect who?"

Aaron slid both hands into his dress pants pockets. "Respect that goes both ways." He let that sink in, noting the senator appeared thoughtful, but not disagreeable. "The government has lost the respect of America's youth and they haven't had enough of ours. You're going to reestablish that mutual esteem as the next president."

The senator picked up a wine opener and twisted the

metal appendage into the cork with quick, precise movements. "How?"

"We want their ideas. We want to hear from them."

Pendleton smirked. "We do?"

Aaron started to laugh, but a picture hanging on the wall behind the senator sucked in every ounce of his attention. Grace. Grace was in the portrait—the family portrait—seated in front of Pendleton, along with the slightly older girl he'd seen at the pancake breakfast. His daughter. Jesus Christ, Grace was Pendleton's *other* daughter? In all his research over the last few weeks, another child had been mentioned only in passing. A budding artist who simply didn't share her father's appreciation for the limelight, but fully supported his political career. There hadn't been any pictures, though. None. Somehow Aaron knew he would have remembered.

The fifth place setting was for her. Acid climbed up through his esophagus, charring the interior, filling his mouth with a smoky taste.

"Clarkson?"

Breathe, asshole. Number one rule in politics? Just keep talking. But...fuck. It was difficult to think, let alone talk. Grace would be there any minute. He *would* see her again, but it could very well lead to his final ruination...because if this nightmare were true, he'd aided her this morning in robbing...her own father.

"Ah, sorry." His hand found the knot in his tie, straightening it. "The demographic we're trying to reach has access to their favorite celebrities today. Twitter, Facebook, Instagram, Snapchat. They've gone from being unreachable to being—or at least creating the illusion of being—peers. Our current president is a celebrity in his own right, as is the first lady." Aaron picked up a wineglass and held it out when the senator extended the bottle, hoping like hell the other man didn't notice his hand shook. "You're not accessible enough. You're their father's candidate, not theirs. You might as well try to reach them through MySpace. But here's the good news: one good sound bite, one good tweet? These days, that's all you need to trend on social media."

"All right, enough shop talk," the senator's wife said, breezing into the dining room holding a covered platter, which she set down in the middle of the table. "Emily will be down in a moment."

Aaron was hyperaware that Grace hadn't been mentioned, especially when Beverley dropped a troubled glance on the fifth place setting, making Aaron's stomach churn.

"Shall we take a seat?" Pendleton boomed, his smile tighter than before. "I have to admit, Clarkson, this idea appeals to me. I'll need the opportunity to bring in my staff for a discussion, but it smells like a definite winner. I think the theme of respect could be interpreted favorably by my older voters, too. Don't want to forget about them."

"Certainly not," Aaron agreed.

When the senator's daughter walked into the room— or skulked, rather—noticeable tension descended over the table, the fifth place setting remaining empty. Beverley passed Aaron a bowl of mashed potatoes, and like that, everyone started to pile food onto their plates without waiting for the final guest.

Grace wasn't coming, it seemed. Unbelievable that he should feel such a distinct ripple of disappointment when her appearance could very well mark the end of his association with Pendleton. The clanging of cutlery tapping against china the only sound being made, glances being exchanged between Pendleton and his wife. Uncomfortable family meals were nothing new to Aaron, but this was different. Something was wrong, it involved Grace, and he couldn't even fucking ask about it.

Everyone at the table ceased their movements when Emily mumbled something beneath her breath, earning a dark look from her father. "We'll discuss it later, Emily. Now is not the time."

"It's never the time, because you're always working." The senator's daughter—Aaron placed her at around twenty-eight—dropped her fork and pushed back from the table. "Y-you can't just keep her out there like a… *prisoner.*"

Oh God. She was talking about Grace. The bite of food Aaron had been in the process of swallowing got stuck halfway down, so he quickly grabbed his wine and washed it the remaining distance. *Prisoner. Prisoner.*

"Sit back down, immediately," Pendleton instructed his daughter, seeming to strive for a lighter tone this time. "Our guest isn't interested in our family squabbles."

"Squabbles?" Emily repeated, trading a look with Beverley, before grabbing her still-full dinner plate. "If she doesn't eat at the table, neither do I."

For long moments after Emily left the dining room, no one said anything. Aaron was still processing everything he'd learned and trying not to panic. Or panic over the fact that he was panicking in the first goddamn place. A sense of urgency with no target had him sliding back his chair and standing.

"My family dinners growing up were never complete until someone started an argument, so thank you for making me feel at home." Aaron laughed, relieved when it didn't sound too forced, and reached out to shake the senator's hand, even though hearing Grace—it *had* to be her—referred to as a *prisoner* sort of made him want to increase his grip until the other man dropped. "We have plenty of time to discuss moving forward and you know where to find me." He turned to Pendleton's wife and nodded. "Dinner was great. Thank you."

"Can I wrap it up for you?" She sounded weary. "You barely got through half."

"No, don't go to any trouble." Aaron pushed his chair beneath the table. "Have a great night. I hope everything works out."

Aaron's first intake of night air outside the house soothed the burning in his lungs, but the relief was temporary. What the hell was the next step? Go back to the cabin, to the company of three people who currently hated him, and attempt to forget what he'd just heard? *Impossible.* He'd climb the fucking walls.

A cool rush of sensation down Aaron's spine made him turn around at the base of the walkway. Behind the estate, across the long expanse of manicured lawn, another, smaller establishment peeked out. A miniature replica of the main house. One window glowed with light, a silhouette barely visible at such a distance. *Y-you just can't keep her out there like a . . . prisoner.*

Was Grace in there?

Voices picked up inside the house, an argument ensuing between Pendleton and his wife. That was Aaron's cue to get the hell out of dodge, since his future employer wouldn't be appreciative of his private discussion being overheard.

Jesus, was he actually considering seeking out Grace right under the senator's nose? He'd made considerable headway with Pendleton tonight, despite his serious indiscretion back in California. And this one would be worse.

A lot worse.

I'm just going to make sure she's okay. Once I know, I'll leave.

Thankful for the darkness, Aaron made for the guesthouse.

CHAPTER FIVE

Grace grimaced at her untouched dinner where it sat on a tray just inside the bedroom door and went back to staring at her distorted image in the window. Her hair hung down on either side of her head in waves that were still slightly damp. When her mother had arrived with the staff hair stylist earlier to wash and detangle her hair, she'd allowed it, even though it had been painful. She didn't regret stealing the money, but hurting her father hadn't sat well. Maybe it never would, no matter their dynamic. But she'd taken the hair washing as penance for her deed. Looking presentable should she happen to draw any media attention would have to be enough.

The trees blew back and forth outside, giving the impression of her face changing shape, again and again. Like one of those haunted house pictures that changes from serene to scary, depending on the angle.

If she were a piece of fabric, she would have been

torn straight down the middle. Not because she'd been defeated. Nope. Indecision, rather, had kept her rooted to the
same spot for an hour. A drumbeat continued to plod along
in her stomach, urging her to complete the mission she'd
organized for herself. The other side of the ripped fabric,
however, was held together by words her father had spoken. Not just tonight, but throughout her life. With one
act, she could repair some of the damage she'd inflicted
on their relationship. But would she feel disloyal to herself
afterward? Wasn't that what she'd been fighting against?

A knocking sound coming from the front entrance
jerked Grace backward where she sat perched on the windowsill. Who could that be? No one in her family
knocked. Her father's security team thinned out in the
evening, usually leaving only a nighttime patrol on duty.
So who was at her door so late in the day?

Fingers curling and uncurling in the hem of her sleep
shirt, Grace prowled out of the bedroom, across the pitch-
black living room, to peer through the peephole. When
Grace saw the identity of her visitor, she rocked back
on her heels, mouth agape. "You shouldn't be here," she
gasped. "Not even a little bit."

"You don't think I know that?" Aaron's growl reached
her through the barrier. "Okay, look. Are you all right,
Grace?"

"Yes," she called, leaning her cheek against the door.
"You can go now."

So much silence passed, Grace assumed he'd left and
wished—wished so *hard*—she didn't feel crestfallen over
it. Not after what he'd said that morning. But she couldn't
help wanting to chase after him. If for no other reason
than to stare into his golden brown eyes and demand he

stare back. Shove his broad shoulders until he complied. Another problem demanded her attention, but the movie star politician kept breezing into the picture and dominating, even though she clearly irritated him. What sense did that make?

Aaron's voice found Grace through the door again and her eyes popped open. When had she closed them? "Can you open the door?" A thud against the hardwood made her face vibrate. "Your answer wasn't very convincing."

Slowly, she went up on her toes to watch him through the peephole again. "Did you bring Old Man with you?"

"Grace, are you being kept in there, or what?" He sounded angry now. "Why didn't you tell me you were the senator's daughter?"

With that, the picture started to clear. Truthfully, she hadn't had to work as hard to keep her identity from Aaron. The times they'd been together, she'd thought there were more interesting things to talk about. "What would you have done differently, if you'd known?"

A beat passed. "I don't want to think about it. I don't like what I come up with when I consider that."

Grace's brow furrowed, her breath catching when he seemed to make eye contact with her through the peephole. Without a command from her brain, Grace's hand reached over and unlocked both deadbolts, watching as Aaron's back straightened, his surprise obvious. She stepped back and allowed the door open a few feet, marveling over the living room's transformation, courtesy of having Aaron walk inside. It went from quiet and empty to rife with life, energy.

Aaron's throat muscles shifted when he saw her, his progress halting just inside the door, that gaze she wanted to hold so badly dipping to her legs and heating. "You have a robe or something you can put on?"

A shiver passed through the lowest region of her belly, warmed and chilled simultaneously by the drop in his tone, but she managed a headshake.

"Of course you don't," Aaron said, whipping off his suit jacket and closing the distance between them in two brisk strides. He seemed so full of plans and purpose until he got close and appeared to realize he'd have to put his arms around her in order to get the jacket on. She couldn't stop staring at his jaw, bunched so *tight*, as his arms surrounded her without touching—not so much as a brush of arms against shoulders—and dropped the jacket around Grace in a plop of warmth. Then he eased back a few steps, looking like the survivor of a tornado. "Better."

"Is it?"

Lines formed between his brows. "What happened to your hair?"

Grace experienced a wave of appreciation, just having someone to talk to about her day—even someone who thought her off. Even someone who was kind of responsible for some of the bad parts. "The hair stylist cut out the ribbons and threw them in the trash. The rest just kind of washed away."

The atmosphere around them went still. Like maybe it was holding its breath. "Are you going to put it back the way it was?"

"I don't know." Discomfort, maybe even grief over having the symbol of her freedom taken away, slid down the walls of her throat, making her speech sound unnatural. "It seems like a lot of work just now."

A handful of seconds passed. "You're supposed to be

smiling and talking about bears and asking me existential questions." He seemed confused by whatever thoughts were moving through his head. "I don't like it when you don't."

"Oh." He'd been very aware of her, hadn't he? Of her *words*. Something compelled her to let Aaron know she'd noticed his qualities, too. Because she had. Way too much. "Why don't *you* smile very often? You have lovely teeth."

The corner of his mouth jumped, as if his body wanted to prove her wrong, but his brain shut the idea down. "I do smile. When it can make some sort of difference."

She nodded, relieved that he'd answered *at all* after the teeth remark. "When you're politicizing."

"Yes."

"Or charming a woman."

Grooves formed between his eyebrows. "I haven't smiled at *you*, have I?"

"No." Her knees turned gooey. "But you're not trying to charm me."

"If I was, I'd be doing a pretty shitty job." He gave her a hot, thoughtful once-over as he raked a hand through his hair. "Smiling is meant to invite people and often mislead them. Make them like you, trust you, want more of you. Those are goals I only have in my professional life."

How could such an astute man not hear the ache in his own voice? "Why?"

"Because it's only a matter of time before they see..." He shook his head. "The smile is a decoy. It's not real. And then they're sorry they ever looked beneath it."

Watching him return to himself, realizing he'd shown a dent in his armor and was horrified by that fact, had Grace holding her breath, lest she release the whimper trying to get loose. With a muttered curse, Aaron marched off, leaving Grace staring after him. When she found him again in the kitchen, it took her a minute to figure out what he was doing. In his hands, he held a pair of scissors, which he'd apparently found in the still-open junk drawer. Concentration evident in his handsome face, he cut strips of his tie, laying them side by side down on the counter. Long, red streaks stark against the white marble like blood. Blood he was shedding in an attempt to fix something he couldn't possibly understand, but maybe sensed was important to her?

Time as Grace knew it suspended itself as Aaron dismantled the entire expensive-looking tie, willing her pulse to quiet down so it wouldn't distract him from restoring a little piece of herself that really wasn't little at all, but huge and personal. She couldn't really keep track of things like minutes over her floundering heartbeat.

When he was finished, he tossed the scissors down on the counter and stepped back, crossing his arms. He nodded at his handiwork, but wouldn't look at Grace. "There. I can get Peggy to string them up...however you had them."

"Would *you* do it?" Grace whispered, knowing she shouldn't. It would have been glorious to feel her new friend's fingers moving through her hair, sifting the strands, but Aaron's fingers? *Oh man.* It was shameful how much she needed to experience it. To imagine them doing something else, such as unclasping her bra or slowly tugging her panties down to her knees. His index finger pushing all the way into her mouth.

His sharp gaze pinned her in place, the planes of his face catching shadows, owning them with his intensity.

"I shouldn't be here, Grace." Despite his statement, he reached out, wrapping his grip around her biceps, and positioned her in front of his much larger frame, wedging her belly up against the counter. "I shouldn't be here. I don't fuck around with girls' hairstyles. Or ribbons, for Christ's *sake*. You hear me?"

With her palms flat on the counter, chest heaving, Grace was grateful Aaron couldn't see her face, positive her mouth was wide open, her eyelids fluttering like a silent movie heroine. "I hear you," she murmured. "Okay."

The kitchen's air stilled, turned expectant, and then, oh God, his fingers were dragging through the crown of her hair. Dividing the thickness. There was no skill to his maneuvers, and Grace gasped mentally at the beauty of it. Had this man ever been out of his depth for a single second in his life? Had she just dragged him into the deep end? How intoxicating…and how good it felt. So good. *So good.* Her scalp tugged as he secured the first slashed remains of his tie. "How many were there before?"

"Four," she breathed. "Like the seasons."

Another tug on the right side of her head, a tight knot being tied. "Speaking of seasons, Grace…" His voice sounded like spikes dragging over concrete. "How many summers have you seen?"

Where before she'd been losing herself to his touch, the right and wrongness of it, now she shot into hyperawareness, his question signaling a crack in the foundation they were standing on. "Twenty-three."

His rough exhale bathed her neck. Relief?

"How many summers for you?"

Another knot was made, this one less gentle than the first two. "Twenty-six."

The grim way he answered made Grace wonder if a three-year age gap was a big problem for him. Sure sounded like it. But that would be ridiculous, wouldn't it? That would suggest he was interested at all. And she kind of thought they'd established he wasn't. He viewed the way she acted, the way she spoke as *not normal*. Then again, Aaron wouldn't be the first man who'd been baffled by Grace, but pursued her anyway, right? One of those guys who shook their heads, clearly recording her comments to laugh about with their buddies later on, but still hoping to hook up.

None of them had ever asked for more bear talk, though. Or mutilated their clothing to avenge her ribbons. *What if he wants me because of how I think and not in spite of it?* That would be really, *really*...amazingly nice. She'd been turned on before, but in a purely down low, physical way. Nothing like the clammy-handed, thick-tongued tingling situation she was in the midst of now.

She became very conscious of her thighs. Her bottom, only inches from Aaron's lap. His chest throwing heat onto her back. How would it feel be horizontal, to have that big chest flush with her spine, sliding up and back? If it felt half as good as the fingers in her hair, the answer was: *extraordinary.*

"I'm not a virgin," she murmured, looking back at him over her shoulder. "I went to art school."

Aaron froze in the act of tying the final ribbon into her hair. With a hasty pull, he finished the job, before taking Grace by the elbow and turning her around. Bringing their faces a breath apart. "Did I ask if you were a virgin?"

"No." His mouth would be so easy to reach. Would he recoil or welcome her? "I volunteered the information."

Her pulse nearly jumped through her skin as Aaron gathered the hem of her nightshirt, turning it slowly in his fist. "What else are you volunteering for?" Before she could deliver an unknown answer, Aaron's head dropped forward, the hand in her shirt releasing the bunched material, lifting to cover her mouth. "Don't answer that. I don't want to know."

"Are you sure?" Grace asked, his hand muffling her question.

For too long, he only stared at her. "I can't know these things about you. I can't..." His lids fell. "I can't walk out of here smelling like you."

Grace's lips parted against his palm, probably leaving condensation in the curved creases. Such a...primal thing for a man like him to say. A man without a hair out of place, without a wrinkle in his clothing or demeanor. *Most* of the time. Right now, in the abbreviated light of her kitchen, her hair freshly mussed from his touch, Aaron had gone back to being the man in the woods. The one who'd treated her words like they carried weight. And maybe, just maybe, kind of liked her.

When his hand fell away from her mouth, Grace realized she'd liked having it there. The kick in his breathing made her wonder exactly how much he'd enjoyed it, too. "How did you know where to find me?"

"I didn't." Was that an agonized note in his voice? She would never know because he cleared it away. "I didn't. Your father is the man I needed to meet with this morning. He invited me to dinner and I...saw your photograph on the wall."

"Oh." He'd had dinner with her father. Likely her mother and sister, too. The image sparked discomfort somewhere in her subconscious, but she chalked it up to jealousy. Aaron had been her secret and now her family was in on it. They were experiencing him now, too. "Was it the picture in the hallway or dining room?"

"Dining room. Why?"

"My mother made us dress in all white for the dining room photo." Pushing aside the unsettled feeling wrought by Aaron dining with her parents, then coming to her door unexpectedly, she lifted her arm to sniff his jacket sleeve. Expensive cologne greeted her—and a hint of dog food. "I spilled grape juice down the front of my dress on the ride to the photography studio, so I had to wear it backwards. Did you notice?"

Aaron huffed. "No, Grace, I was a little busy figuring out what would happen when you walked into the room." His eyes cut to the side. "But you didn't come and..."

She went up on tiptoe. "And?"

"And..." He pulled the jacket more securely around her with an abrupt, no-nonsense jerk. "I started wishing you would. I thought maybe you eating dinner alone some- where was worse than—"

"My dad finding out we know each other?" she whis- pered, positive she'd just elevated a foot off the ground.

"Something like that." He visibly withdrew into him- self. "What are you going to do with the stolen money?"

Grace dropped back down to earth. "Is that why you're really here? To find out where I hid it...for my father?"

An eyebrow rose. "You hid it?"

Dammit. "I didn't say that."

"Oh, yes. You did."

Grace eased out of Aaron's jacket and held it out for him to take, but he only frowned at the offering. She refused to let her hand drop, though. This man confused her. Confused her body. She'd never been attracted to some-one like Aaron before. Someone her mind told her she shouldn't like, while every other vital part of her went heart-shaped with him nearby. He gave her one inch, then dragged her back two. With a past like Grace's, confusion was the enemy, especially when it came to judging a per-son's character. So this was it. The decision she'd been agonizing over before he knocked on the door would be his to make.

And hope willing, his actions would finally give her a solid read on Aaron.

"Here." Grace tossed the jacket at Aaron, who caught it. "I'll take you to the money. You can bring it back to my father. Or you can help me finish my job. It's your choice."

Motors spun inside his head, practically visible behind his intelligent eyes. "What's your game?"

"I don't have one. I'm trying to figure out yours."

"Who says I have one?"

Grace leaned back against the counter, propped on her elbows, realizing too late how her position elevated the hem of her nightshirt to the tops of her thighs. "Um…" Gaze falling to her revealed flesh, Aaron made a gruff noise, rolling his tongue along the inside of his lower lip. "I can't figure out why you're here, when it could mean losing your chance to work for my father."

Their eyes locked and held as Aaron stepped within an inch of her body, his rigid posture suggesting he didn't have a choice. "If you can't figure out why I'm here, hip-pie," he breathed against her ear, "we've got something bigger to worry about than the games we're playing."

God, she hated puzzles, wished everyone would just

speak their minds. Life would be so much easier. It only took a slight turn of her head to bring their cheeks together. Rough against smooth. "If you want me, could you just say it?"

Aaron's laughter was devoid of humor, his hands brushing the hem of her shirt, whispering along the tops of her thighs. "I already knew I was a fucking bastard, but at least I was in control of it." His swallow was audible. "I want to ask you questions, Grace. About yourself. You understand? But answering them the way I hope you will might give me permission." A breeze met her belly, telling Grace he'd drawn up the garment. "But the things I've done would make it wrong of me to take that permission. And normally I wouldn't *care* if I was bad for someone. That *alone* is reason enough to tell me to back off. So even though I want to..." He twisted the shirt tighter and tighter, his breath growing choppy. "Want to watch your eyes go wide, want to watch you catch my thrusts with your hands-off body...I'd buy myself a ticket to hell for it."

Be careful what you wish for. She'd wanted him to be honest, hadn't she? Now there was so much to process. Not an easy task when she was exposed below the waist, Aaron's erection lying against her thigh. *He's heavy.* "Ask me the questions. The ones that'll give you permission." *To get closer. To touch me.*

His exhale was deafening in her ear. "No."

Grace squeezed her eyes shut and searched her mind, remembering his outburst in the morning while she hid in the closet and landing on the likeliest possibility. "I'm not crazy." He stilled, that grip on her shirt intensifying. "You know that when you look at me, don't you?"

Aaron's frown collided with what she hoped was a level look, despite her thundering pulse and his mouth was *still right there. Kiss me. Just do it.* "I see a thousand things when I look at you," he said. "I don't know if I'm landing on the right one."

Her bones turned to liquid, but thankfully the counter and Aaron's body kept her standing upright. "It's so much better when you say your thoughts out loud," she whispered. "Keep doing that, okay?"

As if her mental compelling had finally worked, his mouth came closer. Closer. She could feel his breath on her tongue, didn't care if her parted lips made her seem overeager. She'd thought their kiss that morning would be the first and last, so the possibility of another made her blood dance. *Breathe. Don't take the lead. Let him.* That was how it was done, right? That's what her past love interests had told her when she attempted to explore. But she never got the chance to try the right way, because Aaron stopped. He stopped with only a smidge left to travel, his golden brown eyes—so *alive* and maybe sort of baffled, in that moment—boarded up like an abandoned house as he pulled back.

"Enough, Grace." He let go of her shirt, the material floating down around her legs. "Take me to the money."

An axe fell in her midsection, cutting down the hoard of fluttering butterflies. It happened so swiftly and in tandem with his body being taken away, she reeled, catching herself on the counter. From the corner of her eye, she thought Aaron might have reached out, but she didn't have the energy to confirm.

With doom riding on her shoulders, Grace went to go change.

CHAPTER SIX

None of the Clarkson siblings had never been close to their father.

Except for Aaron.

Lawrence and Miriam had divorced while all four of them were still relatively young. In the beginning, their father had made an effort, picking them up once a week in his silver Taurus to treat them to pizza. And it *had* been a treat, because when your mother is a world-renowned chef, pizza wasn't on the menu very often. Not unless it had truffle oil or a quail egg on top.

Aaron could recall the stunted attempts at conversation while waiting for Lawrence to hand over the arcade tokens, which he'd stockpile in his right pocket like water gathering in the clouds before a big storm. Peggy bouncing in her seat, Rita and Belmont brooding into their sodas at the far edge of the table. Aaron dying for the coins to be distributed so his siblings would bail and he could talk to his father alone, without catching eye rolls from his sisters.

It was the last time Aaron saw his father that stuck with him, though. Belmont hated accepting the tokens from Lawrence, and although Aaron surmised it was due to having a different father, Belmont had never confirmed his feelings on the matter. *Huge fucking shock.* That afternoon, the four of them were playing pinball—the Addams Family version—while Aaron and his father watched from the dining room.

"What do you think of the big one?" Lawrence had asked. "Belmont."

After waiting all week to have ten minutes alone with his dad, Aaron was disappointed his grades or Thursday night's soccer match hadn't been the topic of discussion, but he'd also been curious over the way his father spoke about Belmont. "He's my brother," Aaron said, collecting soda with his straw, capping the end with a finger, and dumping it into his mouth. "Why?"

"He's only *half* your brother." The comment had been offhand, but it made Aaron uncomfortable. At home, they were just a family, regardless if their fathers were different. "You can tell which one of you is *my* son. It's like looking into a mirror."

Aaron cast a reluctant glance toward the arcade. He didn't like feeling proud that he'd been compared to his father, while Belmont had been disregarded. But he couldn't stop it, either. "You really think we're the same?"

"I do." Lawrence drummed a fist on the table. "You don't need games like the rest of them. All you need is yourself. Your *mind*. No one and nothing else. That's how it has always been for me." He sopped up a drop of grease with his napkin. "People like your mother tried to make me into something I'm not. But guess what? If she'd succeeded, she'd have just wanted me to be something new at the end of it."

Aaron loved his mother. And he didn't mind playing arcade games once in a while, but he figured everything Lawrence said made sense. If his father—an adult—said something, it had to be true. "Yeah, I guess so."

"You *know* so." His father held his gaze. "Now run over and tell the others it's time to go."

When Aaron arrived in the arcade, Belmont had been a few pings away from tying the high score record. With his father's approval and being singled out as the best riding on his back, Aaron stuck his foot behind the machine and unplugged the game.

Regret had flooded him right away, burning the skin of his cheeks. He wanted to take the action back. But it was too late. He'd watched his siblings slink back to the dining room, Peggy rubbing circles into Belmont's back. Aaron had started to follow, but his father approached and stopped him, slapping a hand down on his shoulder. "Someone like you doesn't need to apologize. You're just embracing your nature."

Torn between pride and shame, Aaron had only managed a nod. His father's visits had remained steady for another year and sometimes he only took Aaron for pizza, his sisters and Belmont begging off. Aaron told his father everything. About every fight with his siblings, soccer drama, girls. And then one day, he'd never shown up again.

After having Belmont cut him off, Lawrence disappearing had been like déjà vu.

Although he saw one on occasion, he'd never truly gotten either of them back.

Lawrence had tried to instill many lessons—some of which had stuck—but the ultimate one hadn't been intentional. Aaron didn't have what it took inside him to keep people near. So he didn't let anyone nose around. Having his lack of goodness acknowledged was almost as bad as seeing someone he cared about turn their back.

A branch snapping beneath Aaron's feet brought him into the pitch-black woods, following Grace's slight figure as she led him to the stolen campaign money. Get the money, return it to the senator, get ahead. Right?

Right.

"What were you planning on doing with it?"

Why even ask the question? Was he attempting to make this march to the gallows even harder for her? Fuck, this didn't feel right. Nothing had felt right since he'd woken up that morning, but he'd chalked it up to nerves over sneaking into a nationally televised event. It wasn't so far-fetched that he'd experience some tension.

This was nothing like *that*. Grace's shoulders slouched forward, her face hidden by her newly tamed mane. Hair he'd made the mistake of touching and now nothing would ever feel smooth again. Or smell as earthy, the coming home sensation of those strands sifting through his fingers making him feel balanced. What the fuck was *balance* at this point in time?

He might as well be holding a gun to the girl's back. Jesus, he didn't know himself anymore. He wasn't exactly known for being nice to people—on a *good* day—but this mean streak aimed at one specific person was new. Was it because the questions she asked, the way she looked at him...made him look inward a little too far?

"Answer me," Aaron said around the lodgment in his throat.

She tossed her hair back and finally—*finally*—looked at him. Something she hadn't done since he'd almost slipped and kissed her in the kitchen. It broke his stride and made him want *more*. Constant focus. All of it. *Don't think about her upturned face, those damp lips.* His groin ached with the memory and it wouldn't quit its attack on his consciousness. But more than anything, he wanted back the trust she'd displayed by letting him tie ribbons into her hair. Since when did he care about personal trust? "No. I'm not going to tell you what I was going to do with it," she said. "You made your decision. You don't get to know what's behind door number two."

When she started walking faster, Aaron caught up with her, quelling the impulse to grip her elbow. Hurl apologies like water balloons and fuck if he knew what they would entail. "Slow down before you break your neck."

"What a shame that would be," she muttered. "You'd never find the money."

He threw up his hands with a heartfelt curse. "How did I become the asshole when you're the one who stole money from your own father?" As soon as he said the words, regret passed through him like a dark cloud. "Just tell me why, Grace."

Instead of answering, she stopped and pointed toward her feet. Aaron had to hand it to her—she'd done a good job of hiding any trace. Handing over his cell phone—flashlight app engaged—Aaron crouched down and performed the job of digging up what looked to be two pillowcases. Stuffed full of fives, twenties, singles. Seeing the cash in reality made the whole thing seem petty. Like walking through a museum full of fine art and exiting through a gift shop. Especially when he looked up at Grace, finding her still as a statue, eyes fixed on some spot past his shoulder.

And he told himself it was curiosity—even though his bullshit detector went off, loud as an ambulance siren— that had him handing the bags to Grace. He would surely regret the decision in the morning, but just then, Grace was real. The money wasn't. It had no value in the woods, even if tomorrow it certainly would and he'd be calling himself a fool. "All right. Let's go."

Grace split a puzzled look between Aaron and the pillowcases he'd handed over. "Go where?"

"You wouldn't tell me, remember?" He stood, rolling the stiffness out of his neck, brushing the dirt off his trousers. "Look, technically, I'm already an accessory, since I didn't report you climbing out of the window, like I should have. Might as well royally fuck myself—"

Grace threw herself at him, the impact of her body cutting off his explanation. "Shut up, you liar." The words were muffled against his neck. "You can't always explain why something is a good decision, can you? Neither can I. No one can, right?"

Excluding his sisters at events like graduation or Christmas, Aaron had never hugged a girl in his life. Not like this. Not out of happiness, hers or otherwise. On instinct, his arms moved around her, one at her upper back, the other just above her hips. And he tugged the curved little package of her close, just a test. *Just a test.* "Don't you dare get used to this, Grace."

"The hugging?" Her breathy voice sounded right at home in the forest. "Or having you surprise me?"

"Both." *Let her go now. Time to let her go.* "Don't make the mistake of thinking I could be a good man. I will let you down."

Grace stepped out of his embrace with a solemn nod. "But not tonight?"

He couldn't answer that. Couldn't even tell her he'd remain at his current level of decency for one measly night. If that didn't signal to both of them how little they made sense together, nothing would. Hell, hadn't it taken him less than one day to betray his potential new employer? A man who'd overlooked his past transgressions and given him another, coveted chance?

A vision of his foot behind the pinball machine, kicking the wire free, invaded, forcing him to rub his palms down the sides of his pants. "Lead the way, Robin Hood."

Ten minutes later, they were cutting through the cold Iowa darkness in the Suburban, Aaron wondering what the hell he'd gotten himself into. Grace couldn't stop smiling in the passenger seat, reminding him of a nun who'd broken free of the convent. Or she *might* have, if her legs weren't encased to uncomfortable—for him—perfection in purple leggings. Or if he hadn't noticed her distinctly non-holy lack of panty lines when she'd boosted herself into the vehicle. He'd wanted to haul her back out of the Suburban, press her against the side, and yank the purple cotton down to confirm. God help them both if she'd left her house panty-less, with a man whose cock had been painfully distended since she'd answered the door in a see-through T-shirt, her little nipples tenting the white material.

He still didn't have an adequate gauge of Grace's mental state. Or rather, what *other* people had decided about her mental state. Despite his words of frustration earlier—despite her having a handler and eating in a different location than her family when a guest came over for dinner—Aaron's gut told him that while Grace might talk, act, and reason differently, there was a high chance she was better adjusted than he was. But his attraction to her took away his objectivity. Big time. His body had been hot for contact with hers since she climbed backward through the window, so he couldn't trust himself. What if he allowed himself to pursue his attraction to Grace? When he turned out to be a callous motherfucker—and he would—she'd be hurt. And not in the way some women of his experience were offended when he didn't call. No, as with everything else, Grace would react differently.

And the idea of her being hurt made his insides burn.

"Take this turnoff," Grace instructed, breaking into his thoughts. "It's not far."

Aaron steered the Suburban off Interstate 235, turning the windshield wipers on when snow began to fall. Not a lot, just a light flurry, but enough to make someone from California take turns with exaggerated slowness. Something he realized when Grace's soft laugh reached him and he looked over, finding her cross-legged on the seat, pillowcases puffed in her lap, watching him with amused eyes. "Have you ever driven in the snow before?"

"Does yesterday count?"

She pursed her lips. "I guess."

"Try for a little more sarcasm next time." Unbelievable. He actually felt self-conscious. "Do you drive?"

"Not lately. Not since I lived in Austin." She turned in the seat, dropping her feet to the floor. "But when I drove, it wasn't like a grandpa."

"Mario Andretti is a grandpa. Maybe you meant that as a compliment."

"I didn't," she replied breezily.

Aaron caught sight of his reflection in the speedometer, surprised to find himself smiling—without a conscious effort—and quickly dimmed it. "Belmont drives slower than I do. My brother," he explained when Grace lifted an eyebrow. "The mountain you ran into. When you were..."

"Leaving your cabin," she finished, not looking at him anymore, making the back of Aaron's neck itch. "You don't look like brothers."

"We don't act like them, either." He rolled to a stop at a red light, watching the flurries dance along the asphalt, spinning in the headlight beams. "Or maybe we do. He's the only one I have to judge against."

"Turn right at the next light," Grace said, leaning forward to peer through the windshield. "My sister and I were close. Really close. But she didn't...they separated us one summer and things were different after that."

The light turned green and Aaron reluctantly hit the gas, Grace's words ricocheting in his head. "Separated you how?"

"Up ahead." Aaron had no choice but to drop the subject—what the hell was the subject anyway?—when Grace tapped on the passenger's side window, indicating a two-story brick building, tucked back from the road, the front courtyard surrounded by a black, chain-link gate. "There. I'll just be a minute."

Aaron threw the Suburban into Park, scoffing into the

sudden silence, void of the engine hum. "You're not going by yourself. I don't even know what this place is."

He climbed out of the vehicle, rounding the front fender and pulling open Grace's door. She held out one of the pillowcases to Aaron, turned, and started to jump from the Suburban—but a blast of protectiveness had Aaron catching her midair with an arm around her waist, easing her down slowly until both feet were firmly on the ground.

But he couldn't let go. Her breasts were pushed up even higher than usual because they'd dragged down his chest and hadn't had a chance to bounce yet. He tugged her close, tight, and watched them plump, groaning like an agonized bear. She seemed to will his mouth closer with a bat of her eyelashes and his head dropped forward, as if she'd commanded it...and he had no control...none.

The loss of will was so unfamiliar, Aaron released Grace and stepped back as if he'd been burned. A hammer pounding in his head and behind his fly, he pivoted on a heel and made for the gate so she wouldn't see the confusion on his face. Why did this girl continue to inspire such a need to be something he wasn't? For damn sure he wasn't some chivalrous knight who went around snatching damsels in distress out of the air and kissing them, like a scene that played out while movie credits rolled. And the sooner the night ended and he could snuff out any future confusion about his self-image, the better.

Grace drew even with him at the gate, which was locked. He watched in dawning realization that she'd been there before when she reached up and pressed a Call button on a recessed silver keypad, causing a light to come on and a camera to buzz into activity. Grace smiled at the electronic eye and Aaron banked the urge to shove her behind his back. Instead, he peered through the fence for some clue as to where they were, getting ready to hand over a bundle of cash.

Just above the single black door, a small sign was hung, illuminated by a dull spotlight that flickered in the snow, which had begun to fall harder.

YouthAspire.

CHAPTER SEVEN

The name *YouthAspire* triggered some recognition for Aaron, but he couldn't place it. And he didn't have time to ponder it further because the gate clicked open, a light going on at the end of the walkway. Aaron looked down to find Grace's eyes on him, snowflakes clinging to her eyelashes.

"You should go to the door," she whispered, pressing the second pillowcase into his free hand. "Maybe it'll help you understand why I did it." On cue, Aaron opened his mouth to list all the reasons he wasn't walking up to some strange building and depositing two bags of cash—it could be a brothel in disguise for all he knew—but found there was only one factor that seemed to matter, standing there on the silent street. He didn't want Grace going. Not when he didn't know what was on the other side of the door.

"Right. Let's go make me a felon." He transferred both

pillowcases into one hand and dug the car keys out of his pocket, handing them to Grace. "Go wait in the Suburban. Doors locked."

To his surprise, she nodded, floating off to do as he'd asked. Grumbling under his breath, Aaron trudged up the path, swatting snow off the lapels of his jacket as he went. Just before he reached the end, the black door creaked open—and two young girls poked their heads out. Which, obviously, made Aaron stop in his tracks.

"Where is Grace?" one of them asked.

"Out of the way now," came a voice from inside. An adult voice, thank Christ. Both little girl heads vanished and a woman in her mid-to-late forties filled the doorway, taking Aaron's measure with a sweeping glance. A former sea captain, he thought absurdly. "What's this? Where's Grace?"

Dimly, he registered an Irish brogue, but he wasn't exactly in the state of mind to be charmed by it. He nodded toward the vehicle, sighing when Grace waved in the passenger window, all but bouncing in her seat. "There she is," Aaron said, sounding grim. "She asked me to drop this off to you."

Aaron advanced, holding out the bags, just as the two girls appeared again, one slipping between the Irish woman's body and the door frame, the other from between the woman's legs.

"What is this place?"

"Sure, she didn't tell you?" The woman laughed heartily but, in a curious contrast, regarded the pillowcases with trepidation. "We wouldn't be here anymore if it weren't for that one." She whispered something under her breath. "No, we'd be something else altogether."

He rubbed at his jaw. "I'm going to need a little more than that." One of the little girls waved at Aaron, the edges of his mouth lifting to return the greeting with a smile before the response registered. Annoyed with himself and the lack of forthcoming information, he gave them a brisk nod instead. "Is this some kind of orphanage?"

"Eh. Of a sort. We're still figuring out the particulars." The woman shooed both girls away, her demeanor good-natured. "If you don't mind me saying..." She eyed Aaron's wingtips. "You don't seem the kind of man who does anything without knowing all the details."

"You're right." Obviously the woman wasn't planning on taking the pillowcases anytime this century, so Aaron stepped forward and slid them just inside the door. "I'm not."

She was looking down at the bags of cash when she spoke. "Well. If anyone could convince you to take a night off from your scruples, it would be Grace." Snow puffed onto the walkway in the ensuing pause. "Tell her thank you. Tell her to be careful. I needn't see her again for a while, looks like."

Anxious to get back to Grace and begin a new line of questioning, he murmured a good night and strode back to the vehicle, pulling away from the curb as soon as the ignition sparked. *Leaving the scene of the crime. Good God.*

"All right, Grace—"

"Thank you." Her words were accompanied by a blast of cold and white snowflakes, caused by her rolling down the passenger's side window, flinging her right arm out into the night, and tossing her head back. "Thank you," she said again, this time more high-pitched, but still in her usual musical delivery.

She was not from Earth in that moment. Aaron couldn't keep his eyes on the road as they constantly returned to Grace. Moisture dotted her cheeks, although he couldn't tell if the tracks were created by melted condensation or tears—and it didn't matter, because there was so much more to take in. The hair flying around her face like she'd been filmed sinking underwater, then fast-forwarded. It flew and tangled and danced, strands and swaths of his red silk tie catching on her damp face. Her eyes were closed, but she was seeing everything. Aaron could never express the certainty of it. Or the desperation to know what she could see. To hear her describe it.

He didn't realize he'd pulled over, alongside a barren stretch of field, until Grace opened the door, jumped out...and took off running. Panic gripped his throat, but he fought through, all but diving out of the Suburban to go after her. Heart pounding triple time in his chest, Aaron caught sight of her form, illuminated by the still-engaged headlights.

"Grace," he shouted. "Get back here."

His legs turned to marble as she spun around, arms outstretched, laughing up at the sky. Torn. He was so fucking torn. Between worry and...envy. *Look at her*, he had the odd urge to shout. *Just look at her.* The jacket she wore had unbuttoned down the front and that's what propelled him forward—the fear that she would freeze to death. When he reached Grace, it was as though she'd felt him approach, because she threw her arms around his neck, warm breath ghosting down his neck, all the way inside his shirt. "Don't be worried," she breathed. "I can tell you're worried."

He curled his hands around Grace's biceps, setting her

away so he could yank her coat together, buttoning it with unnecessarily rough movements, but they stilled on a dime when she laid her warm hands on top of them, his white breath puffing out between them in rapid bursts. "I don't like surprises, Grace."

"That's a shame," she whispered. "People say I'm full of them."

"Right now, I'd have to agree."

Grace's touch fell away. She stepped back, lifting her face to the sky. "There's so much bad. Happening all the time, around us. I guess I just…" Her chin lowered and the emotion in her gaze almost knocked him back a step. "I like to stop and appreciate when something good happens."

The snow had grown steadily heavier, white flakes landing on her face, her hair, and melting in degrees. His tongue felt thick in his mouth as he stood watching Grace, trying to process the meaning of her words. Afraid he would miss what she might do next. *I'm in a field in a strange place… and I'm not trying to change that.* So unlike him just to stand still and wait. Wait.

"That place." She rubbed at her throat. "It used to be a leadership camp for teenagers. They had a… tragedy and it was almost closed down. But it didn't need to be snuffed out, only changed. You can't throw ideas or people out when they don't work the first time around, right?"

Her forehead wrinkled, as if finding the right words was frustrating, and for once, they were on the same page. "What if all we get are moments, Aaron? Like this. Like back there. We work and *try* and sit and stand and what are we working toward? I think… moments. And we—me and you—got to have one tonight. We got to make a moment for a bunch of other someones. So can we just stop and think about it? That's all I'm doing. I'm thinking in my own way, even if it looks like something else to you. I'm just stopping. And thinking."

He couldn't swallow. Every time he tried, his throat clogged, pressure piling on top of pressure. "Okay," he finally managed. "Okay, fine."

But he wasn't fine when she moved closer. Moved closer to the raw, exposed hunk of flesh, formerly known as Aaron. It was insane. Everything was insane. She was forcing him to consider light and shadows, when he'd only ever dealt in black and white. And she was the light. Shining bright enough to flay him.

He'd operated until now as if people were only hiding selfishness, the kind he didn't bother to conceal. But not Grace. She contradicted everything he held true and it made the earth shake under his feet. She approached him like a lion tamer approaching their target, as if he might get startled and eat her whole. Was *he* the sane one here? Or had it been *her* the whole time? It couldn't be both of them, could it? His thoughts fled when Grace laid her ear over his heart, gasping at whatever she heard. "You feel it, too. You feel the good we did?"

"I don't know."

A smile broke across her face. "That's okay. It's your first time."

"Were you part of that tragedy, Grace?" Aaron didn't know where the suspicion sprung from or how he picked it out among the million questions and thoughts rocketing around his skull. But there it was. "I think you were."

It took him a few beats to realize she wasn't breathing, but she drew in a heavy dose of oxygen before he could shake her. "Moments, Aaron. This is one of them. Come live in it with me." She brushed some snow out of his hair, soft fingertips grazing his ear. "Please?"

Fucked. No other way to describe the situation he'd been sucked into. His body was winded and exhilarated, adrenaline seeping into his bloodstream and warming him, making him hot along with Grace's nearness. He'd been thrown into a vast ocean without a life jacket, and she was reaching out with something resembling help, but it was so foreign and nothing like he'd ever experienced that gripping on to it was difficult. Slipping. It kept slipping. What finally forced him to *hold the fuck on* was Grace. She was in the same ocean. Maybe she was *always* there. What if having him reach out and clasp on was the rescue *she* needed?

Aaron operated from a different plane of consciousness, sliding one hand into Grace's hair, the other around her back. He twined the fragrant, but mussed, strands of hair around his fingers and tilted her head back, watching as her eyelids drifted down, catching snowflakes on their descent. Nothing in his life had ever appeared more vivid, more real, than her panting, parted lips, inviting his mouth down. And he went, because there was no choice to make, melding their open lips together, followed by a wet mating of tongues. A groan he'd been holding in since they'd first crossed paths fell from his mouth like a ten-pound rock. Kisses in fields beneath a light snowfall should be sweet. They *should* be.

Only, he didn't have any idea what the fuck *sweet* meant. Especially when it came to physical interaction with a woman. Nor was he feeling anything resembling such a dainty description. No, with her lips struggling to get wide beneath his, attempting to handle each slanting assault from his mouth, Aaron's cock surged, rousing in his briefs like a prodded snake. But with his eyes closed, he could only see the smiling girl spinning madly in a snowy field—like some mystical fairy—and denial had him breaking the kiss.

"Grace," he growled into her mouth. "We don't make sense. You . . ." God, he couldn't keep his thoughts straight with her body curved around his, tightly, like they'd been glued together. "You see this field and you see a place to run."

"Yes." Didn't it figure with the most insane shit coming out of his mouth, Grace appeared to follow him without a hitch? "What do you see?"

"Nothing. I see *nothing*." His hand cupped the right side of her ass, settling the notch of her thighs over his dick, need spreading like an epidemic. "That's not true. I see a place where no one would witness it if I took you on the filthy ground."

Her head fell back, as if her neck had lost power. "I think that means we make perfect sense," she said on a bursting exhale. "It's so much better when you say your thoughts out loud and I don't have to guess. Have I mentioned that?"

As if an unspoken command had been issued, their mouths met again, worked each other's in a furious, damp slide. Aaron's arm around her back tightened. He was so thirsty for the untamed taste of Grace that he bent her all the way backward, rolling his hips against her without an anchor, no wall to push her up against save the wind. God, *more*. He required all of her against him. How had he gone this long without it?

The wicked spike of testosterone in Aaron must have affected Grace somehow, because she turned into a hot, frantic bundle of sex in his arms, trying to hug his hips with the insides of her thighs. Trying to drive him out of his mind with the soft warmth of her pussy, making him groan every time it brushed his lap. *No condom. I don't have a condom.* The agonizing realization was a blessing and a curse at the same time. A blessing because Grace was better than what Aaron wanted to give her. Which was to pull her leggings down, so he could deliver a knees-buried-in-the-dirt fucking that she'd feel for weeks. A curse, because...Aaron could feel how bad she needed it—almost as badly as he did—even if it would be bad for her.

Beneath her.

Faceless ghosts from another time and place...the sting of being called a betrayer tried to steal his focus, but ignoring them was easy with Grace's mouth under his. The threatening memories only served to make him more aggressive, though, as if Grace could cleanse him, impossible though it was.

"Aaron," she moaned, breaking away from the round of furious kissing. Eyes blind, breath racing, thighs sliding up and down the outside of his legs. "Aaron, oh my God, please..."

Aaron's fingers were working the buttons of her coat before his brain could command him to stop. There was no ignoring her plea for relief; it stole his remaining ability to reason. To remember why touching her, satisfying his curiosity, was bad. Against the rules. With a curse over the heaviness in his groin, Aaron flattened his palm on her stomach, sliding into the front of her leggings. "Okay, hippie." He encountered dampness layered over smooth, hairless skin—a fucking jerk-off fantasy come true. She was a *mess* of want, the evidence wetting her sex, moistening the purple leggings. "*Fuck*, Grace. If I had a condom, nothing would save you now. Not after feeling this." He found the entrance of her body, shoving two fingers far as they would travel, both of their bodies jerking at the perfection of that connection. His groan was so ragged, he didn't recognize his own voice. "I knew you weren't wearing underwear. Maybe you *wanted* help getting dressed. Do you like the idea of me sliding a tight pair of panties up your thighs? Tugging the edges right and left until your lips are covered?"

"Yes." She went up on her toes and the move slid her curves over his muscles, courtesy of the death grip his arm had on her body. But she slipped back down in a boneless drop when Aaron began drawing his fingers in and out. In and out. Stopping to tease her clit with a twisting knuckle, feeling it swell with such tangible pleasure, no reservations. "More, more, more," she whispered, gaze growing so glassy Aaron wasn't sure she could *see* him anymore. And he was nervous without her focus, because he'd been dropping into the middle of the fucking ocean with only her presence to keep him afloat.

"Hey. *Grace.* You need to look at me, dammit." His fingers thrust home and held, urgency climbing up his spine like insistent claws. "Be...here with me. Don't do this to me and just leave."

The green of her eyes snapped, her teeth digging into that full bottom lip, but there she was. She found his forehead with her own, grinding them together just a little, and the pressure was welcome. So fucking welcome. As if she'd known that simple action would calm the foreign war taking place on the soil of his brain. A brain to which she'd found an undiscovered trapdoor and crawled inside. "I'm here. Your fingers feel so good. I can't believe you're touching me like this. I wanted you to." Her gorgeous little body started to shake, her teeth clenching the same time as her pussy started to seize up around his touch. "I wanted to hold your hand in the woods, too. But this is better. *Better.* I'm going to..."

"Christ. Do it. Go on, Grace. Fill up my palm with the best you've got." Aaron ducked his head to suck a trail up the side of Grace's neck, unable to resist a bite beneath her earlobe. Another one. "Girls who get so wet from kissing shouldn't leave the house without underwear, should they? No. And they definitely shouldn't leave the house with someone like me. I don't hold hands. I shouldn't be allowed within ten feet of you." He spoke the words angrily into her neck. "*This* is what I do. I return you home with a dirty secret."

Half of him expected to be pushed off, away from the hottest female flesh he'd even sunk his fingers into. He wished for it, even though he knew he'd come crawling back, begging to finish the job. Finish her off. None of that was necessary, though, because the words he'd meant as a warning seemed to hoist her over the precipice, her walls closing in to milk his fingers in nothing short of exquisite torture. Because fuck, he needed to feel that squeeze, that trickling fall of moisture around his cock so bad, he tilted his head back and growled into the falling snow.

"Aaron," Grace moaned, fisting the lapels of his jacket. One hand slid free, up his throat and into his hair, yanking his head down to engage in an open-lipped kiss. Their tongues didn't touch, thank God, because he might have taken out his dick and begged her to use that tongue where it counted. "Ohhh," she breathed, her body going totally limp in his arms without warning, their mouths disengaging.

And there he was, dipping a girl backward in a moonlit field, her back bent so far that her hair brushed along the ground. As if they'd been dancing, instead of him finger banging her, telling her obscene things to make her come. "Grace—"

"Shhh." She extended her arms up toward the night sky. "Two moments in one night. That's something, isn't it?"

His throat ached worse than he'd ever felt it. "I need to get you home."

With a sigh, she straightened and gained her feet, planting a lingering kiss on his lips and floating toward the Suburban. "Okay." Her eyes sparkled, legs wobbling, as she glanced back at him over her shoulder. "Let's go, Grandpa."

CHAPTER EIGHT

Grace smiled when she crossed her legs in the passenger seat and felt a tug of discomfort at the juncture of her thighs. She hadn't lied to Aaron about her sexual experience. No, she would never do that. But quite some time had passed since her first two years of being semi-experimental in art school—and neither one of the two boys and one girl she'd been physical with had been experienced as Aaron, apparently. When she thought back to those sweaty dorm encounters, she could only recall her thought process. Should I pretend it feels good? Is he or she pretending it feels good?

There hadn't been time for those awkward worries in the field because she'd been struck in the head by a falling lust crater the moment they'd locked lips. She pressed her nose up against the passenger's side window, half expecting to see her prone form, lying spread-eagled in the grass, sending her a thumbs-up.

The image made her laugh as Aaron climbed into the driver's side, starting the engine while casting her a look of concern. "Something funny?"

God, she wanted to straddle his lap and—do *something* to snap him out of the funk he continually fell back into, just when she thought they'd broken free. Maybe a two-finger poke to the eyes, à la the Three Stooges. Or a knock-knock joke in his ear. A kiss. Maybe...maybe that would work. The thought of it caused her smile to fade, the pulse between her legs to pick up again. "It feels like your fingers are still inside me."

Aaron froze in the act of putting the Suburban in gear, his jaw flexing in the near-darkness. "That shouldn't have happened."

Grace had expected him to say that, but she hadn't fore-seen the twinge of pain in her middle following. "Why not?" Needing to move, she tugged the seatbelt across her body, buckling it with a loud click. "Because you're going to work for my father?"

She could hear him thinking in the long pause that en-sued. "Among other things," he said in a low voice, pulling the Suburban back onto the road, into the snowflakes that were beginning to taper off. "You've never asked me why I'm here. What I'm doing sneaking into pancake break-fasts in Iowa. Do you think that behavior is typical of me?"

"No." She tilted her head, regarding his strong profile in the passing streetlights. *Light, dark. Light, dark.* "I guess I was returning the favor, since you never asked me what I was doing inside the school at night."

"Well, ask me now." He delivered the order in a near-shout, seeming to surprise himself, then settling back into the driver's seat with a raked hand through his hair. "Ask me why I needed to be snuck in the back door, instead of walking through the front like everyone else."

"Not everyone else. Not me."

That seemed to upset him, but he didn't comment. Not directly. "*Ask*, Grace."

Her chest experienced a sudden hollowness. "No. I don't want to." Why wouldn't he look at her? Had she imagined that connection they'd forged in the field? "What would it matter?"

"It would. Matter." He steered the Suburban onto the highway, the engine struggling to comply with the request for an increased pace. "It matters what happened to you, too. Whatever the...*tragedy* was. Matters. If you want to live believing life is a series of moments, you have to account for the past moments, too. They don't just fade with the newer, prettier ones."

Heat stole up Grace's neck as she turned in her seat. "Actually, you're wrong. They *do* fade. But you have to work at it. You have to *try*."

"I don't *want* them to fade." She heard his hands tighten around the cracked leather steering wheel. "I don't need to make them weaker for the sake of comfort."

"Is that what you think of me?" Grace whispered. "That I'm weak?"

A touch of horror made it into his gaze as he cast her a glance. "No. I think we've found different ways to be strong. And I think the method I use makes me very bad for you. Everything you feel is so...huge." His throat worked. "I try not to feel anything at all. My way leads to people being hurt. Isolation through alienation."

In the intimacy of the humming Suburban, Grace was

tempted to ask Aaron about what had brought him to Iowa, as a man trying so desperately to regain his luck. Because it was the opposite description of the man who drove so capably, who'd touched her with such skill and had a quick answer for everything. But some intuition told her, *Grace, you're better off not knowing.* And she'd learned the hard way never to ignore her intuition ever again. So she sat back in her seat, staring out through the windshield to regroup. Pretending she hadn't essentially been broken up with by someone she wasn't even dating.

"What is your job going to be for my father?"

Grace asked the question so casually, never expecting the answer to be so catastrophic. Talking politics tended to give her a stomachache and frustrate her. People were people, not numbers and polls and pie charts. Maybe that was why she'd never considered Aaron's position with the Pendleton campaign or given much thought about what he'd be accomplishing, side by side, with her father. But when he spoke, the answer changed everything. Everything. So much so that she was hit by an urge to fling open the passenger's side door at the first stoplight and run for her life.

"My focus will be on the eighteen to twenty-five demographic." His tone had gone from challenging to practiced. "Using the way they think, the mediums they utilize, to bring them over to the Pendleton camp." He threw her a tight smile. "They want to vote for him, they just don't realize it yet."

Ice formed along the inner walls of Grace's lungs, forcing her to breathe in labored drags. Speaking was out of the question. She'd known, on some level, that the Pendleton campaign must be trying to reach the younger voters through various forms of social media—which she didn't personally use—and attempting to make her father appeal to a younger audience. *Of course*, with the presidency at stake, the campaign would employ every trick in the book to get the right hole punched on Election Day.

But she hadn't anticipated it being Aaron's role in the Pendleton campaign. He would essentially be influencing—maybe even tricking—young people into wanting a certain outcome. How was that different than what she'd experienced at YouthAspire? Or on the couch of her psychologist in Austin, who'd fed Grace her parents' rhetoric through patient suggestions?

It wasn't. It was worse, because it was on such a larger scale. Not just a camp full of kids who didn't get enough attention from their parents and were willing to believe anything for positive adult reinforcement. Not just a girl trying to talk through her memories and make sense of them. No, this was everything she'd been fighting to get over. Right there in front of her.

When she'd been sent to YouthAspire at sixteen, back when it had been a leadership camp—a far cry from the youth shelter and recreation center it had recently become—the infiltration of ideas had started slowly. As daughter of a prominent politician, younger sister of a popular student at the local high school, Grace had been a target from day one. The counselors had flocked around her, sat with her at every meal, given her choice of bunkhouse, extra free time. Even at sixteen, she'd gleaned their goal. To bring more registrants the following summer, perpetuate the YouthAspire name, and ultimately, make more money. And she'd wanted to help. She'd wanted to spread the word about their unique teaching format, which included lectures from corporate professionals, workshops designed to increase the campers' understanding of leadership. Teach them how to be a *winner*. How to make the correct *decisions*.

Aaron would be doing the same thing.

God, when she thought back to how *easily* she'd been led, the memories threatened to overwhelm. So much that when the Suburban hit a bump, she startled, palms flying up to cool her cheeks.

"Hey. Hippie." Aaron's concern reached through the fog, but it wasn't a welcoming distraction. She didn't *want* to let him distract her, the way she would have done in the past, as a young girl. With such trust. Making her wonder if she'd learned a damn thing from her experience. "I don't think you're weak. All right? You misunderstood me."

She forced her hands down, laying them flat on her thighs. "I know." How far were they from home? "It's okay."

A beat passed. "You don't seem okay. Should I...pull over or something?"

"No," she said too quickly. "I just want to go home."

Something she never thought she'd say and actually mean, but in this case, home was the lesser of two evils. Maybe not right this second. But the deeper Aaron swam into her father's end of the pool, the more corrupt he would become. And she'd been distancing herself from those who sought to control or manipulate far too long to take another chance. That separation guaranteed she wouldn't make another mistake by trusting the wrong people, believing truths that were nothing more than falsehoods.

When they finally turned down the road leading to

her family home's endless driveway, Grace unhooked her seatbelt. "You can let me out here."

"What?" His incredulity was thicker than the night's dark edges. "You think I'm going to pull over and let you out on the side of the road?"

"You can't very well pull into my driveway, can you?"

"No. I'd thought of that." He sounded grave. "There's a dirt turnoff before your driveway—I almost turned down it by accident on the way over. I'm assuming it leads to the woods near the guest house. Close enough that I can walk you."

She didn't answer.

"You're making me real nervous over here, Grace." The turnoff approached, illuminated by the Suburban's yellow-tinged headlights, and Aaron took it, traveling over the bumpy, familiar terrain Grace had only ever gone over on foot. It did nothing to calm the nerves jangling in her belly. "Did I...Jesus, did I hurt you?" He stamped his foot down on the brake, sending them sliding through mud and snow before the vehicle groaned to an abrupt stop. "Did I?"

Confusion flashed like jagged lightning, unwanted at first, but it snapped Grace out of the paralyzed shock of learning Aaron's political specialty. What he would be doing for months to come. How it was the one thing she couldn't get past. Ever. "No, you didn't hurt me." Her hands were unsteady as she reached down to button her coat, all the way up to her neck. "But you were right before. We don't make sense. You said I shouldn't come within ten feet of you...and I won't anymore. I don't want to."

Grace only looked over long enough to glimpse Aaron's face turning white before she shoved open the creaking door and jumped out. In a million years, she never expected him to follow. Why would he? Since they'd met, he'd done nothing but explain what made them different, remind her they shouldn't be in each other's orbits. So when she heard his feet hit the ground, it startled her enough to spin around. Enough to go still and watch him advance like a wary hunter coming toward a spooked deer. Is that what she looked like?

"Just when I thought I was getting used to your curveballs, huh?" The stilted delivery of his joke—and the stiffness in his shoulders—made it fall flat. "I'm fucking lost here, Grace."

"Why?" Genuine curiosity was the only thing keeping her from turning tail and losing Aaron even more. That's what she told herself. It wasn't the fact that he looked totally bewildered and something about the utter lack of his usual confidence made her chest ache. "Why are you lost? I'm finally *agreeing* with you."

"I don't have to like it," he said, almost to himself. "I need to know what I missed. You were fine one minute—"

"No. You *never* thought I was fine. Everything you've said? I've been listening." She took in a pull of cold night air. "You think I don't know my own mind, and if you knew...if you *knew* how much I resent the insinuation that I can't think for myself, you would have thought twice." Grace tried to rein in the accusation dying to be issued—accusing didn't fix anything—but it knocked free all the same. "Maybe you didn't want me to know my own mind, so you could make it up for me."

Aaron drew up short. "Is this about my *job?*"

"Yes," she whispered, squaring her shoulders in the face of his astonishment. "Partly. I'm so confused by you.

I see one thing—I see and see it—and then it vanishes. And it makes me doubt my own judgment. I've doubted my judgment around someone like you before and it ended badly."

"Yeah. Someone like me." Out of everything she'd said, those three words seemed to have the largest impact. They paled his face, made the lines around his mouth more prominent. "Just like I've been telling you from the beginning, right?"

Grace lifted her hands and let them drop. "Yes."

For long moments, all he did was stare at her, the soft puffs of falling snow sounding at their feet. "But it seemed like you weren't believing it...when I said there was no good in me. Or you didn't want to." He made the statement almost to himself, but it lanced her nonetheless. "You don't even have *some* doubt left?"

"Stop." Stop what? She had no idea. Stop making her question the decision to put distance between them, stop looking so torn up, stop making her throat burn. In an attempt to forcibly remove any temptation to stay around Aaron in the hopes of seeing beneath his exterior, Grace reached up and yanked all four ribbons out of her hair, approaching Aaron just enough to dump them into his palm. "I know you'll be working with my father, and I promise I won't jeopardize that, but we can't be alone together anymore."

Aaron's gaze was riveted by the shredded red fabric in his hand. "How will I know you're all right?"

She started to back away. Before she did the exact opposite and took a flying leap into his arms. Why did he insist on choosing *now* to be so silent and still? "I'm always all right. I make *myself* all right."

The intensity of his answering look nearly buckled Grace's knees, but she forced herself onto the path leading home, counting steps to distract herself. She didn't hear him start the Suburban until five minutes later, when she reached her back door.

CHAPTER NINE

Aaron entered the cabin he shared with Belmont, a hand already extended toward the bottle of whiskey he kept on the nightstand. His fucking head was pounding like a giant demanding entry to a castle—the inside of his esophagus felt like it'd been scrubbed with bashed-up asphalt. The drive home seemed like it had taken place ten years ago, not one single turn or stoplight recalled.

Ridiculous. The whole situation was so *stupid*, he felt a laugh form in his throat. Someone had to be playing an elaborate trick on him. Right? The kind of trick that made his fists shake with their need to plow through a window? Or rip out his hair? Only…no. No one in this world knew him well enough to crawl up inside his psyche and find something to wreck his head like this. Not when Aaron himself hadn't even been aware of the apparent…weakness.

That is what he was dealing with. A weakness. Something about Grace—unbelievable that a mental recitation of her name made breathing awkward—forced him to re-examine himself and his business, and that was a danger-ous idea. You plowed forward, making calls that moved you to the next level. You took steps to ensure you couldn't get burned. And you sure as hell didn't question those tactics or look past the surface to determine what they meant about you. As a person.

Aaron registered Belmont's presence in the room, but didn't acknowledge his brother in any way. Taking the time to throw an insult across the room would mean de-laying his trip to the bottom of the whiskey bottle, and he would avoid distractions at all costs. But that first slide of fire down his throat didn't deliver the liquid salvation he'd been hoping for. Instead, he remembered the maze of silence that had descended in the Suburban after he'd told Grace about his role with the campaign, how she had locked up, that haunted look replacing the joy in her eyes. When he remembered how flippant he'd sounded about something that obviously resonated with her, his stomach threatened to lose his first draw of liquor.

What was it? What had happened to her? The not knowing was goddamn insufferable. That's what it was. Because he dealt in information. He didn't like living in the dark about *anything*. Not just Grace.

Right. Right, you giant, fantastic, fucking liar.

"Did you feel it?" Aaron didn't even realize he'd de-cided to speak until his voice broke the cabin's thick silence. "When we pulled up at the campgrounds. Did you feel that prickle on the back of your neck? Should have left then."

Great. He'd lost his mind. Maybe he fit right in with the Clarksons after all.

Belmont hadn't moved from his epic brooding session, sitting against the far wall in a chair, arms crossed. "Been feeling it most of the trip."

Aaron's head jerked up when his brother actually answered one of his questions. Possibly for the first time since they'd left California. It figured that the first thing out of Aaron's mouth to make zero sense got the response. "Yeah? Well, I don't believe in voodoo. I don't feel prickles. And I don't dance in fields with hippie girls."

The chair creaked as Belmont leaned forward, clasping both hands between his knees, the corners of his mouth turned down. "Didn't mean for her to run into me like that." He cleared his throat, but his voice still contained the usual amount of rust when he spoke again. "She didn't let me get an apology together."

"She's—" Aaron stopped, angry at himself for feeling such a pressing need to reassure someone who hadn't given enough of a shit to speak with him more than a few times over the last decade. "I don't know if she's okay," he said instead, wishing the honesty didn't feel so good. "I *won't* know anymore. When I met her, I didn't realize I'd be working for her father. And it doesn't matter. Okay? It doesn't matter because she finally figured me out. She saw me."

Liquid sloshed in the glass bottle as Aaron tipped it back, hoping this time when the burn hit his belly, he would stop seeing how beautiful Grace had looked with snow in her hair, eyes lit up toward the sky. *You feel it, too? You feel the good we did?* Had he? Maybe for a second? He sure as shit wasn't feeling it now.

"What did she see?" Belmont asked. It took Aaron several beats to gather a vague memory of what they'd been talking about, and oddly, his brother seemed to realize his head was somewhere else. Seemed to understand the affliction, even if he was clearly uncomfortable repeating himself. Talking *at all*, probably. "You said she saw you. What did she see?"

This was the danger zone. Like lying down on an operating table and having his ribs pried open without the benefit of sedation. But miracle of miracles, Belmont was actually conversing with him, and maybe tomorrow he would refuse to admit it, but talking about Grace was making the sudden separation from her easier. When he woke in the a.m., perhaps the whole ordeal would be off his chest, and he could get back to business. "She saw a manipulator. That's what you see, too. I see it when I look in the mirror. I'm good at it. And I *own* it. I'm not ashamed of it."

Belmont lifted an eyebrow, as if to say, *If you say so.*

Aaron pushed to his feet with a curse, taking another long swig of liquor. "You know how freeing it is? Admitting something most people would hide from or make excuses for?" His declarations rang hollow, giving him pause. He'd always thought the first time he'd made those statements out loud, they'd be rife with conviction. Hoping to bolster himself with more whiskey, he brought the bottle to his mouth, but it dropped to his side before a drop passed his lips. "Something bad happened to her. She won't tell me what. But I remind her of it." His laughter scattered about the cabin. "What can I possibly do about that, right? Fuck all, is what. I just have to move forward."

Something about what Aaron had said drew Belmont's full attention. He leaned back in his chair, brow furrowed in what most people would interpret as a scowl, but Aaron knew was just his brother's resting asshole face.

If Aaron hadn't been distracted, it would have occurred to him sooner why his mentioning Grace's unknown tragedy interested Belmont so much. It was similar to his own experience of being trapped in the well at age eight, after wandering off during a school field trip. Four days had passed until he'd been discovered, his voice gone from shouting for help. It wasn't until later, when he'd regained his speech, that Belmont explained he'd screamed so much in the beginning, he'd had no voice left to call out when he heard people walking past later on. For four days. Ironically, with the return of his voice, Belmont had stopped speaking unless completely necessary and brought the pattern into adulthood with him.

"Do you want to leave it like that?" Belmont rumbled. "With her thinking of something bad and coming up with you?"

"I don't have a choice," Aaron said. "And she wouldn't be the only one who thought of something shitty and recalled my face. *You* do it, don't you?" Now that the question was out, Aaron couldn't take it back. Maybe it was the whiskey or dire need for a distraction, but it was out now. "I was the one who found you in the well, wasn't I? At your worst moment, tell me you don't think of my face staring down at you."

Belmont's blue eyes—so different from the golden brown ones owned by the other three Clarkson siblings—seemed to lighten. Or maybe Aaron was just remembering the bright blue sky dredged from his memory bank, how it seemed to reflect off his brother so far below, encasing his curled-up form in sunshine. "Is that what you think?" Belmont asked.

It was too much. Past and present conspiring to wreck

his head. For someone who almost never shined a spot-light inward, the excessive illumination set off alarm bells. Answers were usually his best friend, but in this case, maybe even when it came to Grace, they were the enemy. Aaron propelled himself toward the bathroom door, clos-ing himself in before another word could be exchanged. Thinking fast, he reached over and turned on the shower, before sliding down the wall to the floor and taking an-other long drink of whiskey.

Tonight was an anomaly. Tomorrow he would resume his purpose and ignore the bullshit trying to make its way beneath his skin. It wouldn't succeed.

His final thought before turning off the shower and slip-ping into unconsciousness was of Grace dropping four red ribbons into his palm. And even as he berated himself for the wussy gesture he'd made cutting up his tie, Aaron's hand slipped into his pants pocket to close around them, dragging them out and falling asleep with them pressed to his mouth.

When Aaron awoke to a head full of wet cement eight hours later, he stumbled to the cabin's front door—noting Belmont's bed was empty—hoping a breath of fresh air would calm the roiling whiskey waves in his stomach.

He was greeted by a sea of news cameras, instead.

"What is your name? State your name toward the cam-era, please."

"Is it true you stole thirty thousand dollars in campaign money from Senator Pendleton and left it at a YouthAspire shelter last night?"

"Do you consider yourself a modern-day Robin Hood?"

What. The fuck.

CHAPTER TEN

Grace never watched the news. It wasn't that she didn't care what was taking place outside of her immediate world. She did. And whatever small amount of time was spent with her father—or in the vicinity of his staffers—always resulted in her being educated on world politics. The shortcomings of the current administration's foreign policy. Cabinet changes, Main Street, Wall Street, health care. As if that wasn't enough, when her father had made the decision to run for president, she'd been placed with tutors who'd filled in any remaining blanks, then quizzed her on everything from first ladies to first pets.

So when it came to watching television, she avoided any mention of the upcoming election like the plague. The Discovery Channel usually won her vote—especially programs about bears. Or anything about abandoned structures that had deteriorated over time. The latter made her sad—seeing places once filled with life and laughter being left to rot—so she usually only watched them when something was bothering her, but needed that extra push into a therapeutic cry.

Crying might have helped her unsettled state this morning, but she wasn't ready to let go of the agitation just yet. Her fingers fidgeted in her hair, feeling for the ribbons she'd tugged free last night. She'd only had them in for a few hours; they shouldn't have made themselves feel so permanent. Every time she assured herself severing ties with Aaron had been the smart move—the move that would eliminate any inner conflict—she remembered his concentrated expression as he cut his tie. The way she'd opened her eyes that time as he kissed her and seen his own shut so tight. *So* tight. The heat of his body when he hovered close, the rasp of his clothing, his breath.

Wasn't this what people like Aaron did, though? Create a false sense of security? Make a person feel wanted? *We're in this together. There's no one else. If your family cared about you, they wouldn't have sent you away for two months.*

Grace slumped down onto her couch, gasping under the impact of the unexpected flashback. She'd gone years without hearing that voice, the one that used to haunt her relentlessly, long after it had been silenced. Needing to replace the lingering echo, her hand fumbled for the television remote, her intention to switch on the Discovery Channel losing momentum when Aaron's face greeted her. No...that couldn't be right. She was seeing him now because her thoughts had been full of him all morning. That had to be the explanation.

She reached down and pinched her arm. Along with the twinge of pain came a sinking sensation in her stomach.

It was Aaron. On television, beneath the words *From an earlier broadcast*. She couldn't be imagining his presence on the screen because she'd never seen him so disheveled. Stubble covered the lower half of his face, dark shadows cupping the bottoms of his eyes. His hair...if she didn't find the situation—and her bone-liquefying reaction to his appearance—so alarming, she might have laughed. It stuck out in six angles, like he'd just come from an orgy, filled with handsy women.

For once, Grace didn't appreciate where her imagination went. Didn't like the idea of Aaron being fondled by a sea of hands. Really, *really* didn't like it. Anxious for Aaron's voice, needing it to banish the mental orgy taking place in her mind, Grace turned up the volume and listened.

"What is your name? State your name toward the camera, please."

"Is it true you stole thirty thousand dollars in campaign money from Senator Pendleton and left it at a Youth-Aspire shelter last night?"

"Do you consider yourself a modern-day Robin Hood?"

Grace's hands rose to cover her mouth, her head shaking in slow denial. *Oh God.* She...*they* hadn't planned for the worst-case scenario, but they'd landed smack dab in the center of it nonetheless. The scene outside Aaron's cabin faded, replaced by grainy camera footage of Aaron walking up the pathway to YouthAspire the night prior, two pillowcases dangling from his hands.

This couldn't be happening. How was this happening?

She could read Aaron's mind, knew he was asking himself the same questions. And not for the first time, she witnessed his intelligence without him having to say a single word. *This* was where he shined, even if she preferred him speaking without having a strategy. Saying whatever truth occurred to him without having a chance to censor himself. Yes, she could see engines cranking behind his tired eyes, see the way every reporter in the frame quieted and snapped to attention when he finally addressed them.

"I'm Aaron Clarkson." His charming smile sent white streaking across the television screen. "Although given a choice, this isn't how I would have made my first impression as Senator Pendleton's newest adviser."

A burst of questions and flashes, one of them breaking through as the most prominent. "If you work for the senator, why would you steal from his campaign?"

Aaron smoothed the wrinkled collar of his shirt. "*Stealing* is a strong word," he admonished with a wink, making Grace fall back against the cushions, barely able to recognize him anymore. "The senator is well aware of the donation—it was his idea. Senator Pendleton is a passionate supporter of youth causes throughout Iowa and nationwide. This campaign is about giving back—about earning the *respect* of America's young people—and this gesture was meant to bolster that foundation." Another devastating smile that even had Grace sighing like a lovesick teenager flashed across the screen. "Unfortunately, the senator wasn't interested in taking credit for his idea, so I was the lucky one sent out in the snowstorm to deliver his gift."

An extended silence ensued, but the flashes didn't stop. Without Aaron making any actual poses, Grace had no doubt he would look incredible in every shot. Several questions were fired at Aaron, but he deflected them with a good-natured wave. "If you'll excuse me, I was in the middle of making myself look human." Tentative laughter. "My boss is a stickler for punctuality, so I'm blaming all of you for making me late."

With that, he turned and executed a perfect jog up the cabin steps and disappeared into the cabin, leaving Grace sitting openmouthed on her couch. The beginning of a smile had just started to warm her mouth when she heard the crunch of gravel in the distance. Intuition sparkling in her nerve endings, Grace rose from the couch and looked out the window, unsurprised to find Aaron climbing out of his Suburban in front of her family home. Not the guesthouse. Although, upon removing his sunglasses, he glanced in her direction, igniting a pulse in the southern region of her body. "Yowza," she whispered, pressing a hand to the spot.

When Aaron continued up the porch to her parents' front door, disappearing from view, Grace spun on a heel and ran toward the bedroom, jumping over her discarded boots along the way. A flood of thoughts and reactions to what Aaron had done on national television bombarded one another, but one took precedent. She couldn't allow Aaron to face her father alone. Whatever her feelings toward his profession—and they hadn't changed overnight—the theft and delivery of the campaign money had been *her* idea, *her* actions. Letting him take the fall would be wrong.

Grace threw her double closet doors open and scooped up the first two items of clothing she laid eyes on. Which happened to be a sweater...and tights with a pattern making them look like garter belts. She could change later, though, when her sole focus wasn't being there for whatever went down between Aaron and her father. Making sure she took responsibility for what she'd done.

After slipping her feet into untied boots, Grace flew from the guesthouse, raced across the lawn, and went in through the back door leading to the kitchen. Her mother and sister were late risers and obviously still in bed or they would be drinking coffee at the table, going over the day's agenda. When she heard raised male voices coming from her father's den, Grace slowed her pace on the way through the house. It wasn't eavesdropping, right? She was just taking her time getting down the hallway...

"Give me one reason why I shouldn't have you arrested," her father seethed.

Aaron didn't miss a beat when he said, "Your resurgence in the polls this morning." A light rustling of papers. "You've already gone up two percentage points since the segment began airing."

"Oh, I don't believe this. You're actually here seeking gratitude?"

"I don't want gratitude until you're elected." Aaron sounded so calm compared to how panicked he'd been last night, when she'd explained they couldn't see each other again. How odd, when so much was at stake. His *career*. "Look, they put me on the spot and I ran with what I had. If you don't see the value in that, maybe I should offer my services elsewhere."

Grace realized she'd stopped breathing when her chest started to protest, her father's rejoinder urging her closer to the den. "Even if I was a big enough moron to overlook your unauthorized distribution of funds..." A slam—fist hitting wood—jolted Grace back a step. "Spending time with you in *any* capacity does not benefit my daughter.

Whatever has...happened, I don't want to know. But it needs to end."

That was her cue. With a deep breath, Grace stepped into the doorway, waiting for her father to acknowledge her presence. When it became obvious he was too absorbed in a stare down with Aaron, Grace rapped on the door frame. "Dad..."

If possible, his demeanor went even more rigid. "Grace, this does not—"

"Concern me? Yes, it does." Aaron's expression was guarded as he glanced over his shoulder, but she couldn't focus on trying to read him now. She'd resolved last night to stop trying. Nothing had changed. *Nothing.* That reminder didn't stop her from cataloging every detail of his appearance in one, quick sweep, however. He'd clearly showered and changed since the television interview. Face freshly shaven, hair styled, suit impeccable, he could have been a prince of some foreign country. Every maiden in the kingdom would swoon at his feet while he stepped over them, bored out of his mind. There was nothing boring in the way he looked at her, though. Oh no. She was locked in the prince's crosshairs and a crack of lust's whip tightened her muscles.

Focus. "Aaron...Mr. Clarkson...and I met two nights ago," Grace started shakily. "He didn't know who I was, but we made a deal. He didn't realize keeping up his end of the bargain meant stealing the money. It's my fault. I lied by omission. You know this whole plan was mine."

"Of all places, Grace." Her father deflated a little, massaging the back of his neck with a vigorous hand. "It had to be YouthAspire? After what happened to you there, I—"

"I know. You think I'm punishing you," she interjected quickly, feeling Aaron's attention zeroing in on her father's words. "It's the opposite, actually. I'm freeing all of us from what happened. I wish you could see it through my eyes."

"I'm sorry." He threw up his hands. "I can't. I never will."

Grace nodded, attempting to gather herself, but what Aaron said next silenced her. "I came here with a proposal, Senator. Would you like to hear it?"

Her father ran a hand over his mouth, grimacing when his office and cell phones began ringing at the same time. "Anything to avoid the goddamn fallout I'll be dealing with from the contributors—who could very well want a refund on their donations, *daughter*."

She flinched at the venom in her father's tone, grateful for the way Aaron interceded smoothly, although there was definite tension around his mouth now. "We need to run with this, like it or not. There are news vans lined up down the block looking for a statement from the new, local hero. Not using this to your advantage would be a wasted opportunity." He rolled his neck, giving Grace a fleeting touch of eye contact. Fleeting, but powerful, because he couldn't hide his irritation. At the way her father spoke to her? Yes. But there was more. It was reassurance. And coming from Aaron, it might as well have been a sword battle in her honor. Warmth spun around like a top in her stomach, picking up speed when he spoke again.

"Let's get every available staffer on this. Let's organize committees to find causes—such as YouthAspire—and show voters you're a man of the people. Respect. Giving back. It's your new platform and it will work, if we don't let them get interested in something else first. Because believe me, your opponent it looking for a fucking dinner bell to ring as we speak."

This was good. This reminder that Aaron didn't see people, he saw numbers. Graphs. Polls. Demographics. She needed to remember that whenever his eyes threatened to convince her otherwise. And most of all, most important, she couldn't let the good thing they'd done together last night be exploited. "I want in."

Her father did a double take. "Excuse me?"

"I want to help." She advanced farther into the room, noticing Aaron's gaze dip to her legs. He quickly glued his attention above her neck, but not before he started a race of tingles speeding up her spine. "I know where volunteers and money will be put to the best use. Around Des Moines, especially. I can finally be useful to this campaign—"

Grace broke off when her father held up a hand. "I'm already questioning my sanity by considering Mr. Clarkson's idea. If you think I'm going to reward your illegal behavior and total disregard for the rules, which were put in place for your own good, you have another think coming."

Embarrassment was an emotion Grace rarely experienced, but the easy dismissal of her plea caused heat to bloom in her cheeks. Because Aaron was watching? Probably. Whatever the reason, her recessive stubborn gene chose that moment to go radioactive. Her spine turned to steel, her lungs seeming to expand with a sudden rush of energy. "I never ask you for anything. This is *important* to me."

The office phone began ringing again, but when her father leaned down to answer, Grace placed a hand over the receiver to prevent him. "What are you doing?" he said.

"I'm not asking anymore." Gripping tight to her courage, Grace lifted her chin. "You've kept everything about my experience away from the media, like it never happened. I'm not sure you did that for me, or yourself. But if you shut me up in that guesthouse and don't give me this chance to—finally—do something I'm passionate about?" She wet her parched lips. "I'll go public with everything. Believe me when I say, I don't care who knows. But you *do*. This campaign does."

Grace must have been desperate for comfort, because Aaron's arm brushing against her left elbow forced her to stand her ground, remaining strong in the face of her father's disbelief. And the longer she stood there, refusing to bat an eyelash, the easier it became, until she almost *wanted* to argue more.

Her father lowered his voice and moved close. "Grace, you know why we think it's in your best interest to stay out of the public eye."

"It's not." She shook her head. "I know I'm not polished like my mother. Or accomplished like Emily. But I have something to offer. You have to let me give it."

A deafening pause ensued while her father scrutinized her. She could see the ideas popping into his head, being discarded. Strategies being dissected. Straightening to his full height, he looked over at Aaron and Grace's stomach seized. "You haven't given a shit about propriety so far. Don't start now." He tilted his head in Grace's direction. "Will she hurt or help us?"

Grace became winded, reminding her of the time she'd gotten nailed in the stomach with a kickball. Feeling the remains of her courage slipping away, she pasted a calm expression onto her face and turned to Aaron, who watched her from behind an invisible brick wall. "Help." His tone was brisk as he looked down, began arranging the paperwork he'd stacked on the desk. "If we want your name to stay in everyone's mouth come tomorrow, we need someone who knows the local landscape. The Pendleton campaign has five days remaining in Iowa before the campaign gets back on the trail. I doubt she can do any damage between now and then."

"See that she doesn't." Her father finally answered the phone, but kept one hand cupped over the receiver as he regarded Aaron for one beat, two. "I haven't forgotten what landed you on your ass. Any sign of inappropriate behavior and I'll cut you off at the knees, Clarkson."

CHAPTER ELEVEN

Oh, that *went fucking swimmingly.*

Aaron's internal sarcasm came to an abrupt halt when Grace followed him down the front steps of Pendleton's porch. He only strode *faster* for the Suburban. No way. No, he couldn't handle Grace right now. There were committees to assemble, research to perform, incentives to devise. And if he looked into Grace's sad and brave and beautiful green eyes, he wouldn't give a fuck about any of it.

God, she couldn't be an actual, real person. Who just waltzed in and demanded to take the blame—for anything? In his experience, that was the exact opposite behavior most people exhibited. As if her act of selflessness hadn't been enough to throw him for a loop, she'd actually...made his damn hands shake in there, standing up to her father the way she'd done. For a brief moment, he'd actually considered throwing up the sheaf of documents and shouting, *Oh, the hell with it.* No matter what he did, no matter who he helped get elected or arguments he won, he'd never feel the kind of pride in himself Grace deserved to feel after the scene in Pendleton's office. Not even if he exhumed Abraham goddamn Lincoln and got his corpse reelected by a landslide.

Now, Aaron could get Pendleton into office, no sweat. He hadn't anticipated the pressure of having a new superior, however. No wonder, after his last one had sliced him down the middle with a job termination and a parting shot. *This is how you repay me?*

Aaron swallowed the beginnings of guilt and picked up his pace.

"Hey, could you just wait?" Grace's footfalls fell along the path behind Aaron, but he still didn't turn around. He *wouldn't* until they could no longer be seen from the house. Why? Because she was asking to be eye-fucked. Top to bottom. On top of the battle he'd been waging in the office, his cock nearly giving a full salute to those see-through tights had been just a tad inconvenient. And worse, she could have walked in wearing Mrs. Lincoln's nightgown and his balls would still have filled with weight. Grace simply *did* that to him. Aroused him. Made him wish he'd been born with whatever vital DNA he clearly lacked. The kind that would allow him to witness her level of compassion and understand it. Or recognize the ability in himself.

He reached the Suburban and jerked open the driver's side door, using it like a shield between himself and Grace. Reaching into his pocket, he pulled out a business card and penned his cell phone number on the back, handing it to her. Refusing to witness her reaction to such an obnoxious—but necessary—brush-off, he cut his gaze to the side. There were too many obstacles between them now, and any amount of time spent with her would only tempt Aaron to find ways around them. It couldn't happen. He'd come too far to screw up now. Screw up *again*.

"What's this?" Grace asked.

"My cell number. Do what you can on your end. Get me a list of places, contacts, and their specific causes so I can vet them." He slid his hands into his jacket pockets, but jerked them free when he encountered the shredded red ribbons. "I'll get on the phone and work my own angles, locate resources. We'll touch base later."

"No." She leaned to the right, tossing his business card back into the Suburban like a Frisbee. "I'm coming with you."

Just like that, Aaron's temper spiked so dramatically, he could see the yellow slash of it paint his vision. "*You're* the one. You said we couldn't be alone together anymore. I'm just following the rules." He jerked his chin toward the house. "Those rules are even more set in stone now than they were last night."

God, being this close to her, he could see every nuanced reaction flit across her face. A face that would never be duplicated or even resembled by someone else. She was nervous and excited and trying to be brave, all at once. Brave toward him. Which went another ten miles toward making him a bastard.

"If you leave without me, you'll shut me out. Make a list?" She blinked up at the sky, which rained winter sunshine down onto her features. "I'm tired of being humored. Don't do that to me."

A growl vibrated in his throat, self-preservation clashing with the bitter distaste of picturing her back in the guesthouse, alone in the silence. He tapped his fist against the inside of the car door. "I thought after this morning, after I gave credit to your father for that donation, you wouldn't lend me a hose if I was on fire."

Grace's head gave a slight tilt. "No. What you did, what you said…there was no other way to guarantee the shelter could keep the money." She peered up at him. "Did you think about that? Was it part of your decision?"

Yeah. Crazy enough, it had been. When he'd opened the cabin door and seen the cameras, he'd had two simultaneous concerns. Keeping the hope of a job alive and making sure Grace didn't…lose her moment. He'd actually wanted to punch himself in the face for the mental recitation of those words. *Grace is going to have her moment taken away. Maybe all we have is moments.* Perhaps he'd still been drunk on whiskey, but he'd sobered quick enough, the pleasurable surge of taking charge, solving a problem, overrunning that fleeting goodwill. Thank Christ. "No, Grace. I acted in the only way I could to secure my job on this campaign." He pushed his fingers through his hair. "I thought the pressure was off after last night. Thought you'd finally stopped expecting good things from me."

Her breath had created a circle of fog on the driver's side window, and now she dragged a finger diagonally through the center, as if to say, *Shut up, you bullshit artist.* Or maybe *he* was the one projecting the sentiment. "It was only a question." She dropped her hand and made a move to circle the Suburban. "Shotgun."

In his periphery, Aaron saw the senator move in the window of his den, phone pressed to his ear as he watched

Aaron and Grace, and their obvious impasse in the driveway. He could feel the older man's speculation like a net thrown over his head, ready to drag him up into the trees. Well-warranted concern. "You're putting me in a real fucking spot here, hippie."

She must have taken that as Aaron's agreement, because she tucked her chin down toward her chest, as if trying to hide a smile, and skipped the remaining distance to the passenger door. There was nothing he could do after seeing that, was there? With a muttered curse, Aaron climbed into the driver's seat and started the ignition, smirking when Grace already had her seatbelt buckled, hands clasped in her lap. Her lap, which was almost entirely visible through the sheer tights, her sweater not even long enough to reach mid-thigh. How he ached to draw it higher, over the curves of her hips. To drive down the street with nothing but nylon separating her backside from the seat. And he'd be the only one to know. The only one able to look, to reach over and cup her, stroke her. "You're going to freeze your ass off," he rasped.

Impatient fingers tugged on the sweater's hem, but it only slid back up in a whispery scratch of fabric. "Just drive, Grandpa."

A pained smile threatened, but Aaron banished it and threw the car into gear, feeling pretty desperate to be out from beneath the senator's eyes while getting hard for the man's daughter. Because, yeah. When it came to Grace's body—which he now knew to be responsive as hell—his cock didn't feel like observing the rules. "I, uh…" He turned onto the main road. "I need to take care of a few things, before we get on the phone. Are you okay for breakfast?"

"Yes, thank you." She shifted toward him in the seat. "What few things are we taking care of?"

The royal *we* didn't escape his notice. "I need to find different lodging for my family." Aaron thought of Belmont's marble countenance when he'd left the cabin that morning. At least until Sage came in and perched herself on the corner of the closest bed. As Aaron watched from the doorway, his brother had snatched Sage up like a toy and deposited her onto his lap, all but smothering the poor girl with his arms, face disappearing into her hair. Sage had allowed the treatment without complaint, even appearing gratified by it in some way. Aaron hadn't been able to escape the cabin fast enough. "My brother doesn't do well around news cameras. Or people. Not that he would say a damn thing about it to me."

When they reached a stoplight, Aaron tugged the cell phone from his pocket, preparing to make a call to Peggy on speakerphone, instructing her to get packing. "I know where they can stay," Grace said. "It's a twenty-minute drive north of Des Moines..."

The way she'd trailed off had Aaron examining her face. "What's it called? I can phone them and see if they have openings."

"There's no one to call...but it's open." Grace pressed a finger to her front teeth, the overlapping ones, before she dropped her hand. "Maybe I should bring you there first? It won't take long."

Just like the day they'd arrived, Aaron felt invisible fingers trail down the back of his neck. In the past, intuition had usually arrived in the form of a gut feeling, but since arriving in Iowa, that appeared to have changed. "Grace, tell me where we're going."

She nodded, as if she'd expected the question. "An old campground that hasn't been used in a while. But it's in the preparation stages of housing young people again. Not only as a summer camp, but a year-round place for orphaned children. From Iowa, specifically. It's nowhere close to being ready, but we—Imelda, the Irish woman you met last night, and myself—have been working on making it functional again." Her tone changed, grew softer. "It used to be operated by—"

"YouthAspire?" Aaron realized he held the cell phone too tightly when his palm started to ache, so he threw it down into the cup holder. "I'll take you there, but I can't be in the dark anymore. Maybe you don't think I have the right to ask, but I want to know what happened to you. I'm—"

"I know. You don't like puzzles." She wasn't facing him, but he could see her far-off expression in the window. "When we get there, you can take your turn trying to solve me."

The light turned green, but the car behind Aaron had to issue a beep to get Aaron moving. There was no denying he was anxious to piece Grace's past together, but a warning also buzzed at the front of his skull. *Danger. Caution.* He already felt protective enough of Grace without giving himself more reason. Still, he was unable to stop himself from asking, "Which way?"

CHAPTER TWELVE

Today wasn't the first time Grace had been back at the YouthAspire campsite. No, she'd been meeting Imelda there on a semiregular basis to clean out the old cabins, salvaging what they could and throwing the rest into rented green Dumpsters, which sat in various locations around the main, overgrown yard. They hadn't reached a point where landscaping made sense or could be maintained, but they would. They *would*.

As Aaron drove beneath the peeling YouthAspire sign, once so freshly painted and modern looking, Grace remembered the morning she'd been dropped off, her mother in a rush to make a flight, which would take her to Spain for a vacation with Grace's father. They'd air kissed on accident, laughed about missing one another's cheeks, before having a proper hug. But it had been stiff, impersonal. Two months with the same kids who avoided her in school sounded like torture, and she'd made her opinion known, only to be greeted by patented responses and assurances that the leadership camp would look good on her college application.

Ray Solomon had been the first person to greet Grace, directing her toward the cabin that would be her home. His nearly translucent blue eyes had transfixed her, the falling wave of blond hair reminding Grace of California beaches, puka shells, and sand. So glamorous when she'd grown up looking at the same Iowa backdrop her entire life. He hadn't shown any extra interest in Grace—or any other campers—that first day. Later, though, they'd been his whole world.

As soon as Aaron put the Suburban in Park, Grace alighted from the vehicle, her boots landing on brown grass and fallen leaves. Around them, the camp fanned out, a semicircle of cabins on one end, a massive mess hall sitting on the opposite. At one time, there had been upscale trailers serving as classrooms, but after the incident when Grace was sixteen, they had been reclaimed by their rental company.

Grace felt, rather than saw, Aaron walk up beside her, so she set off for the only clean cabin, knowing he would follow. When they reached the familiar entrance, Grace pushed open the door, indicating the huge interior lined with twin beds, only one of them made up. "I come here to sleep sometimes," Grace explained, feeling absurdly shy about Aaron seeing a bed she often used. "Or if Imelda receives someone new at the shelter and they're not ready to be around the other kids yet, they come here." With a sweep of her hand, she indicated the wall of fogged glass windows. "There are linens in the main office, so we could make up beds for your family. If this is okay."

She turned toward Aaron for the first time since they'd arrived, finding him riveted by the bed, his arms crossed so tightly she feared he'd snap them off. "It's fine. They'll be fine here." His shiny dress shoes made hollow sounds on the floor as he paced the cabin. "You realize, if your father is elected president, you won't be able to sleep in abandoned cabins without a CIA security detail parked outside."

Grace sat down on the neatly made bed, rubbing the flannel blanket between her fingertips. "Yes. I also know I'm going to give them hell."

Aaron's laughter was unrestrained, just for a second, and it was so wide and deep, Grace couldn't help trying to suck it into her lungs. But when he moved to stand before her, he was back to being the unreadable man in her father's den. "Let's hear it, Grace."

She tucked her hands beneath her thighs and breathed. "The summer I came here—I was sixteen—my cabin was the farthest one from the entrance. Making friends...it never came easy for me, but I did it. We kind of bonded over being abandoned here and...he picked up on that."

Aaron became very still. "He."

Grace tilted her head back to meet Aaron's stony eyes. "Before I tell you anything else, I—I think you should know nothing sexual happened. Nothing like that." At her words, he fell back a step, but didn't respond. Since the beginning, she'd sensed his struggle to avoid touching her. Not for a single second would she give him reason to believe he'd harmed her by giving in. Even if it couldn't happen again, she didn't want to tarnish the unique moment they'd captured in the field.

"His name was Ray Solomon and..." Grace trailed off

when she saw a flash of recognition in Aaron's eyes. Not unusual, considering the story had been national news. "All the counselors had a job to perform. Keep the fresh blood coming through the gates. And that meant... influencing us, ensuring we left with a head full of slogans and keys to success. Of course, they only accepted kids who already excelled in school and sports, so they would have the largest impact. Make YouthAspire more desirable, the place the winners chose to spend their summer. But *we* weren't winners, in the classic sense. Not my little group. We were outcasts."

Aaron had propped a shoulder against the wall, stuck back in the shadows, reminding Grace of the night they'd met in the woods. The reminder of Aaron, back before she'd known anything about his job or specialty within the campaign, made her feel comfortable continuing.

"Ray worked slowly, breaking my little group of friends off from the rest of the pack. Earning our trust by telling us these stories... he claimed he'd been like us in high school, not fitting in, not relating to people our age. And then he started in on our parents." A ball of discomfort formed in Grace's throat, forcing her to pause and regroup, balling her hands into fists beneath her thighs. "Our parents didn't call as often as the other campers' parents. Or we'd been rejected, but our parents had begged for the camp to take us off their hands. These are things he told us, over and over. And we were already there, which is something he must have seen. Something that... assembled us in the first place. We were ready to hate our parents and follow him anywhere. And we did. We were just... teenagers."

Grace closed her eyes and thought about their unauthorized meetings in the field in the middle of the night, the five of them sitting in a tight circle, holding flashlights. The way they'd been so dazzled, so inspired by this worldly man who'd been just like them. If he could emerge on the other side of adolescence intact, maybe they could, too.

"The week camp was set to end, Ray started acting differently. He didn't stop interacting with us, but he would snap. He'd get angry at an innocent comment, or if one of us was late to hang out. Away from the rest of camp." Grace opened her eyes to find Aaron had moved closer, his face now visible under the dull cabin light. The rich, golden brown of his eyes was muted, his jaw tight. "Even though there were warning signs—I ignored them, ignored the doubts when they started appearing—we were all in. We didn't want to leave him and go back to the parents who hated us. He'd made sure of that. At least he cared enough to get upset, right?" She forced the tension in her shoulders to ebb. "We snuck out, the night before pickup. We hiked—it seemed like hours—in the dark, until we reached this house. It sounds so stupid now, that we thought we'd live there, playing house, and no one would find us. But they did. The FBI found us the next morning." A humorless smile lifted her lips. "We weren't just campers anymore. We were a senator's daughter, the governor's nieces, and a prominent local businessman's son. And we were being held hostage by a man who'd become unstable after a bad divorce. Lost his year-round job and custody of his children. All in the space of six months." Ray's desperate face flashed in her mind. "He fudged his counselor application and the administrators failed to do the proper background check, which is a major reason the camp is no longer functioning." She paused. "His ex-wife wouldn't communicate with him about reconsidering visitation and had moved without telling him where she was going. I don't think taking us to the house started as a way to get her attention, but that's what it became as camp went on."

Grace gathered the flannel blanket around her shoulders, sighing over the warmth. Someday, just maybe, she could talk about the tragedy without feeling cold, but today wasn't that day.

"We actually laughed when we heard them calling us hostages on the radio. We laughed right up until he showed us the guns, until he pointed them at our heads and ordered us to get down on the kitchen floor." A flash of silver shook across her conscious. "He'd been preparing the house for weeks. To take us there."

"I remember now." Aaron's voice slashed through the darkness, reminding her of metal being cut. "I remember what happened now. You can stop."

"No, I..." She pulled the blanket higher, up to her chin. "I have to complete the story every time I tell it or I'm avoiding."

The muscles in Aaron's throat flexed. "How many times have you told it?"

"A lot." Needing to push through, knowing she wouldn't find relief exactly, but a sense of non-failure to bring the story full circle once she finished, Grace continued. "The hostage negotiator agreed to grant each of his demands for every hostage Ray sent out. A phone call with his ex-wife, an overnight visit with his kids." A lump formed in her throat. "They requested me first, because I was—I am—a senator's daughter." She slid a look up at Aaron. "That part wasn't in the news. Neither was the fact that I didn't want to be released. The officers waiting at the door had to *drag* me out. After I was released from the house, Ray changed his mind. All that law enforcement...he knew they were only biding their time and he'd never get his demands met. And even if he did, they would never remain permanent. So he—"

Aaron sat down on the bed beside Grace, the thin, cheap mattress dipping beneath his weight. He didn't look at her, but their knees touched. Just the barest of grazes, but it gave her a shot of desperately needed warmth.

"He barricaded the doors and set the place on fire," Grace whispered. "Everyone moved at once, trying to get the other campers out, but there was gunfire inside...and nothing could have helped them."

She was grateful for Aaron's silence, grateful that the rehashed events would have time to settle down, like cinders drifting down from a chimney and turning to ash. The stillness of the cabin was something she'd grown used to, having slept there so many nights without the benefit of company, but somehow it felt heavier, more substantial, having someone to share it with.

"I wear the four ribbons in my hair for them." She pressed her knee closer to Aaron's, hungry for human contact. "And I shouldn't have taken them out last night, just because you're the one who put them there."

Aaron's hands met between his bent legs, clasping until his knuckles turned pale. "Don't worry about it."

Grace didn't know if that was possible, knowing she'd negated a kindness because she'd been in a state of shock after finding out what Aaron did for a living. In her haste to distance herself, she'd been callous, and in truth, she'd lain awake for hours during the night, wishing more than anything that she'd just kept the ribbons in her hair. She needed to find a way to make her cold treatment of him right, but now wasn't the time. Not with ghosts of the past sharing the cabin with them. "I didn't deserve to be released first. We were equally important. So I have to build this place better for them. I have to do good for all five of us. To give kids without the advantages we had...a place to succeed where my friends will never get the chance." She blew out a breath and looked at Aaron. "Declaring this place damaged and moving on feels like I'm doing the same to myself. It should be made whole again. It *can* be revived. Will you let me do that?"

CHAPTER THIRTEEN

Don't let her see your hands shaking.

Holy shit. How could he be ... scared? Over something that happened seven years earlier? He didn't *do* scared. Except one vision of Grace on the kitchen floor of some death trap with a gun in her face, and he had to be fucking hallucinating. Because the cabin floor seemed to rise, the walls looming close. He couldn't swallow, couldn't seem to move his legs. They were just sitting there, resembling the appendages he'd been born with, but lacking all function. If this wasn't fear, what was? Nothing could be worse than the sick helplessness he'd felt throughout Grace's entire story, watching as she bolstered herself over and over, while he stood by, knowing she would reject any paltry attempt he made at comfort.

Christ. What had she asked him?

Will you let me do that?

As in, making the camp a better place, in memory of

her friends. He almost laughed, but held back the reaction because it would have been totally devoid of humor. Aaron Clarkson doing something noble. Helping this girl slay her demons. Had he fallen down a goddamn rabbit hole? He wasn't supposed to give a shit about bleeding heart causes and the survivor's guilt of another person. He *didn't*.

He was just ready to rip the walls down if Grace felt guilty for another second about being rescued. Made sense, right?

No, it didn't. Nothing made sense at that juncture, so he would break it down. Put it into neat categories until sense was made. He had a job to do, a career to rekindle. And a relentless urge to banish Grace's pain. Was there a way to accomplish both and keep himself from slipping farther into the confusion Grace inspired? Yes, he could do that. He could get the need for Grace's closure out of his system and send the girl on her merry do-gooder way.

Why did that strategy bring the fear screaming back?

"Yeah." His shoes scraped on the floor as he rose from the bed, pacing away, the warmth of Grace's leg lingering on his own. "Yeah, I can do that. This is our cause. This place. I'll have to figure out a way to convince the senator, since it's obvious he resents what happened to you—to which I say, no shit—but okay. Come tomorrow, we'll start working on getting it done. Now excuse me while I go make a couple phone calls."

His progress toward the door halted when Grace shot to her feet, arms stiff at her sides, those green eyes like glowing jade moons. "I... that isn't what I was asking for. I just meant, let me help you, in general. I—I didn't think..."

Aaron's neck heated. "If you don't like the idea, we can change it—"

She jumped. She actually jumped straight up in the air, hands flying to her cheeks. "I love it. Oh, please don't change anything. I was just so surprised."

He inclined his head, mentally cursing the way his heart decided to make its presence known at such an inconvenient time, walloping his rib cage with thick booms, courtesy of Grace's pleasure. How juvenile. "I'm kind of surprised myself," he admitted, then wished he'd kept his mouth shut.

At least until Grace floated toward him. All shining eyes and rosy excitement, she spurred a lust storm in his stomach. "It's so much better when you say what you're thinking, Aaron."

"You mentioned that."

And of course, it made him want to say *more*. Say *whatever* it would take to get her legs wrapped around his hips. To rock between her thighs until her wetness drenched the fly of his pants. "Get away from me, Grace," he rasped. "It would be just like me to take advantage of you after having to tell that story."

Silence deepened around them. "How can you say that after you just found a way for me to rebuild the camp?" It seemed as if her entire body lifted and fell on a harsh sob. "Last night, you asked me if I still saw some good in you...and I didn't answer. How could I not have answered you?" She shook her gorgeous head. "I didn't mean to—"

Aaron shot forward, capturing her unspoken words with his own mouth. *Guilt.* There had been *even more* guilt in her eyes. Aaron's response was pure denial. *Not be-*

cause of me. Not over me. But as soon as their lips joined, his mind wiped clean of anything but Grace's one-of-a-kind taste. She was juicy, sweet, refreshing, intoxicating madness. He let it pull him down into its depths—*her depths*—gathering up her taste greedily so he could live with the effect as long as possible, even though surely a man couldn't withstand this type of arousal for an extended length of time. He'd want to fuck her again as soon as he came. It was a certainty his body was all too eager to confirm. Yet protectiveness held him in a state of limbo. Wanting—*needing*—to mate with her delicious body while determined to protect her from himself.

Couldn't she sense the past meaningless encounters he wore like gloves, cheapening everything he touched? Couldn't she sense his inability to be meaningful to her? Grace should have someone with substance, not someone who couldn't even garner the love of his own family. Someone who considered the ramifications of his actions and how they would serve as betrayal. *This is how you repay me?*

The voice from his not-so-distant past had Aaron tearing his mouth away with a guttural growl, clasping Grace by the shoulders. *Too hard. Ease up.* "Get away."

"If you really want that, let me go," she whispered.

God, he couldn't do it. Not with her face tipped back, lips swollen and shined up, those eyelids halfway fallen. He'd never in his life had trouble resisting sex. It was always a logical decision based on his needs. This? There was *nothing* cut and dried about it. His attraction to Grace was messy and wild and untapped. Made his chest expand with the effort to contain the expanding of something unfamiliar. Crazy and blinding. His dick needed a good, rough handling from one woman only. Grace. And she wasn't pushing him away. Seemed like she wanted the job, too, her tits sliding up and down his abs with every breath. *Give her one more chance. Show her what she's in for with a bastard like you.* With a muttered epithet, Aaron raked his hand up the back of Grace's thigh, sliding it down the back of her tights, and settling his middle finger in the valley of her ass. "Get away from me," he managed, wedging his straying digit a little more securely, earning him a closed-lipped noise.

"No," she gasped after a few seconds.

Aaron's tether broke. Recapturing Grace's mouth with an obscene amount of tongue, he backed them toward the bed, satisfaction rippling in his middle when she went down beneath him, her legs falling open in welcome. He draped his body over Grace's slighter one, eager grunts leaving his mouth as he positioned himself over her pussy and bore down with his erection. Their groans were pain-filled, reaching every corner of the cabin, breaking off when Aaron got back to kissing that addictive mouth, yanking the oversized sweater up, up to her belly, so he could rock against her sex with only his pants and her tights as obstructions.

"Aaron."

"You were warned," he reminded her with a strangled shout, delivered into the space above her head. "Three times, Grace. That's three times more than I'd give anyone else." He slid up and back in the cradle of her legs, groaning over the rasping friction her tights delivered to his stiff, fuck-hungry dick. "Make it four times. I gave you an out back at the house. You should have taken it."

When Grace should have been trembling or alarmed by

the cut steel in his voice, she only stretched out beneath him like a cat, opening up for him. Almost preening beneath his rough ministrations. "Maybe I should have. But we're here now, so stop trying to scare me." Her fingertips moved down Aaron's chest to the front of his pants, where she smoothed her palm over the curve of his cock, which started him panting like a marathon runner. "You don't really want to scare me, do you, Aaron?"

Christ, her soft words, the sight of her, were choking him up. Her hair was a haphazard display framing her face, those crooked front teeth somehow making him twice as eager to seal their mouths together again. He was a hunter who'd discovered a sprite dancing in the woods and dragged her home, intending to use her body for vigorous relief, but got forgiveness in return. "No, I don't. I don't want to scare you."

"I know," she breathed, unfastening his belt buckle. "I just know."

Aaron's hands were shaking again. *Fuck.* What was wrong with him? Grace, who'd stolen his concrete sense of self, finally lay willing and pliant beneath him. Grace, who must also be a mind reader, because she didn't greet his cock with a gentle squeeze. No, she stroked it like a... "Good girl, good girl, good girl," Aaron grated, driving into her grip as if it were a wet pussy, causing his words to slur like a drunkard's. "How'd y'know what I like, huh? You going to fuck as hot as you're fisting me?"

"Yeah," she breathed, her hand moving, pumping, against his stomach. "With you, yes, I think I might."

He'd never equated sex with honesty before, but hell if he wouldn't always recognize the lack of it for the rest of his life. Life without Grace. It would have to be without Grace, wouldn't it? This couldn't last. "I need to lift your sweater," Aaron said unevenly. "When we were driving, the seatbelt…it crossed right between your tits, and goddamn, you're not wearing a bra, are you? You have any idea the way that material molds to your little nipples, Grace? I kept the window rolled down to make them hard. I *love* them hard." Using his left elbow to prop himself up, Aaron took the hem of her sweater and started to lift, exposing her shuddering belly, the beginning of her rib cage, before letting it drop, drifting his hand lower. Over the opaque tights, beneath which her white panties were visible. "You took our discussion about panties to heart. Remind me what I said."

The hand around his dick turned caressing, almost luxuriating in his flesh, her pupils dilating as she stared up at him. "You said…" She licked her lips, but with a surge of possessiveness, Aaron took over the job, wetting them for her as she spoke. "You said, girls who get w-wet from kissing shouldn't leave the house without underwear on."

"That's right." He gave her mouth a final lick, vowing to return to her sweet, supple lips soon. "Your tits have no such problem, do they? They don't get wet unless they're being sucked. Correct?"

Grace gave a breathy moan, eyes squeezing shut.

"I can't wait much longer to get these tights off, baby." He drifted the heel of his hand over the crotch of her tights, pushed down, before retreating back up to her belly button. "Better give me an answer."

"Yes, wet…" She spoke through trembling lips. "Only when you suck them."

You, she'd said. As in, Aaron. Him. Responsibility swamped his being, bringing with it a fresh wave of lust so extreme, his cock leaked a hint of liquid from the tip, ripping a curse from his mouth, which he repeated when Grace used it to lubricate the tightest, most perceptive jerk job of his life. He shoved his hand up beneath Grace's sweater, fondling tits that had been formed with men's hands in mind. They were small, but plump, conforming to his palm like a sex dream. "You don't leave the house without a covered pussy, Grace, but forget about wearing a bra. These were meant to bounce, meant to be cupped from behind when you're not expecting it. You leave them free for me, understand?"

Aaron made that demand, and then actually glimpsed her tits for the first time, realizing he hadn't done them justice. Round, dusky nipples strained for attention, made even more prominent by her doing a veritable back bend to get her breasts closer to his mouth. She was so motherfucking glorious, his hand went to his pocket in frantic search of a condom, because if he didn't ram his dick into Grace's slick body now—*now*—he would die of neglect.

"No one can hear us out here," he groaned into her neck. "You remember that. Be as loud as you need." His tongue licked out to trace her earlobe. "Don't worry, I'm going to make sure you need to scream yourself hoarse."

Instead of the condom, his hand closed around the ribbons. And it took Aaron a few seconds to realize why his racing pulse, his demanding libido, ground to a halt. Such a severe one, he choked on his own breath. Ribbons. Friends. The camp. His mind dragged him back to last night, when she'd left him in the woods. *I've doubted my judgment around someone like you before and it ended badly.*

Someone like you.

Someone like you.

Aaron jerked back, moving off the bed like a shot. His erection rebounded against his thigh and he welcomed the pain of shoving his hard flesh back into his pants. Leaving it in such a dire state. Maybe it would distract him from the crater rapidly expanding in the center of his chest.

"Aaron..." Grace pushed up on her elbows, not bothering to cover her naked body, not bothering to hide a single thing. Confusion, hurt, sexual need, all playing across her features like a movie reel. "What's wrong? I—I don't understand. Did I—"

In seeming slow motion, both of their gazes dropped to the red ribbons hanging out of his pocket. Something sarcastic, something hurtful, was right on the tip of his tongue. Anything to close himself off, force him back into a familiar version of who he'd been before she'd shown up and rearranged his priorities. Hurting Grace would accomplish that, while putting her back at a safe distance. But he'd *kept* the ribbons. And that fucked him. She was too goddamn perceptive, and Aaron watched in muted horror as she started to cry, seeing every exposed inch of him. Seeing she'd gotten to him.

"Stop crying," he ordered roughly.

Grace jerked her knees up to her chest, in a mirror image of how he'd found her in the cabin closet the day before. Eons ago. "I'm sorry for what I said, and how I acted...I think maybe I was wrong—"

Maybe. "No. You were right." His raw laughter made him want to cringe, made him feel like such an obvious fraud. "If you think I chose this camp to help you in some way, *that's* where you're wrong. No maybe about it. I..." Lame, lame, he sounded so fucking *lame.*

Grace dropped her forehead onto her lifted knees, her body starting to shake with silent tears.

"Please, stop crying." His throat was on fire. "I don't know what to do about it."

"You can hold me," she said, her voice muffled. "You can come back and pretend like we just met... and I didn't say any of those awful things. M-maybe?"

Oh, Christ, that was tempting. It was also impossible. First impressions didn't vanish into thin air. Neither did third impressions, fourth. And after exposing parts of himself to this girl about which he'd barely been cognizant, she'd drawn a comparison between him and a lunatic murderer. Worse, she'd been right. Sure, Aaron hadn't killed anyone. Yet. But he made his living performing mind tricks, the kind Grace had endured at the hands of Ray Solomon. Yeah, she'd pegged him right.

There was a reason she'd refused to ask him about his departure from California. His lack of a job. What he'd done to get fired. Yeah, she could see the ugly in him. She'd *known* it was there all along. What kind of a man lacks enough morality to do what he'd done that night, all those months ago? To harm a family bond with so little thought or feeling. Not the kind of man Grace needed.

Why was he still standing there?

Aaron tugged out his cell phone. "I'm going to get Peggy up here. She can..." His gesture encompassed Grace on the bed. "She'll be better at this."

He walked out of the cabin with his eyes closed, the sound of Grace's tears following closely on his heels.

Chapter Fourteen

Through gritty eyes, Grace watched Aaron's family arrive in a rental van he'd arranged, which they'd used to drive to YouthAspire. Peggy hopped out of the backseat first, holding a hand over her eyes to block the sun, a smile brightening her face. Belmont came next, alighting from the driver's side to assist Sage—unnecessarily, in Grace's opinion—from the back. Grace started to turn her attention away from the pair when Old Man bounded out of the van, running in circles around the courtyard, but gravity sucked her interest back to Belmont and Sage. The petite woman circled behind Aaron's visibly tense brother, wrapping her arms around his waist from the back. And he just kind of... sagged. Like Sage's touch had caused some vital release he hadn't been expecting, which was obvious from the way he propped a hand on the van, head falling forward.

Aaron's voice made Grace jump guiltily from her position on the cabin steps, as if she'd been watching a naughty movie or something. Although, while she'd observed a decent amount of adult film in her time, none of it had ever seemed as...intimate. Grace's cheeks burned when Aaron glanced over, even though there was no sign of their encounter in his no-nonsense expression. No, he looked calm and unruffled, ready to take on the world. Unlike Grace, whose shaky legs had forced her down onto the step an hour ago, and she hadn't bothered to move since. A bear had taken a swipe at her insides, shredding all her organs to pieces, and if she stood, they would all decorate the ground at her feet.

It seemed she'd made a horrible mistake about Aaron. Since taking up permanent residence on the cabin steps, the differences between Aaron and the man who'd turned her life upside down at age sixteen had bombarded her. Since the night they'd met in the woods, Aaron had done nothing but push her away. Even when he'd found out she was the senator's daughter, he'd attempted to create distance between them. God, he'd warned her about himself so many times, she'd lost count. Bad men—the *real* ones—didn't draw attention to their flaws. They overcompensated for them. Or they made those flaws someone else's fault. Aaron did neither of those things. He admitted them and tried to limit their damage.

Grace pressed her curled-up fingers to her mouth, watching as Old Man trotted across the courtyard toward Aaron. Looking surprised at the canine's interest, Aaron scratched at his jaw and crouched down...just in time for Old Man to change course and bypass his owner completely. And when Aaron rushed back to his feet, clearing his throat and checking his cell phone, Grace's legs finally got the desire to move, wanting to fly across the distance and launch herself into Aaron's arms to make up for his dog's disinterest...but she'd forfeited the privilege. The benefit of knowing Aaron would catch her, even if he would chastise her afterward for coming too close. Maybe this time he wouldn't want to catch her at all. Why would he? After she'd done her best to confirm every bad thing he already thought about himself?

"What is this place?" Peggy asked, turning in a circle, her gaze landing on Grace. "Hey, you!"

Grace lifted her hand in a wave, hoping Peggy would be satisfied with the gesture, but manners poked her ribs until she stood and joined the group. "Hi," she murmured, her voice sounding threadbare.

Aaron cast her a speculative glance, but it was fleeting. "You wanted to help, right?" He seemed to strive for a jocular tone, but Grace could hear the doubt blurring the edges as he addressed his siblings and Sage. "Is that, uh...still the case? If you guys want to get back on the road, I can catch up in New York, the way we'd originally planned. It's not a—"

"We're here. We're helping." Peggy looked affronted that he'd suggested otherwise. "Give us the rundown, Captain."

His sister's endorsement didn't seem to convince him. "Bel, come tomorrow, there could be cameras. A lot of people." He shifted his stance. "That's what we're hoping for. That's what we need to make this venture successful."

"Will it be safe?" Grace found it interesting the way everyone's head whipped around toward Belmont at his simple question, but realized she'd done the same. Something about his voice demanded you quiet down and memorize the rocky nuances, give them credence. "For the girls. Will it be safe?"

"Yes," Aaron answered, irritation apparent in his flexing jaw. "You'll be shocked to know I'm as concerned about their security as you."

"I'm not shocked," Belmont said, before turning for the rental van and beginning to unload the luggage, including a doggy bed. Aaron's surprise over his brother's curt statement was clear, but he recovered quickly, shoving a restless hand through his hair. "Right. Long story short, we're going to turn this place into the functioning youth camp it once was. Today is for planning. Tomorrow— when reinforcements arrive—we'll need to delegate jobs and supervise. We're going to need results fast, so maximizing funds and labor is key. We need something to show for our efforts by end of day tomorrow or they could deem this project a waste of time."

Sage angled her body so she could half face Belmont, her steady eyes following his movements. "Who are they?"

"The Pendleton campaign." When Peggy clapped— perhaps for Aaron's work securing the job with her father—Aaron only inclined his head toward Grace. "You've met Grace. Now meet Grace Pendleton."

"Oh," Sage and Peggy mouthed at the same time.

"Yes. Oh." Aaron dug out his cell phone, the vibration indicating an incoming call. "Incidentally, her father is calling me now. Probably wondering where the hell I've taken his youngest daughter. He's going to love my answer."

Grace swallowed a grapefruit-sized lump in her throat. Since the beginning, she'd caused nothing but trouble for

Aaron, and all he'd gotten in exchange was an assassination of his character. "Let me talk to him."

"That's not necessary." Aaron started to turn away, but stopped, digging the red ribbons out of his pocket and holding them out to Peggy. "Could you..." He waved his hand in the space above his shoulder. "She wears them in her hair."

As soon as his sister accepted the shredded offerings, Aaron strode off to answer the phone call, leaving Grace wishing the ground would open up and swallow her whole.

* * *

Feeling himself sink deeper into the inescapable black hole of hurting Grace's feelings, Aaron moved toward the giant mess hall. After leaving Grace sobbing in the cabin, torn between arousal and self-disgust, he'd been desperate for activity, so he'd found himself seeking out an ideal spot for mission control. In other words, a place to station himself with a laptop, a cell phone, and a week's worth of PowerBars so he could pull off this project and move to the next level of his career.

Also known as the original, genius plan he'd made. Back when he didn't have his head buried in his ass and a suspicion he was more capable of...feelings...than he'd originally thought.

Right. Back to business. Already he'd made contact with several media outlets, arranging phone interviews and national news radio call-ins, in addition to granting requests to speak with him directly. Capitalizing on the now-viral video of himself being interviewed looking like shit ran over twice, Aaron had specified any on-camera interviews with him would only be granted with Youth-Aspire as the backdrop, hoping to garner the most airtime possible. And the media were coming, thank God. When they did, he'd be ready.

This whole strategy was unorthodox, to say the least. Throwing every ounce of his weight and expertise behind it would backfire if he failed. In Aaron's early position on the political spectrum, one rarely received a second chance at bat. Now he stood at the plate, armed with nothing but an inconvenient fascination with a girl, his whack-job family, and confidence that felt shaky for the first time.

When the cell phone shuddered in his hand again, Aaron jerked his attention back to the present. *Fake it until you make it, Clarkson.*

Christ, he'd been doing that for a while, hadn't he?

"Senator, how can I help you?"

"We're up another three points in the polls." Pendleton was doing his best to sound even-keeled, but Aaron could hear the beginnings of excitement in the ex-military man's voice. "We want an update."

"We," Aaron repeated, relief filling his lungs with air. More than one person giving their attention meant the campaign staff was finally giving him credit where credit was due. "Who am I addressing?"

"You've got Corbett, my campaign manager, and his staff."

Not too shabby. Unfortunately, the conversation was about to take a fucking nosedive. "In the interest of moving quickly and the campaign appearing focused, I've gone with the best available option, which also happens to be the most convenient." At the top of the mess hall steps, he turned and found Grace watching him, looking sad as Peggy threaded the red ribbons back into her hair. Before he could remember the sensation of smooth strands slipping through his fingers, Aaron continued, his tone deeper than before. "Ms. Pendleton has already made some headway restoring the YouthAspire camp, and with some muscle, it won't be long before we make it viable. With enough resources and local volunteers, we can make it sustainable before the campaign gets back on the trail."

Silence. "You are aware of the camp's history." Not a question. "You can't honestly think it's wise linking my name to the brainwashing and murdering of teenagers."

The blunt description sent acid rising in Aaron's throat, made him want to drop the phone and go shake Grace. Or hold her. Or demand she stop looking at him. Demand she never stop. He was losing his goddamn mind. "The American people aren't cowed by misfortune. Hell, they're fascinated by it. You're not shying away from the past, you're correcting it." No, that was Grace's mission, but he had no choice but to echo it now. Knew she wouldn't fault him, so long as the goal was accomplished. "You're building something strong on a broken foundation. Exactly what you're planning to do as president. No matter what way we spin in, you're doing something positive. Instead of attacking your opponent, you're making him look like a selfish asshole."

There was a round of laughter on the other end, but the acid only grew sharper in Aaron's windpipe as he waited for Pendleton to respond. "Now, as far as Grace is concerned—"

"We'll keep her name out of it," Aaron assured him,

tearing his gaze away from the girl in question. "I spent some time this morning running my own searches through various media outlets, and she's not connected to the name *YouthAspire*. She's so far removed from the public eye, I don't even think her presence here would inspire curiosity. And that's if someone recognizes her, which I won't let happen."

Another beat of quiet made Aaron anxious, but he didn't know why. The answer became apparent a moment later, when the senator spoke again, sounding pensive, slightly hesitant. "And if we were to... allow the media to recognize her. Stop hiding what happened seven years ago and reveal her role in the hostage situation... would that help or hurt us? In your opinion."

Rage blasted Aaron head to toe, so severe, he was forced to lower the phone, bracing both hands on his knees. *Breathe, breathe, breathe. Focus.* He could *not* allow that to happen, no matter what it took. He knew Grace wanted the truth of that day acknowledged, but she didn't understand, had never experienced, a media frenzy. He'd narrowly escaped one himself back in California, or he would never have gotten this second chance. But watching them exploit Grace? Jesus, it would be hell. She was too good to be tainted by their questions, their merciless prying.

Aaron drew a calming dose of oxygen through his nose, lifting the phone back to his ear. And he circumvented the undesirable outcome the only way he could come up with on short notice. "I'm not sure that's the best idea. Unless you think she can handle the pressure of sitting on a couch across from Diane Sawyer." His laugh was forced, but convincing under the circumstances. "All due respect,

I don't know if she can retain the kind of coaching we'd need to put her through it."

Bastard. You're a bastard.

"You might be right." Aaron could hear Pendleton shifting in his office chair. "I've tried creative ways of coaching her before and she's been resistant."

Aaron's stomach went hollow. "What does that mean?"

"We had her in therapy after the camp fiasco and found it was only making her...well...*more.* Wild. Wanting to express herself. So we hired a more suitable one that understood how we needed to direct Grace. Needless to say, it backfired when my daughter found out."

When the phone protested in Aaron's hand, he realized how tight he was gripping it. Directed. Without her knowledge. *Jesus.* On top of the camp tragedy and Ray Solomon, no wonder Grace found him difficult to be around. Another mouthpiece for her dad. Another person skilled in subtle influence. Who could blame her for walking away in the woods last night?

The senator's voice broke into his trance. "I hired you, Clarkson, because you don't have the ability to get squeamish about things like this. I've even considered eventually moving you to Pendleton campaign headquarters in New York, where you could be more effective, going toe to toe with the big boys." A tick of silence passed. "Did I misjudge you?"

"No," he managed, surprise filtering in over the senator's revelation. *New York.* "You didn't. That's my honest assessment."

"You think I'm right to keep her out of the public's consciousness."

Dammit. The man was putting words in his mouth and

he'd left himself no choice but to own them. Even if they were utter bullshit. He knew that now. Knew Grace's unique personality didn't make her a liability, it made her something to be celebrated. "That's right," Aaron intoned, regardless. "You've done the best thing for the campaign." He would have said anything to keep her from being shoved beneath a microscope and dissected for everyone's entertainment, but the words singed his throat on their way out, rubbing his vocal cords raw. "Put me in touch with your speech writers so we can prepare a site visit. Probably not for tomorrow, but the following day. We don't want to put you on camera until there's progress."

"Done and done."

When the line clicked over and another no-bullshit voice answered, Aaron lost himself in the planning, trying not to dwell on the overwhelming sense that he'd just sold his soul.

* * *

When Aaron jogged to a stop at the courtyard's center, Grace dropped the ripped-up piece of floorboard she'd been carrying from one of the cabins, the rotted wood slipping through lifeless fingers. He was...*covered* in sweat. Dripping with the stuff, actually. As he bent forward and stopped his wristwatch, his sides heaving with exertion, moisture gathering in the center of his forehead and dripping to the ground. The gray, long-sleeved T-shirt he wore was so soaked, it clung to his skin in a way that would slap against his flesh if the material connected with muscle. And there was muscle. Ripped flanks and cut triceps. Things Grace had noticed before on other men, but never given a second glance. But on Aaron, who she'd never seen shirtless—which he might as well have been in the gray second skin—the muscles and masculine detail of his body wouldn't release her from captivation.

I almost had sex with that man this morning. Him and his body.

Someone emerging from the cabin in her wake launched Grace out of her hormonal haze...and clued her into the fact that she'd been panting like a horn-dog.

Thankfully, Aaron hadn't caught her staring, but then again, who cared if he did? Grace *wanted* him to know she found him attractive. That she liked talking to him, looking at him. In fact, she was already lonely for him. Was it silly? Yeah, maybe a little. They'd only known each other a few days. But Aaron the jerk was a million times better than Aaron the absent. She'd done that, but had no idea how to fix the wound she'd inflicted. A wound he would almost certainly deny existed if she brought it up. So that kept her at arm's length, right where he obviously wanted her.

They'd been working all afternoon. As soon as the industrial-sized electrical generator had arrived and begun running, not to mention the ten steel Dumpsters that had been dropped off in the courtyard, Belmont had produced a crowbar and hammer from the Suburban and entered the first cabin, grimly relaying the news to Grace, Peggy, and Sage as to which items were salvageable and which ones needed to be trashed. Then he'd proceeded to dismantle...well, everything. Having brought a contractor to the site once before, Grace had been well aware of how little could be saved, thanks to the camp being without upkeep for so long, but watching Belmont swing his hammer, prying floorboards up with a crowbar, had proven difficult. Somewhere along the line, she'd taken ownership of this place and hated seeing parts of it demolished, necessary or not. Thankfully, the cabin frames didn't need to be replaced, which would have demanded the bulk of time and manpower. And the plumber who'd turned the water on that afternoon only needed to replace a handful of pipes that had rusted in their disuse, but for now, they had running water, which was a blessing. Since Aaron would clearly require a shower...

Peggy passed Grace, giving her a subtle elbow nudge, and Grace stooped down to pick up the dropped wood, hurling it over the Dumpster's steel wall. After Peggy followed suit with an armful of insulation, they both stopped, seeming to notice at the same time the sky grew dark.

"Manual labor," Peggy shouted, shaking her fist at the heavens. "This is not what I had in mind when I offered to help my brother. What a total waste of my ample charms."

Aaron reached them, tossing a smirk at Peggy. "Hey, today was supposed to be for planning. You chose destruction. It wasn't assigned."

"We were just sitting around, listening to you sound authoritative on the phone. And you were bow-guarding the laptop." Peggy poked Aaron in the chest. "We couldn't just beg off the first time you actually ask for help."

Without a sound to signal her approach, Sage joined them at the Dumpster. "I think it's been very therapeutic."

"More therapeutic than slapping me?" Aaron asked with a cocked eyebrow, a slight smile easing up the corners of his mouth.

"Hmm." Sage brushed some wood dust off her jeans before answering, "No."

"Y-you slapped him?" Grace croaked, the question emerging before she could stop it. Fire raked through her chest, making it hard to inhale. Aaron's haunted expression when he'd pulled away from her that morning came back, more vivid than it had been in the actual moment. That same man had been struck across the face? By someone *else* who was supposed to care about him? It was too much to take. She couldn't digest it alongside her own guilt. Oh *God*, her eyelids were starting to burn again. "I, um…"

With a backward step, Grace tried to separate from the group, but Sage cupped Grace's elbow, her expression apologetic. "I've apologized. It was…that was wrong of me."

Peggy threw an arm around Grace's shoulder. "You throw four people in a Suburban, then strand them in the wilderness, I'm thinking a few slaps are par for the course." She gave Grace a squeeze. "Aaron can take it."

"Can he?" Grace whispered. "Why should he have to?"

Aaron paused in the act of wiping his sweat-dotted forehead, a move that exposed his muscle-knitted abdomen. He dropped the garment to reveal a frown, but didn't speak or remove his rapt attention from Grace. Not even when Peggy whistled under her breath, splitting a look between Grace and Aaron. "You know what we need?" She gave a single nod. "A girls' night."

Belmont chose that moment to emerge from the cabin. Without tearing her attention away from her own sweat-soaked man, Grace knew Belmont was in much the same condition. Caked in grime, wearing the day's labor like a winter coat, while Aaron resembled more of a sleek, cagey animal. "Girls' night," Belmont grunted. "I don't like it."

"You don't always have to like it," Sage whispered, flushing to the roots of her hair. "Everything will be fine. You'll see."

The mood shifted even more out of alignment. Even though Grace had spent only a limited time in their company, she sensed it was a rarity for anyone to disagree with Belmont. The large lumberjack of a man looked surprised himself, if an eye twitch counted as a reaction. "I'll go with you. I can wait in the Suburban."

Sage tucked a wisp of light brown hair behind her ear. "Can I talk to you somewhere private?"

Belmont stared at Sage in the epic silence, before grunting in response, turning and reentering the cabin. With a deep breath, Sage followed him inside, leaving Grace, Aaron, and Peggy alone once again. "Well." Peggy clapped her hands. "I'm going to freshen up. Grace, do you want to come along?"

Grace grimaced at her dirt-covered clothes. In her haste to throw on clothes and run interference between Aaron and her father that morning, she hadn't planned on physical labor. And especially not going out for an impromptu night out with two girls who looked put together and fresh even after a day of hard work. "Maybe we can put it off until tomorrow night?" She rubbed the bottom of one boot against the toe of the other. "I don't have a change of clothes. I didn't plan on spending the night here, so I have nothing—"

"Spending the night here?" Aaron cut in. "Who said anything about that?"

"*She* did. Just now." Grace swore Peggy's blond curls tightened, alongside the clear surge of her irritation. "And why shouldn't she? She worked as hard as the rest of us. This is her project and there are plenty of places to sleep now." She squared her shoulders. "I have my entire wardrobe with me. There will be something for her to wear. Probably *ten* somethings."

Warmth flooded Grace, along with a heaping helping of excitement and gratefulness. Maybe she was too old to play dress-up, but she'd never had the experience growing up. The idea of Peggy buttoning a row of buttons down her back or trying out shades of lipstick on her mouth? It wasn't an experience she could pass up. "Thank you." Sensing Aaron's scowl, Grace ignored him. "I'll make sure I pick up a few things from home tomorrow."

"Sure, sure." Peggy hooked an arm through Grace's, hip bumping Aaron as they passed on the way to the female locker room. "Tomorrow will be soon enough to deal with everything. Girls' night trumps all else."

CHAPTER FIFTEEN

Grace took a deep inhale of the mingling perfumes sailing on the night air. They were light and fun, not cloying or obvious. Two hours. It had taken *two hours* for three girls to prepare themselves for a night out, but for Grace it might as well have passed in a single eye blink. She couldn't stop running her hands down the black suede skirt she'd borrowed from Peggy, complete with fringe on the sides. Thick, thigh-high tights and a cashmere sweater made the outfit winter in Iowa appropriate, but she could imagine herself wearing it just about anywhere. One of the hipster bars in Austin where she'd always sat in the corner alone, watching everyone else interact. Or maybe at a casual political event, with Aaron's hand on the small of her back.

Bad thoughts. Thoughts she didn't have any right to let form. But there they were. She'd been cleaned up, lotioned down, and dressed in smooth, snug material. After wearing mismatched oversized clothing so long, she felt like a stranger in her own skin. Not in a bad way, just a light-headed, euphoric, change of pace kind of way. Just for the night. And with that feeling came a tingle of permission to act out of the ordinary. *Her* ordinary anyway.

Before they reached the Suburban, Aaron and Belmont appeared out of the darkness, as if they'd been lying in wait. Neither one of them was smiling, both of them with arms crossed. It was the first time Grace had witnessed their obvious brotherhood, and it made her want to push them into a man hug. Although the thought fled as fast as it appeared because Aaron's arms dropped to his sides, that piercing gaze traveling high on Grace's legs, disappearing up her skirt. At least the sensation of his perusal continued on, gliding along the underside of her panties, narrowing her concentration down to a slow inner clench.

"What did you do to her?" Aaron murmured, his attention finally landing on her face. "She doesn't need all that crap on her eyes."

"I like the crap," Grace said, heat sliding from one side of her belly to the other. "The crap is fun and sparkly."

A muscle shifted in Aaron's cheek. He turned his irritation onto Peggy, who appeared to be waiting for it, amused expression in place. "I don't know where you think you're going. There's no bars for miles and they close early."

"I'm sure we'll figure something out." Peggy yanked open the driver's side door of the Suburban, then snapped her fingers. "Ooh, I forgot my wallet. Be right back."

Aaron's sister took off toward the cabin, leaving the four of them standing beneath the bright moon, awkwardness closing in without Peggy to run interference. Aaron and Grace may as well have been standing there alone for all the attention Belmont and Sage were paying them, though, eyes locked on one another.

Wanting to give the two some privacy, Grace crossed behind the Suburban, intending to climb into the backseat, but Aaron beat her there, opening the door and holding out a hand to assist her. Trying to hide her inability to draw a breath, Grace slipped her hand into Aaron's and climbed onto the cracked leather.

Before she could settle onto the seat, Aaron's low, vile curse caught her off guard. "What?"

Aaron's eyes were bright, reminding her of how they'd looked that morning, running the length of her body on the cabin bed. When she'd held his full erection in her hand, stroking it, listening to him growl. Now, in the dark, relative privacy of the Suburban's backseat, Aaron's attention was glued to the sliver of skin exposed between the skirt and her thigh-highs. "Jesus." He ran a thumb beneath the hem, pushing the garment higher, baring the highest part of her legs, just above the stockings. "Why couldn't they go all the way up, like your other ones?"

"I like these better," she whispered, battling the urge to open her knees. To let him look to his heart's content.

"No shit. I like them better, too." He circled his hand around Grace's upper thigh, brushing his thumb over her sensitive flesh, his masculine groan hardening her nipples. "Good thing you weren't wearing these this morning. That little nylon barrier very well might have kept my cock from sinking in where I don't belong." His tongue touched the corner of his lips. "Yeah. You would have been ridden an inappropriate length of time before I came to my senses. I would have had to pull out and lick you wet again at least twice."

Lord above. Grace's neck was trying its best to lose power, her limbs turning to goo. "Don't say things like that," she whimpered.

"What? You don't appreciate hearing my sick thoughts about fucking you?" Aaron stepped back, tilting his head to look up her skirt. "Try living in my mind for an hour. *One hour.*"

"I wish I could. I wish it so bad." Grace pressed the heels of her hands against her nipples, trying to ease the pressure. "But that's not what I meant. I meant...don't say you stopped because you came to your senses. It hurts me."

A ragged sound emerged from his throat. "Ah, baby. It wouldn't hurt after the first minute or so. I'd work you through it, tell you in your ear how tight you feel." He wasn't looking her in the eye, wasn't in the mood for an actual conversation about the issues between them. Maybe he was using sex to distract both of them, but she was too relieved Aaron still desired her body to take issue. Especially when he leaned down and laid a wet kiss on the inside of her thigh, at the stocking's edge. "Keep your naked flesh beneath this skirt tonight, or so help me God, I will be down this mountain like a fucking bat out of hell. Are you hearing me?"

He kissed the opposite thigh, tracing her stocking with a stiff tongue, setting off such a lustful squeeze between Grace's legs, she grabbed hold of his hair, holding him in place. "Why?" she gasped, her stubbornness taking a stab at breaking through to him. "*W-why* would you do that?"

Approaching footsteps had both of them heaving sighs of frustration, Aaron straightening, wiping the back of his wrist over his open mouth, those blazing eyes still riveted on the spot between Grace's thighs. "Why?" Their

gazes finally met, although it seemed as if they were looking at each other through a fog bank. And as the haze
drifted past and cleared, Aaron's expression adapted a
now-familiar impassiveness. "Because you've made yourself my responsibility. If you get in trouble or show up
tomorrow hung over, I shoulder the blame—"

Before Aaron could annoy her straight out of anything
resembling a good mood, Grace lunged forward on the
seat, stamping her lips over Aaron's. Satisfaction thrilled
in her middle when his hand tangled in her hair and he
groaned, trying to deepen the kiss—but she pulled back
before complying became a temptation.

"Shut the fuck up," she whispered against his lips.
"When you met me, I was setting up a robbery. No one
tells me what to do. I'm a little thrown off right now, because I hurt someone I like. And now he's hurting me back
by staying away, even now, when I realize that's not what
I want. I *never* really did. And we're in this place with a
lot of hard memories for me. But I'm a warrior and *you*
don't tell *me* what to do." She snagged his lip with her
teeth, before letting it go. "You might have buried my ribbon cutter underneath a glare, but I know he's still in there.
So just shut the fuck up about responsibility and blame,
Aaron Clarkson. We're in this together, whether you like
it or not."

On cue, the Suburban's engine rumbled to life, capping
off Grace's rambling speech and lobbing her back to the
present. It seemed to take Aaron slightly longer to catch
up, his jaw hanging somewhere in the vicinity of his
knees. Behind him, Belmont boosted Sage into the passenger's side with such a stormy glower, Grace decided she'd
gotten the more desirable male reaction.

With a satisfied nod, Grace took hold of the plastic door handle, lifting an eyebrow when Aaron didn't move out of the way. "Excuse me, please."

Finally, he stepped back, pointing his index finger at Grace. "I meant what I said."

"So did I."

Ignoring Aaron's look of warning, Grace slammed the door shut, surprised to find Peggy reaching back for a high five. "Atta girl."

Grace strapped on her seatbelt with a decisive click. "Let's roll."

* * *

As it turned out, Aaron had been right about one thing. Bars in Iowa did close early. Even Peggy hadn't been able to charm the weary bartender into serving them one final drink before locking the doors. She had, however, succeeded in sweet-talking their way into a bottle of cheap red wine from the bar's supply, which they'd wrapped in a discarded McDonald's bag from the Suburban's backseat. And now passed between them. In a cornfield.

Grace was having the time of her life.

Surrounded by green stalks, drenched in moonlight, they were invisible from the world, every word they spoke seeming to get swallowed up into the ether. Never to be repeated or frowned upon. The last time she'd sat outdoors with girls her own age, she'd been a camper at Youth-Aspire. Maybe drawing that comparison should have been upsetting, but she couldn't have been happier. Taking a bittersweet moment and suturing the knife slashes in its sides with good. Making it okay to enjoy an occasion that would have made her weep in the name of unfairness not so long ago. Another moment to cherish, instead of mourn.

Peggy passed the bottle of wine to Sage, but as the wedding planner had been doing all night, she looked at the bottle thoughtfully without actually drinking from it. "Bel looked fit to be tied when we left."

Sage picked at the bottle's label. "It'll be good for him. He has to learn the world won't fall apart if something is outside his control."

"Oh, I don't know." Peggy fell back, bracing herself on the flat of her hands. "I think it's only having Sage out of his control that gets him worked up."

"Maybe you're right," Sage said. "Maybe I shouldn't have come running to New Mexico. I just—"

"You don't have to explain," Peggy interjected, the white light filtering down from the sky to catch the engagement rings strung around her neck. "I'm glad you did come, though. Saved me from being trapped in the car with two stubborn men. One of them might have been my first murder victim."

Banishing the wistfulness she felt creeping in at watching the close relationship between the two women, Grace reached for the wine bottle and took a healthy swig, settling the green glass between her folded legs. "Would it be all right if I asked...are you Belmont's girlfriend? Sometimes I think it's obvious, but others..."

"No, I'm not his girlfriend," Sage answered in a rush. "He's never even kissed me." Clearly mortified at having revealed that detail, the wedding planner hummed a few bars of the "Wedding March." "I'm sorry I said that in front of you, Peggy. He's your brother."

Peggy made a magnanimous gesture. "Say what you will. We are within the cone of silence." She shrugged. "Either way, it's been like watching a weird kink perfor- mance through double-sided glass since you two met. I think we passed kissing and went straight to edging."

"*Peggy.*" Sage settled back into her cross-legged posi- tion. "What's edging?"

Grace didn't realize she was laughing until her sides began to ache. "It's okay, Sage. I don't know, either."

"Oh, you don't? Pretty sure you've been"—Peggy twirled her fingers in Grace's direction—"starring in your own orgasm deprivation scene with Aaron." Her face screwed up in disgust. "Maybe I'm not as comfortable talking about this as I thought. Stop hogging the wine."

Sage took the bottle from Grace and held it out to Peggy. "Speaking of Aaron..." She pursed her lips as if trying to diminish a smile. "What's happening there?"

With a blown-out breath, Grace stared out over the jagged cornfield outline against the night sky. "Aaron is just...*wow.*" She breathed the word, closing her eyes. "When I saw him, I thought he was a movie star. There's so much *stuff* going on in his head, but I forgot to see it. Or I stopped looking, just like he wanted. That was my mis- take. And now he's shut me out. Stopped giving me those little glimpses into why he's so...hardened. I hate that. It's horrible, trying to make him *see* me again. See *him- self* again." Silence greeted Grace's speech, and when she opened her eyes, the two women stared back in surprise, although she detected a hint of appreciation in Peggy's case. "So, I'm going to seduce him tonight and go from there," Grace finished with a decisive nod.

Peggy, who'd just taken an unfortunate sip of wine, spit

it out on the ground. "Holy shit. Sage, we both need to take a page out of her playbook." Something about her own words made the light fade from Peggy's gaze. "My plan was to show up in Cincinnati—our next stop—and just make the fucker's life a living hell. Maybe I would catch more bees with honey." She tossed her curls back over her shoulder. "Screw it, too much plotting has gone into the original plan. No turning back now."

Before she could second-guess herself, or worry that touching another person too soon might result in them being uncomfortable, Grace reached over and laid a hand on Peggy's arm. "I've had experience making lives hell. There's definitely merit in both."

For a few beats, Peggy only scrutinized Grace, as if checking between her words for alternate meanings. "Whose life could you possibly make hell?"

Grace smiled. "Ask Aaron. I think I'm making *his* life hell."

Sage curled a hand around the wine bottle, lifting it up in a toast. "Not tonight!"

Their trio of laughter cut off abruptly when a strange sound interrupted the night's stillness. They all exchanged a panicked glance, each of them rising slowly to their feet. Grace actually had to bat mist out of the way to get a good look at the surrounding cornfield. "It sounded like an animal."

Peggy edged closer to Sage, the wine bottle forgotten on the ground at their feet. "What kind of animals are out here in the dead of winter?"

Breathing turned ragged, Sage pressed a hand to her chest. "Oh God. All I can see is that movie *Jeepers Creepers* about the scarecrow—"

"Oh my *God*, not helping," Peggy grated.

"Pheasant. It could be a pheasant." Grace nodded, a chill working its way down the back of her neck when the high-pitched gurgling noise reached them again, this time much closer. "Yeah, that wasn't a pheasant."

After that, the sequence of events blurred together. An object shot out of the soupy fog, emitting a harsh gurgle and heading straight for Sage. It whirled around and careened toward Grace. Someone screamed—presumably Peggy, since Grace had been rendered mute in her desperation to identify the creature hell bent on terrorizing them—and all three women went sprinting toward the Suburban, which unfortunately, was a quarter mile back toward the road.

"It's *following* us," Peggy screeched. "What the fuck even is it?"

Sage executed an Olympic-caliber hurtle over a row of corn stalks. "I'm not turning around to find out."

"Get your car keys out," Grace instructed. "Get them out, so we can just dive in."

"Good call, Jason Bourne." Peggy shoved a hand into her pocket, but yanked it back out on a squeal when the animal picked up the pace enough to nip at the back of her shoe. "Oh, shit! *No way*. No way I'm dying in this field and letting my brothers say, 'I told her so' at my funeral."

"Belmont's never even kissed me," Sage pointed out, sounding on the verge of hysteria.

A laugh tickled the lining of Grace's belly, the reality of the situation catching up with her. Someone needed to have a cool head here and the fact that she—the impulsive, headstrong black sheep of the Pendleton family—was auditioning for the role, struck her as hilarious, even as she

slowed her sprint, getting her first good look at their tor-
mentor. "It's ... you guys, it's a turkey."

Peggy shot her a look that said *you're not serious*, but
kept running. "Turkey or wolverine, it's still chasing us.
Should I just stop?"

"No *way*." Grace forced gravity into her tone. "They're
hungry because the corn is running out. Those things
won't stop until they peck your eyes out."

Sage took the lead after that, all but blazing a path
of fire to the Suburban. Peggy—reciting a series of Hail
Marys under her breath—finally succeeded in removing
the keys from her pocket, jangling them in front of her, as
if they might ward off evil. "If Rita was here, she'd be the
first victim. My sister can't run for shit. *Dammit*, I miss
her. If only because her flat feet could save my life," Peggy
said on a strangled shout. "This is so *fucked up*. I should
have married a tax accountant and joined the PTA."

The cold night air and the adventure of it all sent exhil-
aration racing over Grace's skin, wrapping her in familiar
mischief. "No, no, you were meant to be here. You're
meant to go make that man's life hell." Grace fought back
a giggle. "You have to *live*, Peggy. Don't let the turkey
win."

They finally reached the Suburban at the road's edge,
Sage scrambling onto the hood in front of them, Peggy
and Grace following suit. And no sooner were they elevated to safety than Grace collapsed back against the
windshield, laughter wracking her body with such feroc-
ity, she had to hug her sides. Tears blurred her vision when
she opened her eyes to find Peggy and Sage staring down
at her with a mixture of dismay and suspicion, only bringing on a renewed bout of undiluted mirth.

"I'm sorry. I really shouldn't be laughing, but your faces..."

"Oh sure." Peggy's mouth twitched. "Get your jollies at the expense of us two West Coast rubes. That's just... great."

Sage cringed when the turkey began pecking at the front fender. "My life flashed before my eyes and all I saw was other people's weddings." She split a look between them. "I mean, how pathetic is that?"

"It's not," Grace said, squeezing her knee. "It's not pathetic if planning weddings is something you love doing."

"It is." Sage looked thoughtful. "This is going to sound ridiculous, but it occurred to me while we were running from the turkey that I haven't been totally honest." She gathered her legs to her chest. "I came on this trip for more than one reason. Not just to...comfort Belmont. There's something I need to do in Louisiana. I'm going to break off after Cincinnati. I should have told you, Peggy."

It took Peggy some time to respond. "Who says you have to break off? Maybe we can make time to come along—"

Sage shook her head. "I'm better off going alone."

"Sage," Peggy started. "Bel's going to need you in New York."

Based on her lack of reaction, it was obvious the wedding planner had considered that fact already. "We don't have to worry about it now. There's time."

Peggy's hesitant laugh eased the tension. "Yeah, let's focus on getting away from the murderous Thanksgiving dinner."

Wanting to help dissipate the heavy atmosphere that had descended, Grace sat forward, rubbing her palms down the woolen stockings. "We need a distraction. To draw him away while we climb into the car."

"This doesn't seem like your first turkey run, Pendleton."

Grace smothered a smile. "Oh, it is. But hopefully not my last." She blew out a quick breath, emotion clogging her chest. "This is the best night I've had in a long time. I'm sorry if that's the kind of thing I should think, but not say out loud."

Sage and Peggy looked at each other with indiscernible expressions, making Grace almost positive she'd made a mistake. But then, in a move she never saw coming, Peggy and Sage tackle hugged her against the windshield, immersing her in warmth, inside and out. And then they just lay there, huddled together, waiting for the turkey to leave.

Chapter Sixteen

Aaron was making a Herculean effort to focus on the shitload of work that needed accomplishing before tomorrow morning. When the sun came up, there would be scads of staffers, volunteers, interns, and press, all looking at him for direction, and he refused to be unprepared. Unfortunately, every time his attention strayed to the clock in the lower-right-hand corner of his laptop screen, the urge to phone Peggy made his eye twitch speed up to triple time.

Honestly, what could three girls get up to in this low-key part of Iowa?

He never should have asked himself that question, because his mind had conjured up farm boys and house parties and shenanigans in the hay. He'd anticipated them being back hours ago, after discovering how little nightlife was available in the area, but no. Midnight had descended without so much as a courtesy text message from his sister, who would be hearing all about that oversight in the morning.

He knew Peggy well. Knew she'd dressed Grace up like walking sex to drive him fucking insane, dangling her like a carrot in front of his face, before jerking her away. God, her thighs. *Her thighs.* He could smell the combination of her sex and whatever lotion she'd rubbed on them. Could feel the smooth texture against his lips. If they'd had enough time in the Suburban before leaving, if he'd been given the slightest opportunity to lick her pussy, it would have been like sinking into a slice of sun-heated watermelon after two months in the desert.

And she could be anywhere right about now, fresh from telling him to shut the fuck up. Probably being presented with a variety of male options that didn't treat her like a child. Or dry hump her until she was begging, then walk away, leaving her primed and confused. Didn't matter that they couldn't have a physical relationship for a multitude of reasons. His job, her past, and how those two things intersected. The vast difference in the way they lived their lives, treated people, viewed the world. None of that meant shit when Aaron didn't know her whereabouts. Was she safe? Had he finally succeeded in putting the kibosh on any attraction she felt for him?

Shut the fuck up. She'd looked…beyond beautiful when she'd said those words to him. Fierce, sexy, challenging. Why hadn't he yanked her out of the Suburban when he'd had the chance? Instead of spending the night memorizing her voice, her mannerisms, he'd cursed through the process of pitching a tent in the mess hall, aware that sharing a cabin with Grace was bad news, whether or not his siblings slept nearby. Yeah, he was *that* depraved. That desperate to get Grace's thighs up around his waist, to hear her whine for him to pump faster in his ear.

Beneath his laptop, Aaron's cock grew thicker, the heavy flesh pressing against his right thigh. He'd grudgingly resigned himself to self-pleasure, sliding a hand down the front of his sweatpants, when Belmont crouched down in the tent's entrance. Aaron jolted and retrieved his hand with a lightning-fast move, his daydream starring Grace in nothing but stockings busting into fragments.

"Jesus." Aaron settled the laptop more firmly over his arousal, keeping it hidden. "You could have announced yourself."

Belmont didn't comment on Aaron's reproof. In fact, it seemed like the farthest thing from his mind as he stood and began to pace, leaving Aaron with the view of his brother's legs. "They should have been back by now."

Aaron sighed and shoved the laptop aside, his erection waning at the reminder Grace could be experiencing the goofy courtship of some local farmhand named Josh. Or Brady. "Yeah, I know. Peggy won't answer my texts."

"She's doing it on purpose."

"No shit." Aaron watched his brother pace a minute, before climbing out of the tent to go join him. Even after hours spent in the cramped Suburban and sharing rooms in both New Mexico and Iowa, it was weird spending time with Belmont. Talking to him. Their conversations had been sparing and stilted before their mother died, but since then, they'd ceased altogether. He wasn't even sure where to start. Or if he should start at all. "Give them another half hour and we'll take the van down the mountain."

"Ten minutes."

Aaron nodded, relieved someone else was in the mood to be irrational. "Fine. Ten minutes." He leaned back against one of the few cafeteria tables they'd decided to keep and crossed his arms. "If it makes you feel any better, I think Sage is probably the least likely to paint the town red."

"It doesn't."

"Okay, then." Aaron reached into the tent and brought out his electric lantern, setting it on the table behind him. "When did you meet Sage anyway? I'm blurry on all the sordid details."

Belmont stopped his back and forth stalking in favor of staring out the large picture window, out into the forest. "Nothing sordid about it," he rumbled. "She could never be sordid."

Yeah, definitely shouldn't have attempted this brotherly talk. Aaron grabbed his lantern and started to duck down, intending to climb back into the tent and resume his work, but Belmont spoke, halting his progress.

"Peggy asked me to walk her down the aisle. She was marrying the first guy. The Padres fan." He rubbed the crease of his chin. "Sage...she was planning the wedding. And I didn't do well at the rehearsal. Didn't want to hurt Peggy's feelings by saying no, but I'm not...it's not—"

"I get it," Aaron cut in, knowing the rest. Knowing his brother didn't like attention of any manner. Didn't like having the spotlight directed at him, nor did he like being put in a position to interact with unfamiliar people. Basically, Aaron's polar opposite. "You don't have to explain."

"Sage," Belmont continued on, as if Aaron hadn't spoken. "She has this way of...slowing my heartbeat down, speeding it up, slowing it down again. Is that normal?"

Thinking of Grace, how she commanded his senses like a maestro, Aaron sat, running a hand over his stubbled face. "No, it's not normal. But in yours and Sage's case, I don't think it's a bad thing. I think you should let her."

"*No.*" His brother, usually so stoic and unmoved by anything he said, turned on Aaron with dawning horror. "No, I can't."

"Okay," Aaron said carefully. "Why not?"

Again, Belmont circumvented Aaron's direct question. "I didn't mean to...gather her up so no one else could have her. I shouldn't have let myself do that." Slowly, he drew a hand up and laid it over his heart. "She touched me here in the back of the church, and now she decides if it goes fast or slow." Aaron could barely remain upright under the force of the look Belmont dropped on his head. "What if she decides to make it stop?"

This was important. Right there, in the almost dark of the mess hall, Aaron finally had some insight into the way Belmont's mind worked, finally had the chance to aid him in some small way. That was what Aaron did. He was the solution guy. But when it really counted, he came up completely empty. Because he feared there was a ribbon-haired girl out there who might just have the power to stop *his* most vital organ from beating. He might even force her into it. "I don't know," Aaron murmured.

And son of a bitch if that wasn't—by some unseen twist—the right answer. Aaron watched in disbelief as Belmont smiled, a smile so fleeting it could have been his imagination, but it sent a rush of childhood noise blowing through Aaron's consciousness. "Okay." His brother gave a firm nod. "If you don't know, there *is* no way of knowing."

"You have that much confidence in me?" Aaron managed, positive he'd fallen asleep back in the tent and dreamed the whole conversation.

But he couldn't have imagined it, because Belmont's hand on his shoulder was too heavy, too solid. The slight increase of pressure too real as he passed on his way out of the mess hall. When he heard his brother's boots scrape to a stop at the door, he didn't lift his head. Wasn't capable. "I was glad to see your face that day at the top of the well," Belmont said, so quietly Aaron almost didn't make out the words. "I was glad. But I knew I couldn't be the person you looked up to anymore."

Aaron pushed to his feet, intent on demanding a full explanation of that bullshit, but the sound of the Suburban pulling up, feminine voices filling the night, broke them both of the spell. Belmont, the tension draining from his shoulders, nodded at Aaron, who had no choice but to return it.

* * *

Seduction was a tricky business. Truthfully, it went against Grace's nature. She didn't believe in swaying people toward a choice they wouldn't normally make. Distaste for that very practice had driven a wedge between her and Aaron. Which was how she'd drawn the conclusion that fighting fire with fire was her only option. She'd shined a light on their differences; now she would redirect it. Show him where they met in the middle, where they connected. And then she would build on it. Fight one war at a time. She refused to see tonight as a setting aside of her beliefs. Not when they might reach Aaron on the other side of the battlefield.

The light inside the mess hall beckoned, but Grace hung back, needing to garner every spare ounce of confidence in her arsenal. Seducing a man like Aaron—a born seducer himself—wouldn't be easy. If she showed him a speck of doubt or gave him room to shut her out, he would do it. He would retreat so fast her head would spin. That certainty was just one example of how well she already knew him. Setting up camp in the mess hall had been his way of sending a message. You are *there*. And I am *here*.

Not for long, bucko.

Trying to banish the image of Aaron ushering her out of the hall and back to the cabin like an annoying ward, Grace started up the steps. The walls were coming down tonight and she needed to believe Aaron wanted that eventuality. God knew she wanted to feel nothing between them. Not clothing, not hurt, not the incessant *ding-ding* of the bad idea meter. In her experience, risks not taken meant rewards never received. And bone-deep intuition resonated within Grace, a knowing that she and Aaron didn't have a short road, but a long, winding one. If she had to take a shortcut to get them pointed in the right direction, so be it.

With that mission roosting in the nest of her mind, Grace entered the mess hall and walked without hurry toward the tent. *Heel, toe. Heel, toe.* Taking deep breaths, Grace ran shaking hands up the insides of her thighs, beneath her suede skirt, encountering the uncovered flesh above her stockings, remembering Aaron's mouth there.

How his greedy tongue had flattened on her skin, tasting, his full lips sliding back and forth. He wanted her then. He would now.

The red wine still flowed through her veins, making it seem entirely natural to drag a thumb across the crotch of her panties, feeling her nipples plump, her breathing grow short. But the blaring of her pulse was interrupted by the sound of typing. *Clack, clack, clack. Aaron's* fingers. So capable in so many ways.

With a concerted effort, Grace dropped her hands from beneath her skirt, pushed her winter wind-tousled hair over her shoulder, and ducked into the small tent. She'd meant to move fluidly toward Aaron, to negate his chance to list all the reasons why she shouldn't be there, but his appearance brought Grace up short. His lower half was inside a red sleeping bag, but his upper half...*yowza*. He wore a white, long-sleeved thermal shirt that had to be a couple sizes too small, judging from the way its material wrapped tightly around his swelled biceps, his toned chest. As if that wasn't enough to render Grace mute, he wore a black beanie, pulled low over his eyes. Eyes that were sending a clear message toward where she knelt at the tent's entrance.

What the fuck are you doing here?

Yeah. That's what Aaron wanted to project. And he would have been doing a bang-up job if his Adam's apple hadn't gotten stuck beneath his chin, those long-fingered hands gripping the laptop like a shield. Grace could see right through him in that moment, as if he'd stepped in front of an x-ray machine that displayed intention, instead of injury. Right now, his intention was to turn her down.

"I've never seen you in pajamas," Grace whispered. "I thought you'd have your initials over the pocket or something."

"Peggy went shopping for winter clothes. She thinks she's funny." He sat up straighter, going back to staring at the screen. "I feel like some wannabe Instagram fitness model."

"Wannabe?" Grace crawled toward Aaron, noticing his fingers go still on the laptop keyboard. "No, you'd be the real deal."

Without looking at her, Aaron shook his head. "*Grace.*" He'd meant to speak her name like a warning, but all she heard was the gruff desperation. "You need to go sleep in the cabin. I might just be able to explain you spending the night here with two other women present, but this—"

Imagining her courage flowing out behind her like a cape, Grace gently set aside Aaron's laptop and straddled him, taking hold of the hands he lifted to keep her back, stroking his wrists with her thumbs. "Who says you'll have to explain anything?"

"I think we've established I'm a capable liar. You, on the other hand, are not." His tongue stroked the corner of his lips and Grace's nipples puckered to painful points in response. "If you spend the night underneath me, you'll wear your satisfaction like a billboard, baby. Someone asks you about it, you'll blush like a schoolgirl, remembering all the bad things you gave me permission to do in the dark. They'll know I had you. They'll know you got on your back for me and gave me that pussy like a birthday present."

It was all Grace could do not to slump sideways, canaries circling over her head. He was muttering a reproof under his breath, directed at himself. *Filthy bastard. You filthy bastard, talking to her like that.* "You're not making a very good case for me to leave. M-maybe you're having an off night at convincing people to see things your way." She slid her knees wide on either side of Aaron's thighs, watched his attention snag on the flesh he'd licked earlier that night. "I'm not having an off night, though. I know exactly what I'm doing."

"You don't," he rasped, closing his eyes. "I'm not in a nice mood, hippie. Right or wrong, I've been…jealous. For the last four hours and seventeen minutes. Jealous like some sorry-ass boyfriend. You think I'm going to make love to you like some art school chump? You're wrong." He yanked down the hem of her skirt, covering up the exposed tops of her thighs, but in a mind-blowing contradiction, his thumbs slipped up to the edge of her panties, tucking underneath for a single arousing second. "It's not safe for you here. Go sleep in the cabin."

"No." Embracing the shot of bravery, Grace fisted the front of his thermal shirt, drawing him forward, until their faces were an inch apart. "I'm sleeping here. You can try to scare me off as much as you want, but I'm not budging. I know where I'm safe. I know where I'll sleep the best. And I know *you'll* sleep best with me here, too."

His breath pelted her mouth. "We wouldn't be sleeping, Grace."

"After, then," she whispered, releasing the front of his shirt in favor of sliding her hands over his sturdy shoulders. "After you fuck me."

A groan filled the scant distance between them. "You've got a mouth on you tonight, Grace." His teeth dragged over his lower lip. "It makes me think you're looking to be chastised. And if you weren't my boss's daughter, you'd be in the right goddamn place for that."

Almost. Almost. There was a visible crack in his façade, allowing her to peer through his brash attitude and glimpse the vulnerability beneath. The approaching sense of victory was short-lived, though, because lust filled every crack of her framework like hot sand as Aaron's erection made itself known between her legs, swelling, pushing. Grace retrieved her hands and leaned back enough to peel the sweater over her head, baring her naked upper half, the freezing air twisting around her already peaked nipples. "Left off my bra, just like you asked me."

Color bled into Aaron's cheekbones, his nostrils flaring. "Put it back on," he croaked. "You're going to freeze."

Grace ignored his statement, reaching the small of her back to unzip the skirt all the way down, so she could lift the black garment over her head and toss it aside. "Wore panties, just like you asked me."

Was she shaking out of arousal or from the cold? Grace couldn't formulate an answer. The frigid air seemed like the obvious culprit. Obvious—unless a gorgeous, commanding man like Aaron was consuming the sight of your body like a man who ached to give it pleasure, but had both hands tied behind his back. "For God's sake, Grace, you're fucking *shaking*." He spoke through his teeth, his gaze pleading. "I can't watch it. *Please*."

Good man. He's a good man. I've known it all along. "If you want me warm, better let me inside that sleeping bag."

"*Grace*." Without looking, he snatched up the sweater, attempting to drape it over her shoulders, his movements pushing his erection up against the thin barrier of her panties. Even through the sleeping bag, it was a powerful ride, and Grace allowed her head to loll back, a whimper slipping past her lips. Trembling, she was trembling violently, but an inferno erupted from all sides of her being, the contrast slamming together in Grace's stomach, like the Red Sea closing its passage to safety.

With a vile curse, Aaron wrenched open the sleeping bag's zipper. He jerked Grace down into the warmth his body had created, closing the bag again with an angry *zip*. Her bare skin hitting the slippery nylon, Aaron's hard body pressing in from behind, his lap molding to her buttocks at the same time, was so decadent, it knocked the breath clear out of her lungs, dropping her jaw on a silent expulsion. And when his arms crossed beneath her breasts, his voice urgent in her hair, Grace almost climaxed without any further stimulation. Going from the freezing atmosphere into Aaron's embrace was comparable to bobbing among the icebergs to being rescued by an army of towels fresh from the dryer.

"Give me your hands," Aaron commanded, offering Grace no choice but to obey. He took them between his own and made a pained sound, before tucking them between Grace's thighs, which warmed them in a matter of seconds. Their presence so close to her sex warmed everything, really. Made her starkly aware of Aaron's erection nestled between her bottom cheeks, his feet pushing her boots off with hasty movements, abandoning them in the sleeping bag's end. And then he clamped her feet between his muscular calves, warming them through the stockings. "Better, baby?"

Grace wasn't sure she could speak through the pleasure. She was naked, except for stockings and underwear, and gathered so close to Aaron, she could feel the rapid booms of his heartbeat against her spine. Her attempt at communicating came out sounding breathless and dreamy. "I don't think I've ever felt better in my whole life."

Aaron's heaved sigh shifted her hair, before his head ticked back. "What are these tattoos on your neck?" Using his stubbled chin, he shifted the hair aside. "Are these numbers?"

"They're coordinates. That's the exact location of the cabin that burned down," she murmured, a small chisel putting a dent in the sweeping bliss of warmth. "You're the first person to see the tattoo, actually. My hair always covers it." Her pulse spiked with the intimacy they were sharing. "I wear the coordinates so they can't wear me."

The silence lasted so long, Grace wondered if he would comment. Wondered if she *wanted* him to. In the end, he brushed his lips over the spot—once, twice—and God, it was exactly right. "For the love of God, distract me. Tell me where you've been."

She didn't *want* to distract him—she wanted him *present*—but since her body was in a state of pleasure shock, no choice existed but to stall. Until she could turn around and do her utmost to get Aaron naked right back. "We . . . there was a hostage situation."

"*What?*"

Following instinct, Grace turned her face to plant a kiss on his biceps, unfortunately still covered by the white thermal. "The bars were closed, so we shared a bottle of house red in a cornfield. It was the turkey's turf, though. We found out the hard way when he chased us out." Eyes drifting closed, she smiled. "We weren't late on purpose. The last hour was spent on the Suburban's hood playing rock-paper-scissors."

A couple of beats passed. "Why rock-paper-scissors?"

"To decide who would create the diversion," she explained, sucking back a gasp when Aaron scooted closer, driving the ridge of his arousal deeper into the valley dividing her backside. "It started as best out of three, loser distracts the turkey. By the time we ended, it was best out of a hundred." Aaron's fingertips strummed down her belly, sliding back up, making Grace sink her teeth into her upper lip to keep from moaning. "The turkey finally got b-bored and left."

Just when she thought her current situation couldn't possibly get any more amazing, Aaron's body started to shake with laughter behind her. The sensation might have been enough to sustain Grace's happiness for the rest of her life, but the sound...*oh God*, the slow thunder roll of it against her ear, like a drought-ending storm, bathing dry fields and turning everything green...it blew her away. Just sucked her belly in tight, curled her toes, and filled her chest with effervescence.

"It could have been worse," she managed. "It could have been a bear."

The smile—thank God—was still in his voice when he spoke. "Grace. What is this fascination with bears about?"

He'd noticed. "When I was eight, my parents noticed food missing from the kitchen. Not just once, a few times. They didn't suspect me, because I was so young and I was a picky eater anyway." She fell into the hazy rhythm of the story, vowing to lie and pretend she was still cold if he tried to shake her loose. "Then one Christmas morning, a whole ham was missing from the fridge...and whoever had taken it left a trail of grease leading out the back door. And a bunch of little footprints."

"Do I want to hear the rest of this?"

She swallowed a laugh. "They found me in the back-yard, leaving dinner for my pet bear, Nolan. And Nolan was on his way into the yard to get his ham. I'd only seen him at a distance before, but when he got closer... he bellowed." She fit the arch of her foot against his calf. "He ran toward me full speed and my mother screamed, but Nolan changed directions and nabbed the ham instead." Aaron's heartbeat had accelerated against her spine during the story and she gloried in that telling reaction, even as she wanted to soothe it. "I'm not really afraid of the bear. It's more guilt that I stopped feeding him. It sounds silly when I say it out loud."

"You're not silly," Aaron said after a moment, his lips grazing her neck. "I'm glad it was a turkey tonight, instead of Nolan, too. Pissed-off poultry is a lot better than what I was thinking."

"What were you thinking?" *What are you always, always thinking? I want to know. I want you to tell me, so I can lock up your secrets and never, ever betray your confidence, even if I'm tortured.*

Aaron said her name under his breath. "It doesn't matter. Every time I think about you, I land on the same damn conclusion." He started to ease away, shooting a flare of panic through Grace's blood. "You're not the kind of girl who has... short affairs. That's *all* I have. I'm not sure where I'll be next week, but for damn sure, I know I won't be your—or anyone's—boyfriend. I never have been."

He seemed to realize how harsh that sounded, because he pushed his forehead into Grace's shoulder, nudging and staying put. "You deserve someone who can offer the long run, Grace. That's not me. It wouldn't be fair to... set what

I know about you aside for one night. No matter how bad..." He sucked in a breath and blew it out slowly, his erection still prominent against her bottom. "No matter how bad I'd want to turn a blind eye to the right thing. For once, I can't."

This chance was slipping through her fingers, but after Aaron's speech, she was more determined than ever to shatter his defenses. Maybe he didn't realize it now, but he'd just revealed himself. He cared about her. But he didn't think himself capable of offering more. If she could just win this one victory, there would be light on the other side. She knew it in her stomach. She'd do anything to reach that place. Even lie, it seemed. The past might have caused her to doubt, but even the strongest memories and fears that made trusting difficult...they didn't stop her gut from screaming out that the man on the other side of the mask needed her in order to soar. They needed *each other*.

"You're wrong." Grace turned in Aaron's loosened embrace, allowing a chafing of her nipples against the thermal shirt, before pushing a resistant Aaron onto his back and straddling him. "You're wrong. I only want one night." The words tasted acidic, but at least she had his attention. At least he'd stopped trying to unseat her from his aroused lap. "You've said it before. We're too different and...I agree. But..."

"*But what?*" Aaron rasped.

Grace slid down Aaron's body, a merciless drag of ripe female over primed male anatomy, making Aaron's muscular torso flex as he moaned. "I'm attracted to you, even though I know better. It hurts to be around you," she murmured shakily. Truth. That was truth. "I just need you inside me one time and I'll leave you alone. No one will ever know."

"I'll know." His hands fisted at the small of her back. "I'll never *stop* knowing."

She slipped nimble fingers down between their bodies, palming Aaron's rampant arousal. "It's just a moment, like in the field. Give me a moment."

CHAPTER SEVENTEEN

Aaron's willpower capsized like the fucking *Titanic*. He couldn't believe he'd held out even one full minute with naked Grace sliding up and down on his cock. Purring against his throat. Asking for one night. *One night.* There was something undeniably *wrong* about her request. That something was making him anxious, imbuing him with the urge to flip Grace over, take her by the shoulders, and demand to know her game. Or maybe...

Maybe she wasn't playing a game at all. The attraction to him was there, but anything beyond that—any form of relationship—was undesirable to her. Not so hard to believe, right? No. Not at all. Why would she want anything long term with someone who didn't know how to express himself, while she...*God*. While she remained true to herself and her principles, no matter the consequences. How could he assume the most truthful person he'd ever met was lying? That was his shady life experience talking, not his experience with Grace.

He'd underestimated her ability to make decisions before. He'd called Grace crazy while she listened in the closet. He'd questioned her behavior, implied she was abnormal, for crying out loud. No way would he do that again. If she wanted one night with him, he would grasp on to it with both hands and be grateful she'd found him worthy of even a short space of her time.

That permission snapped something loose in Aaron, a green light to devour without holding back. *Take her. Take her. She asked for it. Needs it.*

With an anguished groan, Aaron levered himself up on one elbow, seizing Grace's mouth, licking inside the textured perfection without delay. The taste of red wine and sugar made him drunk, made him wild. Especially when Grace kissed him back with zero restraint, their mouths open so wide, it would be considered crude to anyone watching. But there was no one there. No one to watch him debauch this girl in any way he chose. No one there to shake their head and put another notch on his filthy soul for fucking her sweet body on the goddamn floor.

My hands are too tainted to touch her.

But I can't stop. I can't stop.

Any hope Aaron had of roping his sanity back disintegrated with Grace's next move. With his hands busy in her wild hair, Aaron could only lift his hips in consent when Grace tugged down his sweatpants, releasing his heavy dick into the sweltering interior of the sleeping bag, trailing her fingers over the sensitive moist head, breathing an awed sound into his mouth, swelling it further. "I'm warning you," Aaron grated. "You give me that little I-just-witnessed-a-miracle gasp when I'm slapping my root up against your pussy, it's going to be a hard ride."

"Good," she whispered, looking down at him through hooded green eyes, ribbons and braids falling down around her face. "But...me first."

Aaron couldn't look away from her gorgeous image to judge her intention. But when she reached between their bodies, tugging the crotch of her panties to one side, his cock surged uncomfortably and wedged between their bellies. "What are you doing to me?"

"Shhh," Grace leaned down to feather the reproof over his mouth, licking the seam of his lips, draining him of rational thought. And then she slipped her wet, bare pussy straight up the length of his cock, moaning his name on the way back down. And Aaron forgot the *meaning* of rational thought, let alone the ability to have it. His focus dwindled down to the primal need to get inside Grace's body and work her over until she knew nothing but his cock. How it fit, how it fucked, how every ridge corresponded to pleasure points inside her flesh and exploited them. The monstrous tunnel vision stole his breath, made his hands rough and unmanageable as they kneaded Grace's smooth, cotton-covered ass, the backs of her thighs, urging her to grant him the blessing of another slick ride.

"Again," he groaned, his eyes riveted by Grace's plush, swaying tits. "One more time, then...condom, baby. So hard up for your pussy. You're going to know how miserable I've been. My thrusting dick is going to tell you all about it."

"*Yes.*" Her body loosed an almost violent tremble on

top of him, a sob wrenching from her open mouth, causing concern to penetrate the ferocious blanket of lust wrapped around Aaron's brain. But she slid up again, she slid up with those damp folds dragging on either side of his too-long-ignored cock—and desire dug its claws into Aaron's gut, twisting, drawing his balls up with a shock of pain. Grace kept going, up and down, up and down, faster, faster, the whole of Aaron's erection entering the tugged-aside panties, exiting through the snug waistband, before sliding back in for another hit of paradise. "So good...I can't...can't stop."

The distant quality to Grace's voice tried to drag him back from the brink of forgetting himself, forgetting everything but pleasure, achieving it, holding on to it. But abstaining from someone he'd wanted beyond reason made it impossible to capture or define what was wrong with their actions. What could be wrong when nothing had ever felt this goddamn good in his life?

Aaron reached up, fisting the back of Grace's hair and guiding her down to his mouth, the ensuing kiss voracious, her grinding glides up and down his cock turning into something else. The head of his cock squeezed, followed by his full, aching length...and then he rammed into the back of her pussy. "No..." Aaron growled through the inescapable euphoria of being joined with Grace, nothing between them, but somehow responsibility found a way to grip him around the neck, his words forceful but slurred. "Need a condom. Can't have y'like this."

Didn't matter that he was clean. This...*Jesus*, this was one privilege no amount of atoning for his past, present, and future could earn. No matter how fucking terrible it would feel to pull out of warm, safe...home. The home he could never live in, but would dream about for the rest of his pathetic life.

Above him, Grace's mouth was dropped open, her expression pure, beautiful hedonism. A vision of her dancing beneath the moon, laughing up at the snow, hit him fast and hard in the chest, knocking his determination askew, a guttural shout breaking from his mouth when she fell onto his chest, her hips pumping with breathy sobs, fucking him bareback. "I'm sorry, I know I need to stop," she breathed into his neck. "Help me."

Aaron's hands closed around Grace's hips, intending to ease her off. Just long enough to grab the closest piece of latex protection and get back inside her body. Instead, he urged her down onto his impaling dick, gritting his teeth over the tight journey. "One more time. One." Grace made a sound of relief, rolling her hips and taking him to the hilt, grinding down. "I told you," he said. "I told you I was a bastard."

At that, her half-closed eyes sprung wide, her head shaking in denial. "No, you're not." She treated him to a long, thorough tongue kiss, riding his cock all the while. "Or if you are, you're my bastard." Her breath caught. "For t-tonight."

The reminder of his one-night-stand status in Grace's eyes gave him the surge of inescapable reality he needed. Not just reality, but . . . self-directed anger. That he couldn't be the man to give her more. Make her want to dance every night in a field and compliment her on looking pretty, instead of threatening to come after her, make her sorry. Tonight he could be that man. Tonight he could be the only one she saw, but he would do it right, goddammit. She deserved that much and more from him.

With a growl of determination, Aaron pulled out and reversed their position, turning Grace onto her back with enough force to startle a whimper from her lips. He promptly swallowed the sound, while reaching for the discarded dress pants folded to the sleeping bag's right, knowing there was a condom in the front right pocket. *Need to get back inside her. Now now now.* "That was very bad, Grace," he chided against her mouth. "Like it skin on skin, do you?"

"I don't know," she breathed, licking kiss-bruised lips, grazing his lower one in the process. "That was my first time doing it. You just felt so amazing... I'm—"

"Stop." Invisible pressure exerted itself on Aaron's chest, but with a major effort, he forced away the pride brought on by Grace's confession. The disbelief over her almost apology. "Stop saying you're sorry for letting me test out your hot pussy. I fucking loved it." Finally having located the condom, he ripped the foil packet open with bared teeth. Before he covered himself, though, he slapped the insides of her legs with his heavy, bare length, loving the sound it made, the way her jaw slackened. "Or can't you tell by the way I'm dripping precum on your thighs?"

Grace seemed to hold her breath as Aaron covered himself in latex, the thin barrier tighter than usual around his ready flesh. God, had he ever been this thick in his life? Never. It was as though his body had reached peak wakefulness. Or he'd been half asleep his entire life, waiting for the one body, the one person that magnetized him, brought him out of his self-imposed coma.

Don't think like that. You're damning yourself.

He looked down between their bodies, turned on within an inch of his life to find Grace still wearing the sodden, twisted panties. The ones that had housed his cock as it slid over her clit. With more force than intended, Aaron shoved the underwear to one side and rammed his cock into Grace's entrance, clapping a hand over her mouth to minimize the scream that erupted. His own animalistic groan was barely captured by clamping his teeth so hard into his lower lip, blood could be tasted on his tongue. He was forced to breathe through the heave of release his balls sorely needed and almost produced. Forced to envision finishing without pleasuring Grace to calm himself down. And as soon as the torrid near-requirement to climax passed, Aaron curled his elbows beneath Grace's knees and fell forward onto her body, bucking his hips in cruel slaps, unable to slow down.

"Tight, firm, and giving all at once," he said through his teeth, mouth shoved into the curve of her neck. "You've got a triple threat between your thighs, don't you, baby? I'm beginning to think you wake up like this. Dripping wet. Ready for me to take you down. Lap you up. Make me look at you and think of a dripping hot tongue fucking from behind while you whine into a pillow."

Aaron heard Grace's labored breathing in his ear and realized how much pressure he'd dropped on her slight body. God, he'd lost all self-awareness, every shred of decency. How could he be decent when their connected bodies were the farthest thing from decent? His dick stretched her so wide, he could detect the strain to accommodate him. This high on pleasure, his base would be ruddy, his head so swollen, she would have to work to get her mouth around it. Yet she was wet as hell. *Criminally* wet. All but daring him not to bang the sweetness out of her. *Begging* for it.

The temptation to hand the reins to his depravity, allowing his baser instincts to run the show, was right there, called to him, ordering him to claim Grace hard enough to make an impression that would last beyond one night. But when she wheezed beside his ear, Aaron's heart constricted, a voice in the back of his mind calling him a monster. In a swift movement, he transferred his weight onto one elbow.

"No," Grace protested, banding her arms around his back, face glowing in the lantern night. "Press me down, don't let me move. Take me hard. So hard. I want what you want. I need the *same thing* you need."

Time seemed to stand still, their mouths poised a breath apart, gazes locked on each other. And Aaron felt it. Felt the ground shaking beneath them, rattling the locked cages inside his chest, springing doors open and allowing emotions he didn't recognize—didn't know by name—to run amok. "Grace," he whispered. "It's a jailbreak."

A dazed smile formed, bowing her lips. She reached up and traced his brow with her thumb and he couldn't think or move or get air into his fucking lungs. How was anyone so beautiful? How did the earth sustain the power of her? "It's so much better—"

"When I say things out loud," Aaron finished for her, his tongue feeling thick. "I need you to say more things right now, baby. You're so goddamn, out of this world gorgeous, my mind went blank."

She lit up like an entire city block after a power outage. "Thank you."

More words. More stupid, unrehearsed, dangerous words and promises tried to climb out of his mouth, but he blocked them in. "More, please. Say more."

Christ. Maybe Grace really did know exactly what he needed—a detour into dirty—because an innocent expression descended over her features, the walls of her pussy constricting at the same time. *Hard.* The unexpected contrast made the strength in his arms waver long enough to drop him back down, into the welcome softness of Grace's curves, a groan rippling through his vocal cords. "When you came back from running today..." Her eyelids dropped. "When you stood a certain way, I could see the outline of your...cock."

She whispered the last word, as if in reverence, and Aaron had no choice but to bear down with the fat organ in question, shoving it deep into Grace's pussy, taking his time drawing it back out. "Yeah? Did you think about how it would feel?"

Her nod was vigorous. Earnest. That breathless honesty sent a renewed slide of lust to the hurting flesh between his legs. "I thought—"

Grace broke off on a sharp moan when Aaron drove into her with increased force, the sopping wet panties beginning to tear. "You thought what?"

"I thought I would like it...for you to come and take my hand, and lead me somewhere. Everyone would watch us leave, knowing. And when we got somewhere private, you would push me onto my knees and ask for my mouth." Her voice was hypnotic, like someone in a dream state, even as it shook with each of his thrusts. "I wanted to taste the salt on you. Wanted to feel your sweat drip on my back, my head—"

"That's enough. No more." His voice emerged deep and unnatural. "*No more.*"

"Tell me." She arched her back, spreading her thighs

wider so he could press deeper, tighter, merging them into one machine fashioned from slick, greedy flesh. "Tell me you would have come to the cabin and led me here. It's the truth, isn't it? You would have come and gotten me. Right?"

"*Yes*," he gritted into her hair. "Yes, and if you'd gone home, I would have driven there and knocked on your fucking door again. Banged you against the entry wall in your nightgown. *No one* is going to make you off-limits to me, goddammit."

Too much. He was revealing too much. Presenting a weakness. Her. But he couldn't stop. Couldn't dam the flow of honesty when his body was in a state of pleasure or die, a plane he'd never thought existed. "No one can do that," she moaned, her legs shooting together, toes curling against the flesh of his pumping ass. "No one can make me off-limits."

"You are, though, aren't you?" Rage filtered in, teaming with possessiveness to increase his aggression, until he was pounding into Grace without restraint. "But I have the perfect alibi, don't I, if someone questions me and I don't want to lie?" Aaron dropped his touch between their bodies, stroking Grace's clitoris, her inner walls quickening in response. "Sir, you have my word, her panties never once came off. They stayed up on her pussy and ass where they belong."

She hit her climax like nothing he'd ever seen. He could actually feel himself being milked between her thighs, again, again, *tighter*, again.

"Oh Jesus, baby," Aaron gritted out. "If that's the kind of thing that makes you come, we're going to get along just goddamn fine."

Her fingers raked down his back, finding his ass and rocking him closer, making a sound of pure unapologetic pleasure, grinding his cock into her clenching center until his own limit was hit, pressure building to the point of fucking agony and releasing. *Releasing.* Tearing growls of satisfaction from Aaron he'd never made before, turning his hips into a blur of flesh, desperate to wring every last ounce of perfection free. And still she rolled their bodies together, as if she didn't want it to end. Neither did he. God, *never.* Why did it have to?

"*Grace*," he managed, his weight going dead on top of her sweaty body. Instead of complaining, she banded her arms around the breadth of his covered back, pressing her mouth into his shoulder, whispering words he didn't deserve. Words of praise. Nonsense about white thermal T-shirts and sweatpants. Finally, when he could feel himself wanting to take advantage of the enjoyment she experienced at taking his full weight, Aaron eased to the side, holding his breath when she snuggled in beneath his arm, laying her palm on top of his chest.

"Just say what you're thinking," she whispered.

"I never took my shirt off." He shook his head, mostly because the mundane observation sounded ridiculous after the intensity of what they'd done. "It just seems like a wasted opportunity to feel you everywhere."

God, he was fucking off the deep end. Why didn't that panic him like it should have? Especially when he felt Grace's mouth move into a smile against his shoulder. "Better late than never." She took the hem of his shirt, urging him up and removing it. Then slowly, so slowly, they lowered back down into the sleeping bag, Grace taking her place once again up against his side. Her breasts were firm, but so sweet and soft, the hollow of her belly curving to his hip. "Better?"

Better? Aaron's pulse had slowed to a lethargic pace, while his heart had taken the opposite tactic of complete disarray. Weren't those two things connected? Maybe his mind had hijacked his body. "Better," he said in the century's understatement. "Grace?"

She yawned. "Yes?"

Just say it. She liked when he said things with no forethought. Tomorrow he could go back to being the planner, the thinker, the action guy. "I would protect you from a bear. You're safe from bears."

Her fingertips had been trailing up and down his stomach, but they stilled now, curled into her palm, dragged sideways, and pressed against her mouth. "Thank you," she whispered. "Good night, Aaron."

"Good night."

Chapter Eighteen

Grace hung back in the crowd, pulling on the strings of her hoodie to tighten the dark blue cotton around her face. If someone turned around and glimpsed her, they would surely be alarmed, since she went from blushing and smiling to despair in a seemingly endless cycle. Oh, and then pride would storm in and wipe everything clean, because there was Aaron, the lover in whose arms she'd slept last night, commanding a mass of people, all while cameras whirred and snapped shots of him.

He'd been gone from the sleeping bag when she'd woken up, but there'd been a backpack full of her clothes, telling Grace he'd either woken up early enough to collect garments from her house, or arranged to have it done. The gratefulness had been eclipsed in short order, however, by one question. *What now?* Last night, she'd been chock full of bravery. Seduce this strikingly attractive, razor-sharp man and everything else will fall into place. By not allowing that physical connection, they'd been maintaining a barrier and she'd intended to knock it down. *Had* she?

An answer wouldn't be coming anytime soon, since Aaron was in charge of an army. An army sent to make her dream a reality. She needed to remember that. After coming out on the other side of YouthAspire, she'd tried so many methods to make the injustice of that day right. In her mind, building something positive over a negative was the only thing that made sense. Whether or not these volunteers and staffers knew it, they were there to complete a vision she'd thought would take a decade. Aaron led that charge.

Had she really thought his leadership qualities a bad thing? She might have qualms with how he chose to employ his persuasive skills, but watching him hold the audience captive made her feel...proud. Had she ever felt that way about Ray Solomon or the therapist her parents had hired? No, she didn't think so. There was a note of truth in Aaron's words, as if he believed them. Would make the promises reality. She wanted to believe him so badly, especially knowing that, deep down, he lacked that same trademark confidence in his own character. A belief she'd helped further by letting the past intrude.

Starting that very second, she needed to be grateful for the good happening around her. Aaron taking her words at face value last night and confining their relationship to one evening only mired her in self-pity. Especially considering he'd begun writing his name on her heart the night he'd tied ribbons into her hair and sealed the deal last night inside that tent. But she wouldn't wallow if he decided to cut and run. No. She would just reverse tactics and try again.

Now if only she had a club with which to smack him over the head. And a cave where she could drag him.

As Grace took a deep breath and straightened her shoulders, she couldn't help begging Aaron silently in her mind to come through. For her. For them. And there was a *them*. That certainty sat in her belly like a cement. Even if they had to walk across a series of shaky stepping-stones to find out what they could be . . . she could ignore the rushing river on either side and hold his hand for balance.

"We have bunk bed deliveries coming at noon, courtesy of the Pendleton campaign, so this morning is all about out with the old, in with the new." The wind cascading over the crowd was all that could be heard, apart from Aaron's rich, confident voice. "Cleaning. Now I know it's not the best gig, but if we can get those cabins cleared by midday, beers are on the senator tonight."

A mighty cheer went up around Grace, accompanied by a moment of clarity. Yesterday, her attention had been diverted by Aaron, but here were the differences between them, coming home to roost. She looked around, noticing the volunteers were all young, their choice of clothing current, right down to their Pendleton campaign T-shirts, complete with a new #Respect Twitter hashtag she'd never seen before. Every word out of Aaron's mouth targeted the demographic he'd been hired to seduce, the camera absorbing it like a sponge. His delivery was seamless and undetectable, until his gaze landed on her in the gathering of people and his speech faltered, his eyes clouding over. Just for a second, before he recovered.

"Toward the back of the property, there is a recreation area with a pool, archery range, and stables. For those of you who don't mind the cold, I suggest heading back there and clearing away some of that annoying foliage." He smiled and a feminine murmur floated through the volunteers. "Any questions you need answered can be directed toward the volunteers wearing red shirts—they've all been briefed on the direction we're taking, so please don't hesitate. Let's get this right."

"How is this project being funded?" a male reporter asked, directing his cameraperson to get a close-up of Aaron. "It can't all be stolen campaign money."

Aaron laughed, along with the crowd. "That's how it started. Now we have to keep the ball rolling. Overnight, we've raised thirteen thousand dollars through a crowd-funded campaign." He announced the website, then repeated it. "The senator—who should be with us shortly to make a statement—wants this to be America's project. Not just his. Respect starts at the ground level and we're working to earn yours. Thank you. Now's let get to work."

He clapped his hands, and like that, the crowd dispersed as if they'd been ordered by God himself, which probably accounted for Grace not following suit. Watching them go, she wrapped her arms around her middle, working to maintain the excitement of everything that would be accomplished that day. She was visualizing pristine cabins and a functioning kitchen when Aaron stopped in front of her, blocking out the morning sun.

"Hey, hippie."

Why wasn't he smiling? Shouldn't he be triumphant after what he'd managed to pull together in one single day? The camp had gone from a sad ghost town into a hive of activity. "Hey back."

He was quiet, as if waiting for her to say more. But she didn't know where to start. The dangerous *what now* question sat on her tongue like a spicy mint, begging to be spat out. And now, after having their differences reestablished, there were additional doubts trying to creep back in. If only he were wearing the white thermal and a beanie, she wouldn't feel so thrown. His crisp blue suit made him seem to untouchable, a zillion miles from how he'd been last night.

"Listen…" He slid his fingers along the inside of his collar. "Last night—"

"It was a mistake," Grace rushed to say. Even now when she thought about how inappropriate and downright reckless it had been to take Aaron inside her without a condom, she flushed to the roots of her hair. "I'm sorry."

Aaron's face paled at her apology. "Right. No, you're right. It was. A mistake." He coughed into his fist, looking everywhere but at her. "You'd been drinking and I shouldn't even have let you into the tent. I take responsibility for the…mistake."

"I…" A sharp, invisible object stabbed Grace between the ribs, forcing her to stop for breath. "I only meant the condom part," she murmured. "N-not the whole thing."

His laugh was low and humorless, but his smile dropped so fast, it was a wonder she didn't hear it hit the ground. "Huh." They stared at each other for long moments, the wrenching pain in Grace's side growing unbearable. Maybe she *wasn't* fit to be around normal people. She'd preempted anything Aaron had been about to say by calling their night together a mistake. Now the words had been said from both of them and all progress had been obliterated. "Should we worry…" He stepped close, softening his voice. "Should we worry you might get pregnant? I was…God, I was leaking by the time—"

"No," Grace breathed, the tingle of arousal going a long way in decreasing her pain, but not all of it. "I've been on the pill since college."

Aaron nodded. "Okay." He stepped away, turned around, came back. "Look, Grace. I don't know what the fuck just happened here."

"Me either," she said, gratefulness flooding her chest at his honesty.

This time when Aaron laughed, there was a small note of relief, but his golden brown eyes remained hooded, guarded. "A shipment of medical supplies came in for the infirmary. I think it's a good idea to have the place stocked in case someone gets injured while working." He glanced around. "We have a doctor on hand, but I'm not sure where he's gone."

She noticed a tiny cut on his chin and realized he'd nicked himself shaving. And that little imperfection made her feel closer to him. Made him resemble the man he'd been last night. "You want me to help unload the medical supplies?"

"You don't have to do a damn thing," Aaron answered, suddenly serious. "But I haven't forgotten this is your dream we're building. And I've just walked in and taken over, the way I do with every fucking situation. So please tell me what you want to do. I'll give it to you."

"I want to unload medical supplies," she whispered, overwhelmed in the face of his acknowledgment. Just *him*, in general. He was so present and perceptive and hidden, all at once. Couldn't he tell she just wanted a hug?

"Okay," Aaron said finally. "Anything else?"

She'd hidden the next request so deep, it had always been so far in the future, it took Grace a beat to unearth the idea, dust it off. "I want my name added to the list of campers who were there that day, when the fire happened. I don't want it covered up anymore." Her chest felt lighter. "It's like I'm deserting them all over again."

Aaron was very still. "Don't think like that. It's not the same." He waited for her reluctant nod, his gaze fixating on something beyond her shoulder. "I don't know if I have the power to change something like that, Grace. I don't know that I want to, either." She glanced back to find several cameramen loading their equipment into vans. "They'd turn something good into a circus. I really don't like the idea of that touching you."

Grace understood. She also knew her father had taken her name off the list of campers who'd been duped by Ray Solomon for the same reason. But good intent from those around her didn't diminish the wish. Or make it any less valid. "I understand," she told Aaron honestly, reaching out to squeeze his arm without thinking. When he only stared down at the contact point, Grace slowly removed her touch. "Thanks for what you're doing. I'll be in the infirmary."

As soon as Grace walked away, Aaron was hit with questions from nearly everyone in the vicinity. It took him a moment to start answering, his gaze hot on Grace's back—or was that her imagination?—but he came around in no time, responding in his usual, self-assured manner. It only took Grace five minutes to reach the infirmary, kind of relieved she would be alone with her thoughts for a while. But when she opened the door, a man in khakis was bent over, rummaging through an open cardboard box.

The man—probably in his mid-thirties—jerked up,

holding up both hands, obviously surprised by her presence. "I'm just a doctor. Don't shoot."

A laugh bubbled out of Grace, taking her unaware. *He must by the doctor Aaron mentioned.* "I'm unarmed. You're safe." She entered the medium-sized room, surprised to find it had already been broom swept, two new physical therapy tables lining the back wall, adjacent to a small supply closet. She could see the shelves, bottles, and bandages unpacked and placed in sections. "It looks like you have it covered down here." She started to back down the steps. "I'll just—"

"No," the doctor interrupted, pink dotting his cheeks. "I'd love some company, actually." He dropped a packet of gauze to reach out a hand. "I'm John."

"Grace," she said, shaking his hand, marveling over the everyday gesture. There hadn't been many situations she could recall of late that required hand shaking. It was nice. Like the symbol of a clean slate. "What can I help with?"

CHAPTER NINETEEN

Aaron hadn't seen Grace in an hour and he'd felt every. Passing. Minute. How he'd forced himself to wait the full sixty minutes before going after her, he couldn't fathom. The necessary delay might have had something to do with addressing problems, big and small, organizing a press junket for the senator, appointing a new social media manager, and checking on his family, who were currently off-site completing something he'd envisioned himself, but to which he couldn't devote a damn minute.

Sure. But he could ignore everything and traipse through the woods after Grace to the infirmary, couldn't he? It appeared so. In fact, by the time the squat, log building came into view, he was all but salivating for the sight of her.

This morning had been a misunderstanding and it had been unlike him to let it go unresolved. To let her walk away under the misconception he thought of their night wrapped around each other in the sleeping bag as a mistake. He'd been on a verge of clearing that bullshit right up when she'd hit him with those green eyes. *I want my name added to the list of campers who were there that day, when the fire happened. I don't want it covered up anymore.*

After Aaron's last phone call with the senator, it was clear he'd become open to the idea and the advantages it might provide. The public not only perceiving him as a caring father, but one who had brought his child through a tragedy with hard work. Aaron could actually give Grace what she wanted, to write her back into the history of that day. But now . . . now it would be done with an ulterior motive, whether or not it was Aaron's. He *knew* about the motive. That alone would be enough to sicken him if they let Grace's story play out in the media.

Christ. He used to take pride in this job. He'd felt invincible, watching the cause and effect of his ideas, watching them take root and flourish. But this morning, with beautiful Grace standing there, witnessing his act, listening to him spit out buzzwords and making subtle, yet influential hints that could have monumental effect? Yeah, he'd felt like an imposter. He'd never thought himself capable of anything else. Politics was the only place where being himself wasn't a bad thing.

Was it possible there was more to him, though? Grace might have had her doubts at the outset, but she'd lain with him last night, all curled up and trusting, her breath coasting over his chest. She wouldn't do that with a monster, would she? Once, she'd come close to being devoured by one, but she'd survived and learned. Hadn't she?

Certain his anxiety would stabilize once they were in the same place, Aaron opened the infirmary door, frowning over what he saw. And heard. Grace was on one side of the space, holding a box of bandages—and she was laughing. Not a hint of reservation in the musical sound, just unabashed joy. The cause was a man. That man was not Aaron. Jealousy reached into his stomach and rearranged everything with a merciless twist of its fist. "What the hell is going on here?"

Grace jumped, dropping the box onto the floor and sending bandages scattering in every direction. When the man—who was watching Aaron with confusion—crouched down to help, Aaron got himself to Grace's side first. She analyzed him with a quick look before gesturing to the other man. "Aaron, this is John. He's the doctor."

Recognition dawned—Jesus, he'd only met the guy this morning—but none of the green, cloying mist went away. "I can assist Grace from here," Aaron said, not giving a flying shit about the stiffness in his voice. *If you don't stop looking at her, I'm going to be your worst nightmare.* Part of Aaron was actually disappointed when John backed off with a self-deprecating headshake. He would rather the guy mouthed off instead of being mature. Aaron was simply not capable of the same, knowing Grace had been alone with a man other than himself.

Before John reached the door, he turned around, scratching the back of his neck. "Uh . . . think about what I said, Grace. I'll be around."

As soon as the door closed, Aaron found Grace's eyes and locked in. "What does he want you to think about?"

Her disapproval was clear. "You were very rude to him, Aaron."

"That wasn't an answer."

She knelt down in one quick blur, shoveling bandages

back into the empty box. He'd only seen Grace irritated once before—in the Suburban last night—and just like then, his body quite enjoyed the sight. Wanted the chance to lull her, appease her, any way he could. He had only one option now, however, which was to join her on the floor, gathering up medical supplies. After a few heavy beats passed, she stopped, lifting her chin. "He asked me on a date. I said no. So he asked me to think about it."

Was it too late to go after the fucker? "Well, you've thought about it. The answer is hell no."

She got in his face. "I know it's hell no."

"Why?"

Grace wanted to shove him. He could tell. She lifted her hands to push, but made them into shaking fists instead. "Because I only want to go on dates with *you*." She plopped onto the floor, drawing her knees up. "God, you are such a...*douchebag*."

Aaron's ire plummeted, the bandages slipping out of his fingers. "Dates are at night, right?" His gaze cut down to the ground, his pulse doing pole vaults. "Does that mean...are you definitely on the fence now about having only one night with me?"

Say yes. Say you've reconsidered and I can sleep with my arms around you again.

When she stayed silent, he assumed she was debating the pros and cons, so what she said next was like jumping into a cool lake after escaping a fire. "I was never, *ever* on the fence. I just didn't know how else you'd let me sleep beside you."

"Oh," he croaked, wondering if bones could actually melt. *Let* her? If she'd tried to leave the tent last night, there was zero doubt he would have gotten whiplash going after her. "So you want to go on a *date* with me," he repeated dumbly. "I don't really know what that looks like."

"I don't, either. I've never really been on a proper one. I thought it would be nice with John—he's just a nice man in nice khakis—but then I realized it would make you jealous. And how I kind of wouldn't exactly mind that. Which made me wonder who I am anymore." She shoved at her hair, which Aaron noticed absently had made progress toward being as wild as the night they met, but his focus was on her words. Every shiny, revealing one of them. "I know that was a lot. I know sometimes I say things that make people uncomfortable, so I have to hold back a little."

"Don't," he choked out.

She pulled her bent legs closer, giving him an uncomfortable twist in the dead center of his chest. "I would like to go on a date with you. I want to run my hands all over your back and into your hair, just because. I want you to sit me on your lap to talk about bears. And your dog. You know, Old Man likes you best, that's why he's ignoring you. He's basically *made* for you. I would tell you things like that. You could tell me things back. That's a date, right?"

"No, Grace." Aaron crawled across the floor toward her huddled form. "That would be our date. No one would ever duplicate it."

Her eyes smiled, but she didn't respond. No, she actually seemed nervous about what Aaron would think of her outburst. Truthfully, he was shocked at everything she'd been thinking while he'd been clueless. Wasn't he supposed to be some kind of mental mastermind? Not with Grace.

"Do you hold back a lot around me, Grace?" He sat

down in a cross-legged position, so close her feet were beneath his calves. "From touching, I mean."

"Yeah. From everyone, really. But mostly you." She
lifted one hand, scrutinizing it. "When I was younger, I
found it hard to communicate with words. I mean, I could
talk a blue streak, but people didn't seem to understand
right away. Or they would debate among themselves over
what I'd meant. So I learned to...accompany words with
touches and my point got across better." She let the hand
fall. "When I got older, it wasn't appropriate anymore."

"Said who?"

"Everyone." Her gaze flickered. "But mostly it was the
way people stiffened up every time I tried."

Aaron ached. Oh Christ, he ached all over. Not with
lust, although there would always be a steady beat of that
with Grace so close. No, her pain had climbed over and
sucked him into its dark fold. "Since we're being honest, Grace, I don't like the idea of your hands touching
a lot of people. Especially men. Especially doctors." Her
lips jumped at that. "But if we're alone...and you want
to slide your hands up my back or put them in my hair,
I'm all fucking yours. I'm not happy that I've been missing out."

"We're alone now," she whispered, sending blood racing south to his cock, threatening to steal his patience,
even though the moment required forbearance against his
desire. He sensed that, somehow, but couldn't explain it.

"We'll be alone on our date, too," he said gruffly.
"Tonight."

If the heavens had opened and shined a ray of sunshine
onto her face, it couldn't have been any more brilliant.
Whatever magic was taking place inside him matched the

intensity of it, but not the beauty. Nothing could come close. "Tonight," she repeated. "Does that mean I should wait to touch you?"

"No, Grace. It doesn't."

It seemed like hours were passing as Grace came to her knees, fluid fingers reaching out to grasp the knot of Aaron's tie. As the silk material slithered together, loosening around his neck, Aaron commanded his breath to remain steady, not that it did him much good. Every inhale treated him to sweet, earthy woman, and with her breasts right beneath his nose, sex tried to capture his mind. Fill it with images of his mouth sucking on her nipples while she rode his cock, but Aaron focused. Focused on her eyes and the pleasure she derived from removing his tie. "Are you going to make ribbons out of it?" he rasped.

With those perfectly imperfect teeth sinking into her bottom lip, she shook her head, before regaining that concentrated look. A few seconds later, Grace had finally loosened the knot enough to draw the tie over his head. But the progress of her task stopped short with the silk banded around his forehead. She twisted it to the side and tightened the knot once more, leaving the material dangling down one side of his head. "Perfect," she breathed with a straight face.

It was a weird thing, the mix of triumphant and...silly. In fact, he was sure he'd never once experienced that combination. Ever. And they packed a hell of a power punch. One that moved through him with such strength, there was no other option but to snatch Grace around the waist and drag her onto his lap, her thighs opening to straddle him in a smooth, natural movement. Their mouths met, but they didn't kiss. They *laughed*. Sexual need and humor, at the same time. Another foreign tag team of emotions that nearly knocked him dead. "There I was, thinking Grace was making one of her moments and she's just having a laugh at my expense."

Her warm hands cupped his face, thumbs tracing along his shaved jaw. "Oh, laughing makes the best moments. That was a ten."

"How am I going to top a ten?"

She tipped her head back, humming up at the ceiling. "Maybe we have to come up with a new rating scale."

Aaron leaned in and ran his tongue up the side of her neck, breathing into her ear. "See, now you're talking my language." Planning, as he always did. But different. *Good* different. "Let's split the scale into three. One for Grace's good deeds. One for laughing..." He gave a subtle tilt of his hips that made her lips part. "One for fucking."

The hands cupping his face dropped, clinging to his shoulders. "But last n-night was a fifteen. Already, we can't top it."

He took hold of Grace's hoodie zipper, lowered the bit of metal, pushing open the well-worn material. "Not right now we can't. No matter how tempted I am to take you into that closet to let my cock deal with you." Against his better judgment, Aaron lifted the hem of her T-shirt, baring her tits. "Your nipples are hard. You like the idea of a rough quickie, baby?"

"Yes."

With a groan, Aaron leaned in and sucked her nipples in turn, leaving them shiny and puckered. "No, I'm giving you a fifteen every time. And you love the foreplay, don't you?" Another long pull of her nipples, his hands finding her ass, gripping the taut flesh. "The way you rubbed your pussy on me last night told me all about you. So I'm not taking what I know about your needs and banging you in a closet. That would be for me. Oh *fuck*, would it be for me. I'd knock every last item off those goddamn shelves because I want to ruin any progress you made over the last hour with someone else. I guess I'm a selfish bastard in every way, except when it comes to fucking you. I won't be selfish with your body."

Grace's breath came in quick pants against his forehead, little whimpers escaping when he curled his tongue around her nipples one by one, lapping at them, flattening his tongue to rub them in slow circles. "What if I want to be selfish with *your* body?"

Aaron's head lifted. "That's a different story. I told you not to hold back when it comes to touching me. I meant it, Grace." His voice sounded abnormally thick. "But your father is going to be here any minute. There are things to talk about before I...before *we* take a risk like that."

Yeah, he'd actually just said that. That they needed to have a discussion. About...them. About taking this crazy pairing of a type-A asshole and a genuine bleeding heart who only wanted to bring good into the world. Talk about selfish. But there it was. He needed their relationship to be aboveboard, and whatever she had in mind was the polar opposite. Because holy shit, the excitement and...relief dancing in her eyes were breathtaking. And determined.

"Grace..."

She scooted back in his lap, hands falling to Aaron's belt buckle, the clumsy movements to get it open and unzip his pants making his cock thicken along with his thoughts. "I've been wondering what you taste like since that day you went running." Her hand flattened on his abdomen and slid down the front of his briefs, her thighs tightening the same time as her grip around his erection—*Christ*. A telling sign that she needed the filthy aforementioned fuck against the wall. "When you were sweating and...so mad at me. Is it wrong that I wanted you to take out your anger on me?"

Aaron groaned as her thumb circled his crown. "Depends how y'mean."

"I love that you slur your words when I touch you." She jerked him harder, making his middle quicken and shake. Until she brought his flesh between her legs, rubbing him against the seam of her leggings, and everything twisted violently. "I meant, I wanted you to take out your anger between my legs."

Oh my God. "Not wrong. No...that's not wrong."

With a slow, deliberate smile, Grace eased off his lap and lay down on her belly, compelling Aaron to close his eyes or else lose his shit. Because Grace's bow-shaped mouth being level with his cock, worshiping it with a hungry expression of longing...*fuuuuck*, it was too much to bear. Too much.

Aaron fell back on his elbows. "Come on, show me what selfish feels like coming from a saint."

Her tongue zigzagged up the underside of his length. "I'm not a saint."

She took Aaron halfway to his root, drawing up slowly with a purr, sending every muscle below his waist into a near-painful contraction. "No holding back, right?" His hands flew to her hair, gripping, tangling. "Come on, baby. That's twice now you've talked about liking me sweaty. So get me there. Make me fucking sweat. Just like I'm going to sweat getting you off tonight." He growled in his throat as both of her fists started pumping him, in time with that mouth. "I'm going to work for your come. You like knowing that? Show me. Suck your way down to my sack and make me feel guilty when you choke a little. But not guilty enough to stop asking for it."

Just like the night before, the dirtier his mind went, the more enthusiastic the response from Grace. She fell on him, mouth suctioning tight and working overtime, up and down, until he nearly begged for her to slow down. So he could savor the snug heat of her mouth and throat, savor the knowledge that Grace was the one bringing on his climax. *No one else. No one else. Never again.*

And *fuck* if that scary and beautiful mental commitment and her green, half-mast eyes drifting up his stomach to mingle with his gaze didn't propel him past the finish line, ripping the orgasm from a deep, untapped area of his body. He threw an arm over his face, roaring her name into the crook of his elbow, his eyes wide open, but seeing nothing except pitch-black. Back arched, stomach clenching, his legs shook violently as wet desire rippled out of him, painting the inside of Grace's exquisite mouth. "*Jesus*, baby. Ohhhh, you're so fucking hot. I needed this. *I've needed you.*" His voice cracked. "Thank you. *Suck it down.* Oh my God, thank you."

Aaron didn't come back to himself until Grace crawled up his prone body, tucking her head beneath his chin, her tits heaving against his shuddering stomach. "I needed that, too."

His lethargic laugh was rife with disbelief, but he sobered quickly, the feel of Grace in his arms too important to make light of. "They broke every rating scale when they made you, Grace."

For a moment, they were both still, until Grace tilted her head to press kisses along his neck, assuring him as she always did when he spoke outside his comfort zone. "I think about you almost every minute of the day. I want that to be okay."

Invisible hands closed around his heart, making the pumps feel labored. "You're not alone."

Grace sat up, a blush decorating her cheeks, and she went about the task of arranging his clothing back the way it had been. With delicate fingers, she zipped his pants, smoothing a hand up his fly to refasten his belt. And he let her. He watched her through a dreamlike haze and...let her. Allowing someone else to perform such an intimate process would have been beyond him a matter of days ago, but now it was just something inside recognizing the needs of another. Grace. The consuming responsibility of allowing that need to be met. Being fulfilled in return.

"Hey." Aaron sat up when she was finished, taking her chin between his finger and thumb. "I would go to sleep with you right now, if I could."

"I know." She rocked forward on her hands and kissed him, sliding their damp lips together. "Now, get back to work. You have a date tonight."

I'm in love. I'm in love with you, Grace. I'm... "Fucking right I have a date," he managed. "You think I could forget?"

A few minutes later, with a final look at Grace over his shoulder, Aaron walked out into the cold, allowing a smile to form on his face.

* * *

Grace's influence must have caused Aaron to grow a conscience, or unearthed the one he'd buried, because conversing with the senator after having Grace's mouth working between his thighs wasn't easy. Not by any stretch. He schooled his features and recited the Gettysburg Address in the back of his mind while they went over poll numbers and Aaron updated Pendleton on the camp's progress, which the influx of college student volunteers had actually put ahead of schedule. Deliveries had been made, checked against receipts, and unloaded. Local restaurants had donated food and beverages for the workers, the news media was having a field day with not only the senator's involvement, but human interest stories about some of the volunteers who'd actually attended the camp as youths.

As anticipated, the media was quick to sink their teeth into the story of four—not five—girls who'd been victims of Ray Solomon and the fire that had taken their lives. Aaron was grateful to have Grace removed from the public eye while the questions were fired at him and the senator, and he hoped the story would take a backseat to the rebuild sooner rather than later. To be on the safe side, he took Peggy and Sage off the project he'd designated for them to work with Grace and keep her away from the cameras. The Pendletons might have kept Grace out of the spotlight, but Aaron's number one rule was never underestimate the media. He wouldn't start now when Grace's comfort was at stake.

Goddamn, he could barely concentrate under the newfound need to protect her. Maybe because he'd never experienced the urge, but there was no ignoring it now. It had been brought on by the flood of admitting how he felt.

Love. What the fuck was he supposed to do with it? He'd barely gotten through asking her out on a date, knowing it could breed commitment. When it came to his job, Aaron knew what was expected of him. Success. He didn't know how to achieve that with another person. Everyone in his life, his parents, siblings, knew he could be counted on for logistics, but sure as shit not affection. Grace...she needed more than the plan man. She deserved *everything*.

Okay, asshole. Regroup. First step was getting used to loving someone. That was enough of a feat for now. After tonight, after their date, he would go from there. No decisions needed to be made while the ground beneath his feet was still quaking.

The senator's hand clapped him on the shoulder, bringing Aaron out of his boiling mental stew. They were sitting in the makeshift office Aaron had set up in the mess hall, going over his upcoming statement to the press, taking what the speech writer had written and putting Aaron's specialized spin on it. "Okay," Pendleton boomed. "I've got my marching orders. Let's go make the evening news."

"Better yet, let's get your name trending," Aaron said, his words sounding empty and insignificant when they should have filled him with adrenaline.

"Sure," Pendleton said absently, gathering the numbered notecards. "I have to hand it to you, Clarkson, you're worth your weight in gold. You talk a big game and you back it up. Not a lot of people in this field can deliver on both."

Aaron stood, shaking the senator's hand. "Thank you, I appreciate—"

"That's why I'm sending you to New York." The silence from hell ensued while the quaking under Aaron's feet turned into an eight on the Richter Scale, the destruction of buildings blaring in his ears. "You've gotten the ball rolling at YouthAspire, put the plans in place, and my team can take it from here. We need you at headquarters, where you'll be more valuable, not in the mountains of Iowa."

This was everything he'd wanted. Hell, his family was staying in Iowa to help him, but the master plan was to meet in New York anyway. Nothing had changed...except Grace. But she was a whole motherfucker of a game changer, wasn't she? Grace wouldn't be in New York. She would be *here*, out of his reach. Saying words he wouldn't hear, needing to touch him and not having the option.

He was going to be sick. His stomach was curling in on itself, preparing to expel the contents of his breakfast, and perspiration was forming on his brow.

"Have to say, Clarkson, I thought you'd be over the moon about this."

And that's when he knew the senator had an ulterior motive for sending his ass out of the state, away from his daughter. God, he couldn't even fault the man. Fathers didn't allow their daughters to attach themselves to men with Aaron's reputation. Especially men who aspired to the presidency. There might have been a sliver of a chance for him and Grace if he hadn't done something so unforgivable in California. Something that had meant exactly nothing to him could keep him away from the person...who meant everything.

It would have been so easy to say no when he'd answered that knock on his apartment door. So easy to rebuff the polished proposition. But he hadn't. He'd let a woman use him as punishment for her unavailable husband. Now he and Grace were going to be separated by half a continent because of something he'd done without any emotion or thought of the consequences.

"I know this is about Grace." He barely got the words past numb lips. "But you don't understand—" *I love her. I would die before hurting her.*

"Oh, I understand how men like you operate. You won't be operating with my daughter." With concise movements, Pendleton tucked the notecards into his coat pocket and strode for the door. "I want her home by tonight, sleeping in her own bed, instead of God knows where, with you. And I want you on the road in the morning. Those two things don't happen, you don't keep your job. Are we clear?"

Aaron's eventual nod could have come from a stone statue for its stiff reluctance, but he had no choice. Not when he knew the chances of him giving her the healthy, loving relationship she deserved were slim to none. What would he offer her anyway without a job to his name?

As soon as the door closed behind the senator, Aaron dropped like a boulder into a folding chair, staring at the wall but seeing only Grace. He'd promised her a date, and he wouldn't let her down. He wouldn't hide the fact that he was leaving Iowa prematurely, but the revelation could wait until the end of the night. Until then, he would savor every moment.

CHAPTER TWENTY

Grace didn't see Aaron again that afternoon. With the rumor of free beer passing among the volunteers in excited murmurs, they began to disperse, leaving the camp in a state of suspended animation. Jobs were halted and instructions for the following day passed on through the appointed supervisors in red, who were also quick to remind the students and staffers not to show up too hungover the following morning, as the real work was only beginning.

Aaron was nowhere to be seen as the volunteers piled into vans and hybrids, faces lit up by their cell phone screens as they chatted excitedly. Grace tried not to panic that he'd canceled their date. He wouldn't do that. No, he was probably holed up somewhere, working on something spectacular for the following day.

Grace was caught in the middle stages of dressing, sitting on her bed in the cabin with Old Man curled beside her, still trying to come down from the buzz of everything that had happened during the day. The camp's functionality had grown by leaps and bounds in the matter of twenty-four hours... and then there was Aaron. What they'd done in the infirmary. Or what *she'd* done, rather. Wanted to do again at the earliest opportunity. Fingertips pressed against her lips, she remembered the way Aaron's happy trail had looked, descending from his belly button. Black, masculine hair that didn't match the rest of his polished appearance. No, there was nothing smooth about the way his abs had swelled up and dropped with sudden intensity, a physical symphony conducted by her mouth. Those hands in her hair...

She hadn't brushed it since then and she wouldn't. At some point, her locks would need detangling and those knots would be a trial, but tonight wasn't for worrying. It wasn't her first date, in terms of going somewhere with a member of the opposite sex. But it was her first time wanting to sprint toward the event like an Olympian. Her first time labeling an outing a *date*. If Aaron meant everything he'd said that afternoon, she didn't have to hold back around him... at all. How was she going to handle the sudden liberation of everything she'd struggled to keep inside so long?

Didn't matter. Grace's lips curled into a smile. *Didn't matter.* Aaron wouldn't let her feel awkward or out of place. He might even be a little awkward himself. And if making that wickedly intelligent man act awkward wasn't something to look forward to, she didn't know what was.

Grace looked up from buttoning her shirt when Peggy and Sage straggled in, looking like they'd been off-roading in a convertible. Peggy's curls were weighed down, clearly having lost the battle with exhaustion. Sage just looked shell-shocked. Belmont filled the doorway behind them, watching the wedding planner with anxious concern that immediately became a fifth presence in the room.

"Told you not to push yourself." Belmont slapped his fist against the doorjamb and kept it there. Old Man leapt off the bed to go butt his head against Belmont's legs, but the extra-large man only managed an absent nod before zeroing back in on Sage. "You're limping."

"I'm fine." Contradicting her statement, Sage whimpered as she fell onto her bed. Which made Belmont look like someone had unloaded a round of bullets into his gut.

Belmont pressed his forehead against his propped fist and breathed. "Back in New Mexico, you promised me you would cut your bangs when they started to cover your eyes." Old Man started to yowl. "If I'd been able to see your eyes, I would have known you were tired. Cut them tonight."

Sage squared her shoulders, as if preparing for battle. "You can't just order me to cut my hair."

Tense moments passed with Sage's words hanging in the air. They all held their breath when Belmont entered the cabin, his boots thunking on the wooden floorboards. He moved slowly, but his lack of speed was more intimidating than if he'd broken into a dead run. He came to a stop in front of Sage, who seemed to have no choice but to tilt her head back to maintain eye contact with the towering Belmont. Color leached from the room's atmosphere as Belmont reached a hand out, brushing Sage's bangs to one side, the way a giant might take care with a kitten. "Please," Belmont said in a gruff voice. "I need them."

"Okay," Sage whispered, giving a wobbly nod. "Okay."

Grace swore none of them breathed until Belmont left the room, the absence of his bulk making the cabin's interior feel triple in size.

"Well. I'll get the scissors," Peggy said, pulling her suitcase from beneath the bed. "You're all dolled up, Grace. You got something special happening tonight?"

The way Peggy asked the question, Grace knew Aaron had shared their plans. And why did that send a flock of birds winging in her belly? She was the girl Peggy's brother was dating. "What have you guys been up to all day?" Grace asked, instead of answering. "I didn't see you around camp."

Peggy and Sage exchanged a sly look. "Oh, we've been here and there. Behind-the-scenes-type stuff. Real hush-hush."

Sage still appeared to be in her mesmerized state. "Aaron is still up there."

With a gasp, Peggy launched a balled-up sock at Sage's head.

"Up where?" Grace questioned her, picking up the socks that landed at her feet, tossing them back to Peggy. "Where's Aaron?"

"I'm right here."

Hel-lo. That deep voice held the signs of strain, probably from repeating himself and issuing orders from dawn until dusk, but the scratchy quality only affected Grace more, sending a mudslide of lust and anticipation crashing through her middle. God, the way it would sound in her ear…

And all those thoughts hit before he stepped into the cabin. When he did? *Yowza.* The tips of his hair were still wet, the dark ends sticking out from beneath the black beanie. He wore a heavy jacket, but it was unzipped so she could see the thin gray sweater beneath, the way it highlighted the definition of his muscular upper half, the flat stomach disappearing into his snug-in-the-right-places jeans.

I can't handle him like this. Dressed down and comfortable. Like she could tackle him onto the grass without worrying about ruining something expensive. Throw in his unwavering stare from beneath the edge of his beanie and Grace wouldn't have minded if their date started and ended back in the mess hall tent.

There was more, though. His eyes were warm. So much warmer than she'd ever seen them, and finally, the softer edges of him were visible. The humor that had slowly gone from biting and sarcastic to conspiratorial. But still so Aaron. Right now, he was looking at her as if they shared a great secret together and she wanted that. Wanted to communicate in ways no one else understood. Maybe they already did.

"Yeah…" Peggy's smug voice popped the fantasy bubble over Grace's head. "You're going to want me to shop for you more often, Aaron."

"You might be right," he murmured, coming toward Grace, propelling her heart into an erratic tempo. She expected Aaron to hold out a hand and pull her to her feet so they could leave. Instead, he stopped between her bent knees, leaned down to plant his hands on the bed…and French kissed her in a slow, leisurely fashion. Right there in front of his sister and Sage. It wasn't over fast, either. No, it went on until Grace's supply of oxygen ran out. "Ready to go?" Aaron asked, pulling back, his gaze glued on her mouth.

"I don't know," she breathed. "Yes."

The edges of his lips ticked up. "Didn't think I would kiss you with an audience, did you?"

"No."

He made a warm noise in his throat, then leaned in to speak quietly against her ear. "As soon as we've been on this date a respectable amount of time, I'm going to return the fuck out of that favor you gave me today." His lips grazed her lobe, sending a shiver down her back. "Those tights are going to be very easy to tug down...for what I need to do. Is that why you wore them?"

Grace was already nodding, her consciousness dwindled down to Aaron. Nothing and no one else existed but this dynamic man crowding her on the bed, making risqué plans in her ear. "Yes."

"Why aren't you touching me, Grace?"

She didn't realize her eyes had closed until they popped open, the rush of pleasure pausing at the concern in Aaron's voice. That same pause allowed her to notice her hands, which were balled into tight fists to keep from reaching out. But she didn't need to keep herself in check, did she? No sooner had the reminder been made than Grace shoved both of her hands under Aaron's jacket and yanked him forward, causing him to lose his balance and land partially on top of her, making the mattress groan.

But he only laughed that new, spectacular laugh, dropping a hard kiss onto her mouth. "Better." With a regretful sigh, Aaron gave Grace's forehead a nudge with his own, before standing, taking her hand to pull her off the bed. He glanced over his shoulder and gave a wry smile. "Turns out there is something that can make my sister stop talking."

Scissors clearly forgotten in her hand, Peggy visibly shook herself. "Grace, what have you done to my brother?" She shared a baffled glance with Sage. "Seriously, did you hypnotize him?"

"Something like that." Aaron threw an arm around Grace's shoulders and led her toward the door. "Don't wait up."

* * *

Aaron wouldn't think about parting ways with Grace after their date. In fact, he hadn't even told his siblings they were hitting the road in the morning, because he knew they'd give it away somehow. Grace was more perceptive than people gave her credit for, and *nothing* was going to ruin her night, so he'd shot Peggy a quick text to be ready for departure just before leaving camp. And was now staunchly ignoring the incessant buzz of his phone.

Every inch of his body was riddled with pain. And it had nothing to do with the physical labor he'd thrown himself into after his phone call with the senator. No, it was a direct result of the catastrophe taking place inside his sore rib cage. The ache radiated out, delegating pain to other parts of his body, knowing the inexperienced organ in his chest couldn't handle it all.

But Aaron had a lot of experience with avoidance. Tonight might be the biggest test of his skill set, but he needed the memory of Grace, too. Needed it to be untouched by his dread over the upcoming good-bye. Now, as he helped Grace out of the Suburban, Aaron drew on every ounce of his capabilities, pushing aside anger in favor of memorizing Grace's curves as they slid over his body.

Grace tugged gloves out of her coat pockets and put them on, her breath puffing into the air. "Where are we?"

"Good," Aaron said, relief easing the tightness in his neck. "You don't know it. I wasn't sure, since you grew up here."

She looked around the flat courtyard, still white from the snow they'd received. Up ahead lay an old barn, lit up from the inside with a soft glow, music flowing out through the open windows. "I think I've been to this place, but never during winter. What is it?"

Aaron took her gloved hand, marveling over how easy the action felt, even though he'd never held a woman's hand before. "I believe the technical term used was *jamboree*." He blew warm air into their joined grip. "I asked some of the local guys where they were bringing their girlfriends tonight. And then I did the exact opposite." Their footsteps crunched in the hardened snow. "I hope that's okay. I really didn't feel like talking to anyone but you."

Grace ducked her head, but not before Aaron caught her smile. "That's better than okay."

Already, Aaron could tell he'd underestimated his ability to withstand Grace's blushes and smiles and breathy responses. It took a superhero level of willpower not to throw her over his shoulder and lock them in a room together somewhere. *Mine tonight. Don't want to share.* "So, I…" He sucked in a fortifying breath. "I asked Sylvia, the older woman who donated lunch, where I should take you."

"You did?" She laughed into the sleeve of his jacket. "I wish I could have heard that conversation."

"No. You really don't." He shook his head, remembering the way Sylvia had asked if he was planning to propose. "My mother was a chef. I think maybe that's the only reason I—"

"Felt comfortable talking to Sylvia?" Grace stopped and faced him. "I didn't know that about your mom. The little things you've told me...she sounds like someone who would be easy to miss."

Aaron really wanted to keep walking and dismiss the uncomfortable topic, but Grace's expression was so earnest, he didn't want to let her down. And hell, talking about his mother couldn't be any worse than *not* talking about her. "She left us this journal," he heard himself say. "I have it. It's in my suitcase and I can't even read it."

"Why not?" Grace murmured, stepping forward to lay her head on his chest.

He stared toward the barn, noticing the lit-up trees for the first time, extending from the barn's far side, down through a grove of glowing trees. The Winter Walk. The reason he'd brought Grace there tonight. "I'm afraid to read what she said about me," he finally answered, his voice distant. "I don't want to confirm what I already know."

It was the kind of confession he would have regretted if Grace had gasped or chided him for being ridiculous. But she didn't. She merely slipped a hand up beneath his sweater, gliding it around to his back, leaving a warm path in its wake. "You're not so difficult to see, Aaron. Your greatness isn't so hidden your mother wouldn't recognize it."

He melted toward Grace, dropping his chin onto her head, wishing rather futilely that her touch could go farther down than his skin. "I don't know. I think you want me to be good so much, I'm doing it involuntarily."

She pressed a kiss to his throat and he felt the smile transforming her lips. "I'm not so powerful."

"Ah, Grace. You're the most powerful person I know." He sank both hands into her hair, lifting the fistful of strands to his nose and inhaling. "I need to kiss the fucking breath out of you, but if I get started, there will be no cider drinking. Definitely no Winter Walk. Sylvia will be very disappointed in me."

She went up on her toes to bring their mouths together, puffs of hot air clouding the area between them. "I'll kiss you extra later."

That familiar right hook of need caught him low in the stomach, tightening his muscles. "You're the one who'll be getting kissed." He snagged her upper lip, sucking it into his mouth. "Tell me where I'm going to put the kisses."

"Um."

Goddamn it. No going back now that he was started. As long as he avoided putting his tongue in her addictive mouth, he might be able to go through with the date. But Christ, he needed a dose of Grace's body up against his own. Just a reminder to his starving body he would give it relief later. Aaron's hands dropped to the smooth mounds of Grace's ass, lifting until she wrapped her legs around his waist, fitting her pussy against his bulge. "*Um* is not an answer," he rasped.

Her green eyes took on a mesmerizing glean as she gave a long, unhurried roll of her hips. "There. You'll kiss me there."

Aaron shoved his forehead into the crook of her neck. "That's right. *Jesus.*"

"You asked," she breathed, warming the back of his neck. "I love when you ask those kinds of questions."

"Do I ask them often?"

Even though he couldn't see her face, Aaron could feel shyness descend, hear it in the quiet, breathy quality of her tone. "Yes, when we're...touching." When she swallowed, he felt it against his lips. "Like it skin on skin, don't you? You've got a triple threat between your thighs, don't—"

"Stop it, Grace," he ground out, reeling under the unexpected impact of having his words from the night before repeated back. Against his mental will, his hands were jerking her ass closer, grinding her sex against his cock. "Actually—fuck, I must want to be tortured—but I've been meaning to ask you something else."

Her fingertips slipped through his hair, nails creating exhilarating trails along his scalp. "What is it?"

Can I fuck you, right here, standing up? Wrong question. But a valid one. "Why are you bare between your legs?"

She lifted her head, zeroing in on his eyes. "Do you like it?"

"I *like* breakfast. I *like* John Wayne movies." He licked the cleft in her upper lip. "I want to build a fucking shrine to your pussy. There's a big difference."

Grace's smile turned a wrench in his chest. "The day I stole the money...the woman who came over to cut and clean my hair...she asked me if I wanted anything waxed. And, I don't know, I thought I would give it a whirl." Her gaze fell to his mouth and shot back up. "Maybe in the back of my mind, I thought the kind of women you like would have it done. Was I...right?"

Because he could see the answer mattered, he trapped the humorless laugh in his throat, where it joined the nonstop ache. But nothing would keep the truth suppressed. Not with their bodies interlocked, breathing in time with each other, surrounded by cool nighttime air. "You think I have the ability to look at you and remember anyone from before? Before Grace?" Her mouth parted, cheeks warming with color. *Wow.* He was a total bastard. How could he say that kind of thing to her, knowing he would be leaving? "Did it hurt?"

Grace stared back at him blankly until he tilted his hips, reminding her of their conversation. "Oh, the waxing." She nodded. "Like a motherfucker."

Aaron's bark of laughter echoed off the packed snow, the towering trees. "I guess I have a love-hate relationship with this hairdresser I've never met, huh?" His lips lingered against Grace's cheek. "She ruined your beautiful hair, but she made your pussy nothing but slippery for me."

"My hair's not ruined," she whispered, a slight tremor in her delivery. "It's back to normal now."

His mouth twitched at Grace using the word *normal* to describe her hair. "I need to get you inside this barn soon, Grace." He turned and trudged toward the big structure, Grace's legs still wrapped tight around him. "I can't decide anymore if I want to pin you down and just *talk* to you...or fuck you. Or, Christ, do both at the same time. I'm not even sure if that's something people do."

"It can be something we do," she whispered, her words dropping like shiny pearls between them. "You just have to want it."

His stomach lurched. "I wish wanting something was enough, baby." Sensing Grace's curiosity, he forced himself to smile. "Let's go get our jamboree on. Whatever the hell a jamboree is."

CHAPTER TWENTY-ONE

There was always something fascinating happening behind Aaron's movie star mask. *Always*. But she'd never sensed resignation in him. Never seen the relentless wheels behind his eyes stall and spin in the dirt, as they appeared to be doing now. *I wish wanting something was enough, baby.* Until he'd said those words, Grace would have sworn nothing could make her wish the date were over before it started. So she could be one-on-one with Aaron, warm flesh pressing together, listening to his ragged breaths, hearing his groaned truths in her ear. That was when his walls officially came down. She knew that now. And while tonight he was treating her like some long-lost princess who deserved the date of her life, she only wanted the experience with Aaron totally present.

Grace curled her fingers in the neckline of Aaron's shirt, ready to tug the material for his attention, but he released her. She slid down his body a split second before they were bathed in warm, yellow light. Above her head, Aaron's hand pushed open the barn door, violin music coiling in the air around Grace, forcing her to turn around.

Her lungs imprisoned the breath she tried to draw. How? How had she lived mere miles from this place and never known of its existence? Strings of twinkling white lights were strung from the rafters, swaying in the breeze they'd generated by opening the door. The scents of pine and cinnamon beckoned her into the warm interior, her feet moving involuntarily. People were everywhere. Locals, obviously, wearing their familiarity with one another like snuggly sweaters. Hands were being shaken. Hugs given. Pieces of pie being passed around. Oh, and there was dancing. The music's tempo had picked up at their entrance, almost on cue, drawing couples to the makeshift dance floor, where fathers spun around their daughters, the older guests regarding them fondly. On the opposite side of the barn, women handed out desserts, granting huge dollops of whipped cream and ladling cider.

A few people sent curious glances in Grace and Aaron's direction, but their expressions couldn't have been more welcoming. And when Grace's attention landed on an older woman in an *Iowans Do It in the Field* apron, she knew it was Sylvia. Especially when the woman dropped the stack of Styrofoam plates in her hand, face breaking into a smile when she saw Aaron.

"You brought her!" Aaron bent down so the petite woman could throw her arms around his neck. "I was half worried you might cave to the peer pressure and take her out for...I don't know...*beer*." She gave ladylike gag. "Well, let me see her."

Aaron settled an arm around Grace's shoulders, pulling her into his side, and Grace tucked the sensation of belonging to someone away for a rainy day. "Sylvia." He paused, looking down to run his gaze over her. "This is Grace."

"Such a lovely name," Sylvia said warmly. "And the beauty to match."

Grace managed to tear her attention away from Aaron's rapt expression long enough to shake the woman's hand. "It's lovely to meet you." She gestured to the barn as a whole. "I never knew this was here."

"Well." Sylvia leaned in with a wink. "We like to keep it quiet. Just friends and family, once a year. But my mother started the tradition, so I get to invite whoever I darn well please."

"Lucky for us," Aaron murmured, dropping a kiss onto the top of Grace's head. "The place looks great."

"Oh, as if you've looked away from Grace long enough to spare it a glance." Sylvia laughed, splitting a thrilled look between Grace and Aaron. "Now, listen. Here's what we're going to do. I'm going to put a cup of hot cider in each of your hands, and Aaron, you're going to take Grace out back through the grove. Remember? We talked about this."

"I remember," Aaron responded with a solemn nod. "We're ready when you are."

As soon as Sylvia was out of earshot, Grace made a wistful sound. "Are we really going back out so soon? This place is incredible." She braced her throat with a hand. "It's awful that I don't know anyone here. This is my hometown."

"Now you know Sylvia. That's a good start." Aaron

pushed one of the red ribbons out of her face. "You should come back next year."

Grace didn't have time to wonder about the hollowness to Aaron's voice. A group of locals in Rudolph and Frosty sweaters approached, recognizing Aaron from television and asking about the progress of the camp. To her surprise, Aaron labeled Grace the expert on all things YouthAspire and let her update them. At first, her words were stilted, but their encouraging smiles and Aaron's arm across her shoulders made it easy quickly enough.

Somewhere along the way, she began to flat out enjoy herself. Watching the children bob for apples and being asked to settle a tie, sharing a piece of pecan pie with Aaron, listening to a grandfather tell stories about the first annual jamboree, back when he'd been a child. By the time Sylvia found them again, Grace's sides hurt from laughing...although the awareness of Aaron's proximity never left her. How could it when he didn't take his eyes off her once, as far as she could tell?

Sylvia pressed fresh cups of cider into their hands and cocked an eyebrow as if to say, *Ready?* Without waiting for their nods, she shuffled them through the parting crowd of curious onlookers toward the barn's back exit. After a dramatic pause and an audible exhale, Sylvia slid open the groaning door. And if Grace thought she'd been taken off guard by the glowing, holiday-happy barn, nothing compared to her internal reaction to the grove.

Magic lay in front of her. No other description fit the winding path, surrounded by ancient trees, covered top to bottom in lights. Every single color she could fathom, seemingly in every shade. Reds, greens, pinks, blues. A couple of laughing children ran down beneath the overhanging branches, but apart from them, the snowy walkway was deserted.

"Aaron?"

His hand smoothed back and forth along the small of her back. "Yeah?"

Grace couldn't look away from the glow. "I think you broke another rating scale." Unable to stand still a moment longer, Grace reached for Aaron's hand, twining their fingers together. They walked side by side into the grove, the cold somehow less biting within the trees' embrace. Even their breath seemed to remain in the air longer, hanging there, like white spun sugar. Behind them, the barn door slid shut, muffling the party sounds, but leaving them the gentle cries of violin strings. There was a rush underneath the wind, as if there were a rollicking stream nearby, even though if one existed, it would surely be frozen.

Before she could get too far, Aaron pulled her to a stop, taking her cider and setting it down on the path's edge, along with his own. "I don't dance, Grace." He contradicted his words by stepping so close she had to crane her neck to keep eye contact. Placing one hand on her hip, he clasped the other against his shoulder. They started to sway in a slow circle, not a breath of air separating them.

If it were possible for someone to explode, shooting rainbows and unicorns in every direction, that's what Grace would have done as they danced beneath the ethereal tree light to string music. "If you don't dance, what do you call this?"

"An illusion." There was a smile in his voice. "We're not actually dancing right now. You're imagining the whole thing."

"I see." She pressed her lips together to hold in a laugh.

"I have been told I let my imagination run away with me. So...what are we *actually* doing?"

Aaron's lips glided over the knuckles of her lifted hand, along the seam of their combined grip. "You're the one with the imagination. I'd rather you decide."

With a big inhale of Aaron's unique scent, Grace closed her eyes and let her mind drift. And in such a fairy-tale setting, it wasn't hard to do. "Maybe we're really playing hide and seek with those kids. But they can't find us, because we climbed to the top of the highest tree."

"And now we're stuck. We can't ever come down."

Grace allowed her lids to lift. "See, you have an imagination, too."

She could see that playfulness trying to break through in Aaron...and he let it. That was the most extraordinary part—Aaron giving up the fight. He laid his mouth on her temple and continued to sway her. "We wouldn't have to come down. I'd build you a tower up in the sky." His lips quirked against her. "We'd let your hair grow until I could use the ribbons to climb down and get supplies. Like ice cream and toothpaste."

"And dog food for Old Man."

Aaron's low laugh shifted the strands of her hair. "I'm making a mental note to put a doggie door on this sky tower."

"Perfect," she murmured, feeling weightless. "After that, all we'd need is time."

But the comfort slowly dissipated when she connected with Aaron's stare. It was penetrating, possibly a little agonized, and once again Grace got the distinct feeling Aaron was holding on to something important. Watching her closely, he eased Grace back into a dip, bending her so far, the tips of her hair trailed on the snowy ground. No sooner had Aaron pulled her back up than their mouths were hovering, so close, so very close, mutual heavy breaths making their mark on the air. "Grace, I..."

"Yes?" she whispered when he didn't continue.

"What do you want to do? In the future?" He gave a quick headshake, as if he knew the formality of the question was unworthy of the moment. "Do you have... plans?"

She wanted to demand to be let inside his head, but in the short time since meeting Aaron, she'd learned to trust her gut. And her gut was telling her not to push. That patience would be rewarded quicker. "I never got a chance to decide. My father decided to run for president, and it's been all about the campaign since I left Austin. But now I think I'm finally getting breathing room." As they turned in a slow circle, Grace stared at the myriad colors being cast down on the snow. "I want to stay here until the camp gets up and running, then I want to move on."

They stopped moving. "Move on where?"

"I don't know." She smiled, thinking of the possibilities behind those three words. "Places I'm needed. Places I can help. They're everywhere." She'd always thought stating those dreams out loud would feel more like soaring, but while being held in Aaron's arms... maybe it was premature, but there was more than just herself to consider now. Their paths might not be destined to intersect beyond the foreseeable future in Iowa, but pretending she didn't hope they did? She wouldn't do that. She wouldn't lie by omission. "But right now, you're here—"

"Shit. Grace, I can't do this." His arms dropped from around her in favor of plowing through his hair, leaving the cold to rush in from all sides. "I don't know what I was thinking, keeping this until the end of the night."

"What?" Grace managed around the claw of dread sinking into her jugular. "Keep what?"

Aaron stared down the path for a few heavy beats. "Your father is sending me to New York earlier than expected." Their gazes met, wind rushing through the gap separating them. "Tomorrow morning."

Around Grace, the colors whirled with a kaleidoscope effect. "Tomorrow? But the camp—"

"Yeah, I screwed myself there, didn't I? Set it up so well, pretty much anyone can walk in and run the rebuild. I made myself obsolete."

Grace realized her hands were twisting the material of her coat, and with an effort, she pried them free. She'd thought they had a couple of weeks together before he left to fulfill his mother's wish in New York. So shortsighted of her. Of course her father would want him in New York sooner, where he'd set up Pendleton campaign headquarters. Their poll numbers had gone through the roof since Aaron arrived, and he would be most efficient around more cameras. More people and action. But another more undesirable notion occurred, knocking the remaining wind out of Grace's sails. "He's not sending you away because of me, is he?"

His massaged the center of his forehead. "Yes. That's part of it." Grace almost buckled under the reality of her father's interference—once again—in her life. This time, grinning and bearing wouldn't be possible. There was something big between herself and Aaron and cutting it short...it *scared* her. She was scared. Aaron interrupted her train of thought by capturing her chin, lifting. "I'm sorry. You have no idea how much." Eyes burning, his hand fell away. "I need to get you home."

Disbelief plowed into her midsection. "Already?"

A muscle moved in his cheek. "I must not be as big a bastard as I thought." He took her hand, but made no move to leave. "I can't sleep with you tonight, knowing full well I'll be on the road while you're still in bed tomorrow morning. It doesn't feel right, hippie. Not with you."

He started to tug her up the path, but she resisted. "And you can't finish our date, either?"

"No. I can't," Aaron grated. "This was a bad idea. Every second I stand here with you, I'm making it harder to walk away. You're—God, *look* at you. You're brighter than the fucking lights and I have to drive away. More than that, I should be happy about it. This campaign job was the only thing I cared about until now."

She absorbed that. "I've ruined you."

"No. Never." He turned her hand over in his palm, scrutinizing each of her fingers in turn. "But there's no way of being sure that I wouldn't ruin *you*. And, Jesus, as much as I'm dying to take you somewhere and taste you all over, to hold you through the night…" He paused to release a shaky exhale. "I'll feel twice as fucked up over leaving. I'm *leaving*, Grace. And maybe it's a good thing we won't have the chance to find out how you and I would have played out."

Grace's blood had slowed during his words, making her feel light-headed. "Do you believe that?"

"No," he whispered. "Fuck no, I don't believe that."

What were her options here? To beg him not to leave Iowa? Ask him to travel around the country, sleeping on cots, living one day at a time, as she'd always dreamed of doing? Aaron was no more suited to that life than she was cut out for life on the campaign trail. Or the fast-paced, high-powered New York beat. There was so much in store for Aaron there. He was already taking the political scene by storm, rising to fame, along with the poll numbers he commanded at will. Furthermore, Aaron hadn't asked her to come to New York. It was an option that didn't exist, so why was she thinking about it, instead of living the way she'd chosen? Living for the moments, because they were what counted. They were what would be remembered.

"You're treating me like I can't think for myself again."

Aaron did a double take. "How so?"

Until she'd said the words, Grace hadn't realized the truth behind them. How his white glove treatment scalded her pride. Or maybe it was her fear of waking up tomorrow and not experiencing what Aaron made her feel. Whatever the reason for her sudden surge in determination, she had no choice but to go with it, because a giant sinkhole had opened in her stomach, sucking away her ability to be rational. *Leaving. He's leaving.* "You're assuming I can't handle our last night together." She tipped back her head to stare into the lights. "You think I'll fall apart any more or any less tomorrow if it's on the heels of us sleeping together? Well, I won't. I'll probably miss you the same amount, no matter what." Her breath sailed out in a trail of white. "A lot. I'm going to miss you a lot."

"Grace..." She heard him swallow. "I didn't even know I was capable of missing *any*thing until I found out I was leaving you. I haven't even packed yet and I'm... panicked." He massaged his chest. "I think. I don't know what missing someone is supposed to feel like. Sharp? Huge? It's a Grace ache. It won't *stop*. But—"

"My father is right to send you away from me?" she interrupted. "If that's what you're going to say, please don't."

His gaze cut to the side. "All right. I won't."

Her body reacted to the misery in his voice, a painful throb forming in several vital regions. Center of her chest, mainly. But also the spot where her thighs joined. God, she didn't want their last memory together to be cast in sadness or resentment. She'd pictured their date ending in a tangle of straining bodies, wet kissing, moaning. If she'd had some time to prepare, maybe she could have trailed a finger down his stomach and suggested they end the night the best way, like a worldly woman might. Which she clearly was not, because her body was shaking under the weight of Aaron's good-bye.

Grace felt for one of the ribbons in her hair, rubbing the silk material, praying for her elusive maturity to return. The longer she stood there, the more guilt she heaped on Aaron for following his dream, building his career. A career he was born to excel in. She was being selfish wanting him to stay behind and...build her a tower. Live there with her forever. But she could have tonight. He'd obviously *wanted* to give her one more night, hadn't he? Before his chivalry had kicked in?

Yes. Maybe if she closed her eyes and concentrated hard enough while Aaron moved inside her body, she could remember it with perfect, punching clarity. Hold on to it always. He wanted that memory, too; she just needed to remind him how much.

"Okay," she breathed, surprised her motor skills were

functioning well enough to hold out her hand. "Take me home."

Aaron didn't move for long moments, staring at her from beneath the darkness of his furrowed brows. Just as Grace readied to drop her hand, Aaron latched on and walked her back up the path. In tacit agreement, they bypassed the barn, crunching through the heavier drifts of snow on the barn's perimeter. Hearing the sounds of joy emanating from within only made the journey harder, if such a thing were possible.

They reached the Suburban, and too quickly, Grace was forced to let go of Aaron's hand. He unlocked the passenger's side door, gripping her elbow and guiding her into the seat, before extending an arm across the console to start the Suburban's ignition, unlock the doors, and get the heat running. After that, silence fell like heavy theater curtains, only growing denser when Aaron made no move toward the driver's side. He always loomed in his largeness, his overwhelming energy, but as he stared down at Grace, he was massive. Unavoidable. And when he reached across her body to lock in the seatbelt she'd neglected to engage herself, she couldn't hold in the effect of having him so close, so desolate.

As if they moved on their own, Grace's hands lifted, palms curving along the shape of Aaron's cheeks, moving down to his jaw, back up. His gruff curse pierced the quiet, his lids falling to hide his eyes. His endurance of her touch didn't last long, though, his masculine hands finding her face, thumbs sliding along her cheekbones, along the bridge of her nose, the curve of her upper lip. All without looking, as if he might be cataloging Grace's features and didn't want the power of sight detracting from touch.

"I don't know why, but..." Aaron eased closer, wrapping Grace in his warmed scent. "I'm so fucking worried that when I think of you, I'll think of you huddled on the closet floor after I said those horrible things. But that shouldn't be. Not after I've watched you dance in the snow and...moan underneath me." His fingers raked into her hair from the bottom of her skull, letting loose a flood of tingles down her back. "I think maybe I *want* to stay fucked up over this. I think that's why I won't think of you and be happy. The pain will mean you were real."

"That's either the best or worst thing you could say to me." His laughter dropped like a boulder into the crook of Grace's neck, followed by a heavy inhale. She could feel the effort it cost Aaron to keep his touch above her neck, and every moment of that struggle was met by a growing one, low in her own belly. "When I think of you, you'll be climbing up to our tower in the sky, ice cream in hand. That's the real you."

His grip flexed in her hair. "That guy is going to vanish when you're not around to see him."

"No. He was there before I came along. He'll be there after." Grace turned her head, bringing her mouth up against Aaron's ear, a deep, male groan warming her neck at the brushing of lips and lobe. "He could be there tonight, moving inside me."

Grace felt the rough shift in Aaron happen. Finally. His abdomen was hollowing and shuddering against her stomach, his energy tightening like a bolt. With that change in Aaron's intention, her lungs filled, relief and rightness and arousal clamoring in from all corners. She didn't want him to remember her on the closet floor. She didn't want their parting to be sad. In fact, she refused. *Moments*. Something told her there had never been more important ones to capture.

One of Aaron's hands remained in her hair, but the other had fallen to her knee, his breath beginning to pelt her neck, ear, shoulder. "No. No, I think I'm already losing whoever you think I am, Grace." His hand coasted up her thigh. "That other guy knows he should take you home and leave you with a good-bye kiss on the cheek. But me..." He cupped her feminine flesh, pressing the heel of his hand against her mound with a harsh sound. "That guy wants to fuck you in the backseat."

CHAPTER TWENTY-TWO

Aaron was too aroused to hate himself. That would come later, landing like cement blocks on his shoulders. Right now, he was all about funneling every goddamn, inconvenient ounce of regret into pleasuring Grace. Her thighs were spreading on the seat to accommodate his touch, telling Aaron the need was far from one-sided. Words. He'd spoken more words to her than anyone in his memory, but none of them were adequate. Christ, he didn't even have a handle on the meaning behind them yet. That understanding could come in fifty years, for all he knew. In this moment, this physical ache for Grace was what he could grasp. So with an invisible iron manacle fashioned around his throat, he dove for the lifeline.

"Yes, I want that," she whispered, both of them reaching for her seatbelt at once, mouths shoved together without kissing. Just breathing, breathing, panting, promising without words how big and bad they were going to orgasm each other. In that moment, even with lust building to a crescendo beneath his belt, Aaron knew he wouldn't feel a fraction of that desire ever again, with anyone else. Before Grace and After Grace. Two distinct periods of his life, slicing him right down the middle, severing his heart in the process.

As soon as the metal slid free of its hold, Aaron jerked Grace off the seat and out of the Suburban, frantic for the pressure of her pussy, growling as it dropped onto his hard cock. "Can't believe I won't get my fill of this." He was off balance and hungry and staggering under the atomic blast of need, so Grace's ass hit the car with more force than intended, but he could only manage a muttered apology before he was dry humping her giving body against the car door, the impact rocking the whole damn Suburban with rusted groans. "How long do you think it would take, huh? Before I could go five minutes without getting hard for your pussy?"

She whimpered under the force of a rough thrust. "I'd never let you find out."

Good God. Had he once thought this girl fragile? No. Grace was benevolent and seductive and fierce. She was life. She was everything. "Sounds like you're getting cocky now." He pressed his forehead to the frigid car window, delivering a merciless pump of his hips. "You should be. That's a tight, slippery ride you've got between your legs, baby. Going to bury my tongue so deep in it, your legs will shake for a fucking week." She got a little wild at that, grinding into his drives, confirming Aaron's suspicion that she had a dirty streak. "When you think about me, you think of that. Think of me stroking off somewhere, trying to grip my dick as hard as your pussy grips me when you come."

"*Aaron.*" Her head capsized, falling back and bumping the window. "I need you. I need you inside me."

"Not half as bad as I need it." Aaron paused in his assault on Grace's body long enough to open the ancient door and lift her onto the leather seat. Already the windows were fogged up from the heat he'd turned on, creating a sense of total isolation no one would be able to share with them. Aaron rolled the door shut and joined Grace on the cracked leather, taking a moment to savor the way she watched him as they removed their jackets—all wide-eyed anticipation—before he gripped her ankles and flipped her face down on the seat. "Push up. Show me my ride, Grace."

The rapid rise and fall of her back—that show of nerves and excitement—turned him on to such an extreme level, Aaron had no choice but to unbuckle his belt and lower his fly to ease the confinement of his pulsing cock. And all the while, he watched Grace gain courage, watched as she flattened her palms on either side of her head, hips lifting, back bowing to give that perfect tilt. There was no stopping himself from sliding a hand into his jeans and granting himself a series of brutal strokes, not bothering to hold back his sexually charged grunts, well aware that her breathing got increasingly shallow the longer he kept her waiting in that position.

In reality, only a few seconds passed before Aaron grew impatient to touch, to see every inch of the body his own had become obsessed with giving relief. Releasing his rigid cock, he tucked his fingers beneath the waistband of Grace's leggings—panties, too—and whooshed both garments down her thighs, leaving them bunched at her knees.

"Oh my God," she breathed, a tremor moving down her back. "Oh God."

"We're not fucking in a sleeping bag this time, are we?" Mesmerized by the smooth, succulent shapes of her sex, her ass, Aaron trailed a thumb downward between her cheeks, unable to stop it from lingering at both entrances, applying light amounts of pressure. "You can't hide anything from me now."

Without giving her a warning, Aaron clutched the insides of her thighs, pushing them open. "Please..."

"Baby, you don't have to beg for a goddamn thing." Satisfied that her position would give him enough access to taste her the deepest, he slid each of his hands over their own personal ass cheek and squeezed, watching the shadows shift along her flesh, watching the way her feminine lips seemed to strain toward his touch. "If this is my only chance to eat your pussy, I promise, it's going to be thorough. First, though..."

"First?"

"First." Aaron pushed the shirt up Grace's back, exposing the gorgeous curve of her spine, and he trailed his tongue up the entire length, ending at her nape. "Tell me if I'm wrong. But when a girl is hot enough to bend over and show a man both ways to get inside her, she doesn't mind having her ass slapped." With his left hand, he gripped her taut backside until she moaned. "Would you agree with that?"

"I...I don't know. I've never—"

Swat. "Now you can say Aaron's done it." He released a pent-up breath as Grace whimpered. *Fuck,* he wasn't going to recover from this. The way her flesh gave that sweet little reverberation, her bottom lifting in a silent plea for more. That was his Grace, always eager for new experiences, new sensations, greeting everything with open arms and he wanted to *give and give and give* until she was overflowing. He delivered another slap with his palm, coming up from below, feeling his cock thicken in the loose opening of his jeans. But nothing—*nothing*—compared to the way his mouth salivated, dying to make a meal of her already glistening pussy.

One more slap of her tight backside was all he could manage before he threw his weight down onto one elbow, shooting forward to bury his tongue in the beckoning flesh, licking through her seam to find that nub. The one begging for ownership, someone to take care of it, rile it up and soothe it down.

Needing more access, more *Grace*, Aaron used his right hand to push apart her ass cheeks, growling into the separation, laving the pearl at the top of her pussy with his tongue, saying a thankful prayer to the God of cunnilingus when she pressed backward against his mouth. Goddammit, if he had time, even just one more day, he would give this beautiful girl whisker burn between her legs from too much oral. The taste of her was an intoxicant, turning him into a drunk trying to get every last drop of whiskey from a bottle.

"I'm going to—" Grace broke off, her body beginning to shake. "Don't stop, please, please, please..."

If his tongue wasn't busy feeding his new addiction, he would have reminded her begging wasn't necessary. If anyone should be begging, it was him. She was unreserved and unrepentant in getting herself up against his mouth, the kind of reaction he'd only ever fantasized about in a girl. No holding back or pretending he wasn't fucking great with his tongue. Just all-out, relief-seeking, hip-writhing glory, and he could have mouth-banged her for a month straight without coming up for air. And all that was before she climaxed and her pussy cinched up around his tongue like a designer belt, her breath choking off, her thighs turning to thin, shaking columns of lithe muscle. Grace's taste was better than the last drop of whiskey, it was the elixir that granted eternal life, and he lapped it up like a greedy motherfucker who would die unless he absorbed every ounce.

He only stopped when her Grace's hips listed to one side, rebounding off the leather seat. She was sobbing. Sobbing his name, God's name, and damn if she wasn't still begging.

No. That was *Aaron* begging. The word *please* scraped from his raw throat, echoing off the frosted windows. He made a desperate grab for Grace's shoulders with one hand, liberating his cock with the other. "Please. Please, I need to fuck what I just tasted." Folding his legs beneath him, Aaron applied protection taken from his pocket, then braced himself on the roof and front passenger's seat, very nearly spilling his come when Grace performed a little scoot onto his lap, both of them slick with sweat and her pleasure. "Reach behind your well-spanked ass and slide me home. You're wet enough this time to take it without three pumps from me to get it in."

His last few words were slurred, his power of speech compromised by the smooth palm encircling his sensitive erection, the look of praise she sent back over her shoulder. A look that made him want to deliver another spanking, following by round two of his tongue between her legs. But as she sank down with slow devastation onto his thickness, that desire drained along with his will to ever leave the snug perfection of her pussy.

"Oh, fucking Christ, Grace, don't move. Just…" Aaron breathed through his nose, attempting a mental battle with the swelling in his balls and failing. "Stop clenching, baby."

"I c-can't," she whispered, bracing her hands on the window she faced, leaving behind prints as they slipped down, down. "I think I'm going to—"

"*Jesus*," he growled as Grace tightened up around him with her second orgasm. Or maybe just a continuation of the first. Not that it mattered because Aaron was going to die either way. Die trying to make it last. "Fuck it. Go on, baby. Ride it out. I can take it. I *need* to take it."

Saying and doing were two different things, though, and Aaron should have known by now to expect the unexpected with Grace. She threw herself back, head falling onto his shoulder, working up and down his hardness with hypnotic lifts and drops of her hips. The husky moans coming out of her were pure fucking decadence, capturing his senses and pulling him down into inescapable fever-lust. He was caught between letting his seed power into her rocking pussy or holding on any way he could, prolonging what would signal the end. *The end. No.*

Aaron didn't realize he'd sunken his teeth into Grace's shoulder until she cried out, throwing a hand back to tunnel fingers through his hair. "Yes," she urged. "Yes. More."

Operating on instinct, Aaron surged forward, flattening Grace—facedown—on the seat, bearing down with his starved body. His open mouth traveled over her neck and hair, delivering hot gusts of breath. "Might as well have your name tattooed on my cock because you own it, you fucking own it. Sent to ruin me, weren't you? Ruin me and then get taken away. I'm going to die without you. I'm going to *die*."

He heard the words coming out of his mouth, couldn't take them back. He didn't want to. But any kind of response from Grace would obliterate his slim chances of escaping intact come tomorrow morning. When he would leave without her. No, he couldn't deal with her reassurances or, hell, maybe even a suggestion that it didn't have to end. God knew it did. He couldn't keep expanding to let more love for Grace in or he would implode and take her down with him. He wasn't built for love. Not Grace's kind.

She opened her mouth to say something, but Aaron slid a palm beneath her face and covered it. Regret lanced his chest, even as the relentless yearning for *release, release, release* stole his last remainder of sanity. Or he thought it had. Until Grace's hand covered his, holding on tight with understanding. And that's when everything—except for stealing every second of pleasure from Grace—slid away into an abyss. His body rolled over her, stomach gliding over the swell of her ass, delivering blow after blow between her legs. Rearing back and pounding into tight innocence he should never have been given and would never have again. They were one person united in the grinding, slapping, and abusing of flesh. Straining, gripping, grunting, Aaron holding on as long as humanly possible. "I might be leaving, but I'm yours. Wherever I am, I'll be yours, baby, hippie, Grace. *My* Grace. *Your* Aaron."

She turned her face away from Aaron's covering hand,

whispering the word *yes*, and completion rose like a hot tide around him, robbing the oxygen he'd stored in his lungs, slaying him with the sharp knife of pain due to the magnitude of his orgasm, how long he'd held back. Agony twined with bliss, pressure slowly—too slowly—draining and shattering him under the loss of misery. The gaining of more relief than he'd thought possible. *Complete. I've never been complete until now.*

But the very reason he'd abstained from release rose up like a monster to terrorize him in no time, Grace's heated body cooling gradually beneath him, in some macabre symbol of his own upcoming death. Because in the morning, he would leave behind the man he'd become, the man Grace saw, and go back to being the person everyone hated. Including him.

CHAPTER TWENTY-THREE

Aaron stared through the front windshield of the Suburban and watched Grace walk away from him, getting smaller and smaller as she wound through the trees. Last time she'd walked away—in the very same spot—he'd all but dove out of the driver's side door to get an explanation. There had been no words exchanged between them this time, however, just Grace leaning over to kiss his white knuckles on the steering wheel, before opening the door, letting in all the cold, and taking the heat of herself away.

Cold. That's all his brain would acknowledge once she finally disappeared from sight completely. *That's all, folks.* If he squinted enough, he could probably see the ghost of himself—the man she'd woken up—trailing behind her. It would make sense for him to be dead, his soul moved to a higher plane, because he'd never felt less alive. Lethargy started at the top of his skull and draped down, like an unraveling blanket with weights strategically sewn into the edges. Down, down, down, until no amount of mental commands or attempts at motivation could make him put the Suburban into gear.

He needed to leave. Belmont, Peggy, and Sage would require the Suburban to continue their journey to New York while he hopped on a plane. But the draped blanket kept pulling, dragging, turning Aaron into an immovable object on the seat. Driving away would be the final step in leaving Grace behind, moving on, pretending like she hadn't come out of nowhere and made the world seem like a not-so-shitty place. If innately good people like her existed, were people like him meant to balance the scales? Even the odds? Because his every action now felt like a direct attack on all the positivity she represented and living like that going forward...fuck, he was going to be empty. So empty without her.

But Grace wouldn't be empty. She'd remain full and loving, especially without him around. His career, the cynicism he'd developed, would only taint her beauty and no way in hell could he live with that knowledge. One day, he would look over at Grace and find her watching him, watching him in that way that said, *How does he live with himself?*

And she didn't even know the worst of it.

All you need is yourself.

You're just embracing your nature.

Someone like you.

Aaron flinched as his father's words crept through his mind. The man had called Aaron's methods from jump street, hadn't he? Here he was, leaving behind the woman he loved in order to further his career in New York. It was almost poetic.

Anger and righteous self-disgust rose like a dragon from its cave and breathed fire down the back of Aaron's neck. His hands tightened into shaking balls, arm muscles flexing until he swore—he hoped—they would rip straight through his skin. Acid mixed with frustration in his throat, the deadliest cocktail ever concocted, until the taste made his mouth fall open, forced him to suck in air to hit his scorched insides with coolness. It didn't work. His fists met the steering wheel, one after the other, following by his head.

"Grace."

It was a shout in his head, but only emerged as a broken whisper. For long minutes, he simply gawked at the wretched man staring back, trapped among the speedometers. Until finally his eyes closed, visions of Grace dancing in the field twirling like slow motion ballerinas in his head. The image was too happy, though, and he didn't ever want to feel happiness again. It would only be watered down, a fucking imitation. So he stamped out the dancing source of life and conjured a darker image of Grace, legs drawn up to her chest on the closet floor.

"That's where you'd have put her eventually...right there...again."

Maybe next time it wouldn't be his words that hurt Grace. It could be a *lack* of communication. Or an inability to recognize when she needed affection. Or getting sucked into his career and not having enough time for her. A thousand different possibilities—and none of them would pack as much of a punch as his past. It lingered in the air like the smell of gasoline, making him nauseous.

When sleep rose up and began to steal Aaron's consciousness, he let it come, welcoming the merciful numbness.

* * *

It had been so long since Aaron slept late, the sunshine that blinded him upon waking was almost more disorienting than the steering wheel stuck to his forehead. A sharp ache speared both eye sockets as light rushed in, blinding him, bringing both of his arms up to block the intrusion. And then he remembered the previous night and both appendages fell like someone had shot them off.

Christ. He had to get out of there, before someone on the senator's security team made their way out into the woods and *actually* shot him. And even Aaron could admit that his physical safety accounted for only a small portion of dawning common sense. Mental safety was definitely in the lead. Last night, his course of action had been clear, but this morning everything appeared twice as stark, similar to the cold, frozen ground surrounding the truck.

Beside Aaron on the seat, his cell phone vibrated. Peggy. Probably wondering where the hell he'd gone. Wondering when he was returning to camp with the Suburban, where all three of them were likely packed and ready. To leave. Just like he would be leaving Grace. Watching Iowa get smaller from the window of an airplane. Knowing if they ever saw each other again, the bond they'd built would be replaced by formal greetings and…distance. So much distance.

Aaron's stomach heaved violently and he barely got the driver's side door open before the meager contents emptied onto the leaf-strewn ground. *Jesus.* Jesus, he was a shaking, fucking mess. Tremors gripped his hands as he climbed back into the truck and turned over the ignition, swiping at his mouth. Once again, the sun assaulted his vision, so he reached up to flip the visor down—

His mother's journal fell out, bouncing off the steering wheel and landing in his lap. *What the hell?* He'd left the notebook locked securely in his suitcase—had it sprouted legs and walked by itself into the Suburban? When Aaron noticed it was open to a specific page somewhere near the middle, his eyes narrowed. Someone had either been reading the journal in their spare time, or they'd left it in the sun visor for him to find.

Maybe he was stalling because driving out of the woods meant leaving Grace, or maybe he just wanted to burrow inside his own misery and never leave. Whatever the reason, Aaron picked up the notebook and started to read the familiar, loopy handwriting of Miriam Clarkson.

I've never denied being an arrogant woman. Mostly because it's true. I'm a prize asshole when I choose to be. Maybe one day the culinary world will change and it won't be so male dominated, but I've busted my hump to achieve greatness—without assistance—and sometimes I like to revel.

My arrogance gene skipped three children but landed splat on Aaron's psyche...

Aaron took a deep breath through his nose, letting the journal fall against the steering wheel. Here it comes. He always knew it would. *Just get it over with.*

But Aaron's arrogance comes with a lemon twist. While I tend to rejoice in my inflated confidence, Aaron uses it to guard every other part of himself. You (whoever is reading this—have you lost weight?) will be shocked to know, I take the blame for this. I can pinpoint the day Aaron started turning inward. The day Belmont came home and shut the door in his brother's face, and never really came out again, was hard on everyone. Aaron, a fixer by nature, took it harder than anyone. Even his brilliant mother. Maybe because I was so busy assuring myself everything would straighten itself out, I couldn't see the branches of my family begin to grow crooked. Not crooked in a bad way, just diverted to a harder path.

Aaron was born to rule the world, but if I'd paid closer attention, if I'd been as good a mother as a chef, I would have seen. He didn't really want the world. He just wanted the world to spin the direction that would make everyone around him happy. And when that didn't happen, when that couldn't happen, he was forced to settle on just appeasing himself. Sometimes I look at Aaron and try to figure out if he's really satisfied with that isolating cycle, though, and I wonder. Has he merely carved out a way to keep from being closed out again? Can anyone blame him?

Here's the good news. Men who were born to rule the world eventually figure things out. Perhaps they decide the world is a relative concept. Maybe it's a person or a small place or every goddamn inch of the planet. Whatever it is, it's theirs. Aaron never

stopped coming back no matter how many times
his differences were pointed out or scrutinized. He
never stopped being a brother or a son because the
going got tough. He stuck it out because that's what
a ruler does. They rule. My son rules.

Aaron fell back against the driver's seat, seeing nothing
and everything at once. Flashes of those looks from his
mother. Looks he'd always interpreted as disappointment
or...bewilderment over his strident, no bullshit outlook.
Miles away from his siblings, who wore their feelings like
colorful party masks, even if they couldn't voice them.
Had Miriam been...proud of him? Had she been disappointed in herself, instead of him?

My son rules. His throat constricted until he choked,
and even though no one was with him in the Suburban,
he attempted to disguise the sound with a cough. Fuck, he
felt so light. Out of nowhere. Like he'd been inflated with
helium. And he didn't *want* to be alone in the Suburban.
He wanted Grace to be sitting beside him so he could hand
her the notebook, let her read the words that were making a valiant attempt to give him some kind of...peace.
He wanted to say, *You were right. She saw good. She saw*
good, like you, hippie.

But he couldn't do that, because Grace wasn't there. A
giant void sat where she should be, smiling at him with
pink lips and green eyes. The wrongness of her absence hit
him like a battering ram, square in the chest. His mother
had been wrong about one thing. Aaron didn't want to
rule the world. Not the one he'd created around him. Not
alone, either. He wanted Grace to show him every facet,
every corner of *her* world, so he could rule it beside her.

With her. Always with her. And if Grace saw good in him, Aaron trusted her to be right. He had to trust the ability to hurt or taint or disappoint her didn't exist inside him. *Please don't let it exist.*

Aaron couldn't feel the notebook in his hands. It slipped through his numb fingers and fell into the well, wedging beneath the gas pedal. Or at least he thought so, because he was already busy fumbling with the seat-belt that had remained attached the entire night. He cursed through his fumbles—ready to rip the nylon strap to get out of the car, if necessary.

Need to get to Grace. Not going anywhere without Grace.

CHAPTER TWENTY-FOUR

Grace shoved two fingers up against her forehead, praying the pressure would keep the room from spinning. She'd been foolish the night before, coming home and opening the bottle of red wine her sister had thoughtfully stocked in the kitchen months earlier. Her plan had been to consume one glass, just enough to stop the agony from expanding in her veins, making an explosion seem inevitable. A blast that would end with parts of her body all over the room. *It appears she just... exploded.* That's what the coroner would say to her parents as they swept her up in industrial-sized dust pans from Costco.

A hysterical laugh bubbled from her lips, escalating the throbbing in her temples until she felt sickness rise in her throat. She bent forward, positioning her head between her thighs. Breathe. Breathe.

It was difficult—really difficult—considering all the eyes trained on her. She'd been woken by her father and

asked into the living room, surprised to find half a dozen
staffers loitering there. Even now, after they'd been talking
for five minutes, she'd gathered no real information about
what they wanted from her. What could anyone want from
her, the morning after she'd had her heart sliced apart?
It hurt to be awake, let alone communicate. Had she said
hello? Offered them coffee? No...no, she was in a
bathrobe trying not to cry or throw up or explode.

That was all.

Where was Aaron? Had he left already?

A pitiful sob shot from the pit in her stomach, but she
caught it with a balled fist, sitting back up and focusing on
her father. Her father, whom she recognized less and less
every time she saw him. Weren't fathers supposed to notice when their daughters were sick and...help? Do something to make it better? Because she was sicker than she'd
ever been in her life, only none of the symptoms were visible. She wished they were. She wished for *wounds*.

"Uh..." Grace pulled her bathrobe tighter, crossing her
ankles the way she'd been taught, but rarely ever did.
"What is this about? Can you start over?"

Her father's shoulders drooped with a dramatic sigh.
"I'll just get to the point quickly, since we're not in a listening mood this morning." Tempering her outrage with
patience—not easy with a pounding head and a dry
mouth—Grace gave a quick nod and her father continued.
"The tragedy at YouthAspire. For years, you've been asking to have your presence that day acknowledged. I want
to give you that. More than that, I want you to come out
of the shadows. To take more of a visible role in this campaign."

A few of the cobwebs cleared, just enough to allow

hope and...confusion to trickle in. "I don't understand. Now? This morning?"

"That's how things work in this world, Grace. Timing isn't always convenient, but when an opportunity is handed to you, taking it, seizing it, is key."

Was he making a speech? Grace panned the room, taking note of the air of expectation. The paused animation. As if they were all waiting to spring into action, her father included. She suddenly wished for Aaron so bad, tears boiled behind her eyes. What was going on here? "You've never wanted my name associated with what happened. Why..." She swallowed, dreading the answer to her next question. "How did you want to proceed?"

"Well." He straightened his tie. "I think you know everything I do these days will be pounced on by the media, so we believe the best course of action is to approach the reveal head on." He took a few steps in Grace's direction, crouched down, and took her hand. "I don't want you to feel hidden away anymore, so I've arranged for a quiet interview this morning. Nothing flashy or over the top. We've already approved the questions and they're nothing to be afraid of." He patted her arm. "But if you don't want this—"

"No," Grace rushed to say, startled by the rare display of affection. "I guess I just don't understand what everyone else has to do with this."

"Grace." Her dulled senses wouldn't allow her to decide if her father's tone was warm or...patronizing. "We have to handle everything delicately, make sure we send the right message to the public."

"I don't want to send a message," she whispered. "I never needed that."

A knock on the door. The way everyone reacted with suspicion made Grace hyperaware of the thick tension in the room. Had it been like this since she walked in? What did they *really* want from her? Another, more insistent knock, followed by a familiar voice shouting her name, sent Grace's heart into a tailspin. She shot to her feet, kicking off a renewed round of hammering at the front of her skull, but she was too relieved, too...high to care. High on the sound of Aaron *being there*.

Her father didn't look the least bit excited at Aaron's arrival, nor did he look surprised. Grace didn't have time to examine that reaction, though. Letting Aaron in, whether or not she looked like flaming shit, was first and foremost in her mind. He wouldn't care how she looked. He wouldn't care. But when she attempted to bypass her father's stiff form and head for the door, he wrapped a hand around her elbow. "Go let him in," her father instructed one of his security detail. "Sit down," he said to Grace, before softening the command with a smile. "Please."

Seeing no choice but to sink down onto the cushions, Grace kept her attention trained on the entryway, waiting for a glimpse of Aaron. She got it a moment later when he rounded the corner, searching her out with wild eyes. Grace's anxiety spiked over his dishevelment. Wearing the same clothes as last night, he looked pale but determined. Until he saw the room full of men and drew to an abrupt halt, visibly bristling.

Golden brown eyes, no less brilliant in their exhaustion, seesawed between her and the gathering of suits. "What the hell is going on here?"

Anger showed in her father's expression. "My daughter

is not your business, Clarkson. Not anymore." He checked his watch. "Don't you have a flight to catch?"

Aaron didn't bother to answer, clearly still stuck on his initial question. "She's in a robe, in her own living room, surrounded by men. If that's not my business, it should at least be yours."

Caught up in the situation, she'd forgotten about her abbreviated attire, but looking down now, she noticed how her hands clenched in the material, holding it over her breasts and neck, grip shaking.

"But while we're on the subject," Aaron kept going, his gaze transferring to Grace and reassuring, softening. Softening in a way she'd never seen. "It's up to her if she still wants to be my business."

Grace started to rise again, ready to dive over the couch to reach him. Maybe his meaning—*be my business*—was still slightly unclear, but she *knew* Aaron. She knew the look on his face meant something big. Something *huge*. And she needed to get close, to help him let it out. Her father put a staying hand on her shoulder, and although she attempted to brush him off, what he said next kept Grace rooted to the spot.

"All right, Clarkson. You were given your chance to make this easy, but you're putting me in a spot here." The room braced expectantly, including Aaron, who she could see was trying to cover his sudden nerves. *It's okay*, she wanted to shout. *Everything is okay as long as you're here.* But her father popped the dialogue bubble she was trying to send Aaron's direction. "I don't mind admitting you've become valuable to me, Clarkson. I need you on my payroll. But when you stepped into my family's affairs, you crossed a line. I'm just going to see you back to the other side, so we can resume business. Nothing personal."

Her father's hand felt like caked cement on Grace's shoulder, so she sidestepped, watching it fall away slowly, as if it drifted through water.

"Grace." Her head came up at her father's prompt. "I'm trying to give you what I—as you father—have wrongly denied you so long. I shouldn't have made the decision to erase your name from something that turned you into such a strong young woman. Aaron is here because, as someone who works for me, he doesn't think shedding light on your experience a wise political move."

"That's bullshit," Aaron ground out.

Grace's father tilted his head. "Are you denying that when I suggested bringing Grace's experience out in the open, you claimed she couldn't handle it? I believe your exact words were, 'She can't retain the kind of coaching we'd need to put her through.' You asked me if I could honestly imagine her on Diane Sawyers's couch, which incidentally is where she'll be sitting this morning." The ensuing pause was deafening. "Did I fabricate anything you said?"

Beneath Grace's feet, the ground turned to rubber. Or was it her legs? Standing became an effort, but she refused to allow the twisting in her heart to continue, banishing the weakness. *Don't break.* She wouldn't break. Not when Aaron was imploring her so desperately with his eyes, ignoring everything but her. That connection between them was so strong, her father's accusations had only made the tiniest ding on the exterior.

"I said that to protect you, Grace. I didn't want them to throw you to the fucking sharks. I still don't." He shifted, hands lifting, as if trying to grab the invisible lifeline extending from him to Grace. "I'm sorry for saying those things. I'm sorry, but you know I didn't mean them."

Warmth slid down Grace's spine. She *did* know. Both her heart and gut were screaming a reassurance at her, louder than the dissension in the room aimed at Aaron. And she was going to do something she hadn't truly been capable of since Ray Solomon. She was going to place her trust wholly and irrevocably in a flawed human being. Come what may, they were in it together. Forcing Aaron to see the good in himself had made Grace realize something. She'd spent a long time learning to trust her instincts again and now was the time to believe in herself. By believing in Aaron.

She'd doubted him once, comparing Aaron to a monster, and it had been the worst mistake imaginable. Hurting him again was out of the question. This man she loved couldn't have fooled both her head and her heart. And when she nodded at Aaron, allowing a small smile to turn up the corners of her lips, he fairly staggered toward her. *I was right. I knew I was right.*

"Aaron was fired from his last position in California, Grace. Are you aware of that?" Aaron's forward progress slammed to a stop and so did Grace's pulse. *This.* She'd forgotten about this one little mystery. The one she'd suspected all along had been Aaron's main reason for pushing her away. Without thinking, Grace reached out and tugged her father's jacket sleeve, intent on asking him to stay quiet, to tell him that whatever it was didn't matter, but he plowed ahead regardless. "He slept with his boss's wife. A *senator's* wife."

As she watched, Aaron grew haggard, defeated. His

eyelids dropped to hide any access she had to his mind, shoulders deflating. A hand came up to cover his mouth and he turned away, already gone. She could feel the absence of his energy so profoundly, it hurt worse than last night's good-bye. As far as the information her father had imparted...she didn't like it. She hated it. *Loathed* it. The idea of Aaron with anyone beside herself? It didn't compute. It didn't feel real. It *wasn't.*

It wasn't real. He hadn't been the Aaron *she* saw when he made that poor decision. She felt it deep down. Furthermore, he'd tried to tell her what happened. She hadn't let him. And now the very wedge he'd tried to drive between them was being driven into his chest. Wounded to kill. Was she naïve believing he'd changed...for her?

No, she wasn't. She *knew* him. They knew each other. She wouldn't be deceived here.

"This is what he does, Grace. God knows I'm benefiting from the way his mind works, and if I wasn't so keen to make a difference in office, in this country, I would find another path to success."

As if her senses had been sharpened with a whittling knife, she could hear everything, every inflection in the spoken words. The phony resignation in her father's voice. The ease with which he cut another man down. To benefit whom? "He probably hasn't even acknowledged to himself what he's done, sweetheart. He has insinuated himself with a member of my family—same way he did at his last position—and used your plight to his own advantage. It's unconscionable. Unfortunately, it's also politics. I'm sorry you were his target this time around. You weren't his first and you probably won't be his last. You'll be safer with him in New York."

"Stop," Grace rasped. "Just stop."

Aaron jerked when she spoke, his gaze searing her in all its blazing pain, before it went completely blank. Blank. As if he'd never truly been there to begin with. As if her father had spoken the truth and he'd finally dropped the act. No. *No*, she wasn't going to be duped. Not again. Not like the last time.

The haze she'd woken to dissipated fully, and her father's presence—the staffers' presence—began to make perfect sense. The memories of the event she'd lived with for so long...her father was going to gain an advantage from it.

A surge of indignation whipped in Grace's blood, attempting to overtake the pain of her father's betrayal, but before she could order everyone out of the guesthouse, Aaron gave her one final look and began backing toward the exit. Confusion and denial made Grace hesitate...and holy hell, it cost her.

Grace's father slung an arm around her shoulder, jerking her up against his side, whispering parental comfort into her hair. The staffers closed ranks around her. All the while, she shook her head, watching Aaron get closer to the door. "No."

The sound of the front door clicking shut caused an eruption of rage, the likes of which Grace had never experienced. With a strangled scream, she shoved out of her father's arms, slapping his hands away when he attempted to haul her back. *Prevent her from leaving.* "You." She swallowed the lump in her throat, aiming a finger at the older man's chest. "After everything, after Ray Solomon, after influencing my therapy sessions...you would try to manipulate me like this again?" A shuddering sob broke past her weakened defenses. "You're my father."

Grace vaguely registered the surprise on the staffer's face, directly beyond her father's shoulder. Not surprise at the accusation, surprise she'd been astute enough to make it. "Yes, I'm your father," the senator continued. "Your manipulator just left. I'm trying to protect you."

"No," she whispered, shaking her head. "You've never even let me sit behind you—with my own family—during a single one of your speeches. Now you suddenly want me in the spotlight?" She forced back the moisture threatening to spill from her eyes. "I don't buy your sudden compassion. I don't buy you."

To his credit, something in her father's eyes dimmed, his Adam's apple sliding up and down. There was regret there, but he was too late. And if Grace didn't hurry, she would be, too.

The brevity of her attire forgotten, Grace spun on a bare heel and sprinted to the front door, throwing it open and weathering a blast of cold air. She immediately spotted Aaron, head down, striding toward the haphazardly parked Suburban. Just the sight of him and the vehicle she'd grown to love sent Grace's pulse into a frenzy. "Wait," she said in a strangled whisper, racing down the steps. "*Wait.*"

Aaron's shoulders stiffened, but he didn't stop walking. If anything, he moved quicker, unlocking the driver's side door and yanking it open. "You should be inside, Grace. You've got nothing on." His knuckles were white on the door handle. "Go to your sister or mother—whoever will help—and borrow their car. Go somewhere until I can handle this somehow, do you understand?" His big back was rigid with tension. "You'll freeze, Grace. *Go.*"

A flashback to the night in his tent, when he'd voiced

a near identical command, invaded her mind. "If you want me warm, you better hold me."

The look Aaron turned on her was so full of disbelief—and anger—she fell back a step. "Are you serious?" He spoke through clenched teeth, any sign of the man who'd danced with her in the forest...vanished. Gone. "Were you listening in there? All those things your father said were true. *All of them.* And do you know the worst part of it?" Eyes blazing, he didn't wait for an answer. "I felt *nothing* for that woman. I didn't have to say yes. It never even occurred to me that it was wrong. A married woman with children and it never even entered my mind, Grace. Not once."

"How about now?" she threw at him, ignoring her jealousy and sadness and sympathy. "Look at me and tell me you haven't *hated* yourself for it."

A white heave of breath obscured his face, but she caught the answer in his glassy-eyed anguish. The one she'd already known. But he wasn't ready to voice it out loud. "Are you really still standing there waiting for me to deny I'm a bastard? A betrayer?"

"No." Grace watched him through the condensation hanging in the air, her throat hurting over the self-hatred in his tone. "I'm waiting for you to come inside and be none of those things with me. You weren't ever supposed to be them. And now it's over. Let it be over."

His laugh was devoid of humor as he turned in a circle, tossing a punch into the driver's side door and denting the metal. "You know why you make it sound so easy, Grace? You *want* it to be."

"What's that supposed to mean?" There was a tremble in her voice, due to the cold in the air, in him, and she watched Aaron react. Watched him struggle with her bare feet in the snow. And when he tore off his jacket and dropped the warmth on her shoulders, Grace's heart soared and soared. He was in there. She just had to reach him. "Tell me what you meant."

Aaron was still for so long, Grace could see her opportunity slipping away. Could see those ever-present wheels spinning behind his too-intelligent eyes, the ones that she'd seen soft with affection and rife with lust. None of those qualities were present now, though. Only calculation. And the brief, flying past of regret threading through the golden brown, before he buried it deep, along with a dagger. "You see the world better than it is. You trust the wrong people." He stared over her head, a wrinkle between his brows. "Your father was right. It's not even conscious anymore. I see a way to get what I need, and I take it. I'm—" He turned and climbed into the driver's seat, ramming the keys into the ignition, movements jerky, unnatural. Off. "I'm the monster you accused me of being, Grace. And you were easy prey."

Even as agony seared her middle, she managed to reach out and prevent the door from slamming. "Well, you were right about one thing. You're a liar."

There. When Aaron's head whipped around, his body tensing, she saw him. The man she loved and all his naked self-doubt. But that man she wanted with her whole being was gone too fast, closing the door between them and driving away, leaving her broken in the snow.

CHAPTER TWENTY-FIVE

Aaron hung up his cell and tossed it aside, not caring where it landed. For the first ten minutes of the drive, his sole focus had been on sending a ripple through the newswire. Wanting to give Grace some time to leave her house—and himself some time to think of a better idea—he'd called and pushed the televised interview with Grace back two hours. Thank God they'd recognized his name and assumed he held the proper authority with the Pendleton campaign, because he hadn't even been questioned. They'd even been grateful to have the later flight arranged on their behalf. A flight Aaron had booked on his own credit card without hesitation.

With the task completed and his focus no longer diverted, Aaron's head was back on fire. That had to account for the crackle and burn of every thought that tried to germinate as it went up in smoke. He could only see Grace. The tears in her eyes, the redness of her nose. The cold

climbing up her feet like red ivy. The confidence she'd re-
tained in him before he'd taken a machete and hacked it
to pieces. Fuck. *Fuck.* Hoping to numb himself or put out
the flames engulfing his skull, Aaron rolled down the car
window, allowing freezing air to whip through the interior,
icing his skin, slowing the rush of blood.

Turned out, being cold was worse. Far worse. It gave
him too much clarity. What had he done? *What had he
done?* Left her standing there, looking devastated. Crying
as he drove away. Oh God, he'd been right last night. He
was going to die. The rupture happening inside his rib
cage was not something a person could survive. It was too
malicious, and yet he welcomed it. *Kill me. Finish me.*

Who got to continue living after laying a blow on
someone so forgiving? One final blow so she would do
them both a favor and finally, *finally*, stop believing he
could be something other than the morally corrupt prick
that performed mind tricks. His mother's journal might
have given him hope, but then again, Miriam hadn't
known how low her son could stoop, had she? Grace had
found out, though. Why the hell hadn't she turned away
from him? The revelation of what he'd done to earn the
boot in California obviously hadn't been enough to damage her faith, but it had reminded Aaron she could be
misplacing it. And he loved her too much to let that happen.

So he'd tried to drive her away. He'd insulted their relationship by calling her easy prey. And apparently he'd
even lost the ability to *lie* effectively, because she'd seen
right through his bullshit. Still believing the good in him.
God.

His leaving would take care of that error. His flight to

New York would be rescheduled as soon as he reached camp. He'd be back to business and even more ruthless than before. Whatever humanity he'd been holding on to had been left at Grace's feet back in the snow. The world hadn't seen the half of what he could do.

To Aaron's left, the red notebook full of his mother's thoughts caught his eye and he scoffed. Falsehoods. Lies. *You weren't as brilliant as you thought, Mom.* The silent insult toward his mother resulted in a flash of shame, but he flipped it the bird and moved on. No time for any more thinking. Or *feeling*. He'd done too much of that lately and look what it earned him. A ticket to mental hell. *Don't think. Don't think. Don't feel.*

Aaron could see the newly erected entrance for Youth-Aspire ahead, one he'd watched cause Grace to flush with pleasure just yesterday, and a roar poured from his mouth, vibrating straight down through his thighs, his toes. No way to keep the thoughts out. No way to do it.

He braked hard just inside the swaying, wooden over-hang, noting absently the scheduled volunteers hadn't arrived yet—too early—and fell from the driver's side, landing on his knees. Gravel dug into the heels of Aaron's hands as he stood, bones aching, head splitting with a vengeance. His stomach pitched under the nausea, but there was nothing there to expel, resulting in a dry heave.

"Aaron?" His sister's voice sounded like it came from a mile away. "Aaron? *Jesus!*"

"Where's Bel?" Was that *him* talking? He sounded deranged. His fingers felt along his lips to confirm the strangled shout came from his mouth. "Where's my fucking brother, huh? *Where is he?*"

"Here." Aaron spun around to find Belmont leaning against the rental van, suitcases stacked at his feet. Arms crossed, blue eyes narrowed to slits. "Need something?"

"Yeah." Aaron pounded his chest with a bunched fist, images of Grace moving across his vision like a never-ending reel of torture and joy and torture and joy. "Hit me. Knock me out."

Belmont remained unmoving. "No."

"*Do it*," Aaron bellowed, enjoying the raw discomfort it caused his throat. "I've never asked you for a goddamn thing in my life. Have I? I'll never ask for anything else. Just stop me from thinking of her. I can't do it when I'm awake. End it, please, just fucking end it." Aaron lunged forward, delivering a two-handed shove to his brother's chest. Belmont's arms uncrossed, irritation coloring his expression as he rebounded off the van, but he didn't give Aaron the knockout he desperately needed.

"She'll still be there when you wake up," Belmont said.

The truth was like nails sliding down a chalkboard. "I'll deal with it then. Just not now." Another brutal shove, harder this time. Another. "Do it. Knock me out. I'm *begging*. Is that what you want—"

Belmont moved so fast, Aaron didn't have time to prepare before his brother's arms were wrapped around him in an unbreakable steel hold. Instantly, Aaron's limbs turned useless, along with his mouth, both paralyzed by shock. His brother was hugging him? Why? Aaron allowed himself to register the sense of...solidarity. Or support. Or something...welcome. And good. Until he realized the rage and self-disgust toward himself had quieted in his mind and that was bad, that was bad. Grace rose once again, twirling up out of the misty ground like a fairy, her smile dazzling in the moonlight. *Shhhh*, she said, holding a finger across her lips.

Aaron breathed long and deep through his nose, hesitating a beat before placing an arm across his brother's shoulders. Just in time for another figure to crash against his back—Peggy—if he recognized that muffled, feminine cry correctly. And because it felt right, he reached back and used his free arm to draw his sister close, feeling her cheek nuzzle his back.

Aaron had no idea what the fuck was going on. But the pressure bracing him from both sides was holding him together like glue, and he wasn't sure if he would have survived otherwise. "I don't know what to do," he rasped. "I always know exactly what to do."

Belmont grunted. "What do you want?"

The answer to that question required zero thought. "Her."

"Who's stopping you?" Peggy murmured.

"Me," Aaron answered, his tongue feeling heavy, lethargic. "I've seen and done too many shitty things to be good like her. Good *for* her."

"Maybe you've seen and done enough shitty things to know you never want to do them again," Peggy said, her hold tightening.

Aaron sensed Belmont's nod, the rumble in his chest going off like distant thunder, unfamiliar when up close. "The things from the past...they make you the best one to protect her against them in the future."

Grace clutching her robe around her neck inside a circle of suits almost collapsed him. If he hadn't come back, she would have faced that situation alone. Correction, she *was* facing it alone. Right now. He might have stalled the process, but the senator was a determined man. Tomorrow would be another day, another tactic. Aaron knew the game better than anyone. How to chop at someone from ten different angles until they toppled like a tree. The notion of Grace going through that threatened the relative calm his sibling sandwich had foisted on him.

"I can't—"

Sage cut Aaron off by joining the group hug, suctioning onto his side with a gentle humming sound. "Stop saying you can't, Aaron."

His sigh was heavy, but he was shocked to feel hope trickle into his aching chest. Not yet. He couldn't hope yet. Not after leaving her crying in the cold. *Fuck.* "I can't bring her to New York. Not with this job." His mind raced for a solution but, for once, came up empty. "My only option is to quit and then what the fuck do I have? What do I offer her?"

"Ask her," Peggy said. "You should be asking her."

"I left her." His legs tried to buckle, but the group held him up. "*Twice* I left her. Christ."

Aaron felt a figure weave through his legs, a wet nose slipping up his pants to snuffle at his ankle. He leaned back to find Old Man watching him from the ground, head tilted, but very still. Then the animal turned, trotted toward the Suburban, and waited by the driver's side door, his usual state of boredom intact.

Sage and Peggy's giggles shook the group, as if they were sharing one body. "I think he just offered to be your wingman," Peggy said.

Maybe it was ridiculous, but finally having the dog's faith got Aaron right in the damn throat. Everything about the moment did. Despite years of being an asshole, he still had his family and their vote of confidence. His mother's was there, too, shining down from the Iowa sky and warming his neck.

Grace's faith was there, too. The best person he knew was positive *his* best was yet to come. He wanted to believe her. So much his lungs burned. His misdeeds had come out of the shadows this morning, but she'd staved the demons off for both of them. Could he join her? Could he be better, forever, for her? God, yes, he could. He needed to be a better man for Grace—and himself—with every inch of his soul.

"I don't know where she is," Aaron rasped, hating everything about that statement. "I told her to take her sister's car and leave—make sure she did without being followed—but I have no idea where she would go."

"Yes, you do," Belmont contradicted. "You know."

Needing some space to think, to pick through the wreckage the last hour had created of his mind, Aaron eased free of the four-way embrace, shoving a hand through his hair, steeling himself against the sudden loss of unexpected support. "Jesus, Bel." The brothers looked anywhere but at each other. "You couldn't just knock me out?"

"Next time."

Peggy and Sage shoved at Aaron's shoulders, but there was no heat behind the gesture. No, their hearts were all in their eyes, so concentrated, he couldn't handle it. Not with so much at stake. "I *know* her. I just..." Moving toward the Suburban, Aaron braced his elbows on the hood, capturing his head in his hands. "I just need to think."

Which wasn't easy, because it meant letting the endless footage of Grace flood in, the opposite of what he'd been attempting on the drive to camp. Letting her in was agonizing. Seeing those beloved images while unsure if the damage he'd done could be repaired...it hurt like a motherfucker.

Like a motherfucker. Grace saying those words to him the night before came sliding in on a deluge of longing. Aaron could feel her legs wrapped around his waist, hear the catch in her voice, so telling in terms of the way he affected her physically. The way they affected each other. Aaron pressed his thumbs into his eye sockets, seeing Grace sway into his tent, eyes bright from drinking wine and having an adventure. So alive, so ripe. So Grace. A sliver of light crossed over her naked back as he warmed her inside the sleeping bag...and that's when he remembered the tattoo.

Coordinates.

I wear them so they can't wear me, Grace had said.

Oh my God. I love her so hard. No one has ever loved this hard. And it's mine—I want it. I covet it. I never want to let it go. Never let Grace go again.

Aaron's hands shook as he turned, facing the south edge of camp. "I know where she is."

* * *

Grace picked through the forest, climbing on top of a tree stump to look around, judging her location. She hadn't been back to the site of the burned-down cabin in a while, and after so much time passing, growth continued to creep in, covering up the spot as if it had never happened. The hike, the search, were serving to occupy her mind, but they were doing a terrible job. The tip of her nose hurt and her eyelids felt heavy, but crying wasn't an option. If she let the tears start, she might sit down and get overtaken by branches and roots, just like the ash-covered earth where the cabin had once stood. Where her friends had perished.

This isn't how love is supposed to feel. It was such a stupid thing to keep repeating in her mind, but it was solid. It was something she could say without wanting to scream up at the sky, startling the birds from the trees. They were words she could meander through while waiting for Aaron to reason everything out.

Because if she let herself consider the other option— that he'd actually left for good—lying down on the forest floor would be too tempting to resist. Animals could make their homes in her hair, hikers could use her body as a landmark or a bench. At least she would be useful in repose. Right now, she felt anything but.

Whether her father's motives had been self-serving, she'd let him down. She'd walked away instead of seizing her one chance to be the well-oiled cog in the Pendleton machine. No going back now. Or if she did go back, the option of being useful to her father would probably never present itself again. Moreover, she didn't want it to. She wouldn't allow what had happened eight years earlier in that forest to be exploited, along with herself. Especially when her heart was already so exposed, so fresh from Aaron's rejection.

No, not a rejection. Just a delay. He *wouldn't* leave. He would figure it out.

A dreaded sob wrenched from Grace's mouth and it moved from head to toe, giving her no choice but to plop down, into a mix of snow and leaves. Her palms landed on her knees, face up, and she watched in a daze as white flakes landed on them, dissolving as soon as they touched down.

"You've gone and done it now," she whispered. "Now you'll never get up."

Even as Grace said the words, she attempted to stand, knowing the snow could get worse and she couldn't be stuck in the woods in nothing but the thin leggings she'd thrown on in her haste to leave the guest house. Using a tree and the tread of her boots for assistance, she rose, feeling like the fall had aged her ten years. She needed sleep. She needed...what? Right now, she could only focus on reaching the tragedy site. After this morning, after the suggestion had been made to use the horrific event for political gain, paying her respects seemed vital.

Feeling pretty confident she would find the spot over the next rise, Grace squared her shoulders and climbed over a log, continuing on the overrun path.

"Grace!"

Euphoria crackled in her veins with such exhilarating intensity, Grace lurched forward, clutching the center of her chest. "Aaron." Her voice emerged as a croak. No way he would hear her. She tried again, but only a whisper emerged.

It didn't matter, though. Didn't matter, because he burst through the trees a moment later, looking like an escapee from hell. His eyes were red and bloodshot, shirt untucked, hands outstretched in her direction. So different from the cool, indifferent man she'd met...how many days ago? Hadn't it been at least a year? Wouldn't feelings like the ones churning and pumping inside her take a millennium to develop?

Aaron's gaze raked over her, a choked sound punctuating the air between them. "Oh...God. Baby. I hate when you're cold. What are you doing out here?"

Grace swallowed, tugging Aaron's jacket—the one he'd given her back at the house—tighter around her body, sighing as his scent wafted up. "I could ask you the same question." She wanted to run to him, get caught up in his heat, but not yet. Not until she knew he wouldn't leave again. That his head had finally caught up with the heart she'd fallen in love with. "How did you know where to find me?"

He crunched forward a step, hands balling and flexing at his sides. "The numbers on your neck...the coordinates."

"Oh." A twist beneath Grace's breastbone stole the breath from her lungs. "You remembered them? After only seeing them once?"

His humorless laugh sent a plume of white into the air, obscuring his face. "I remember every mark on your body," Aaron answered gruffly, coming closer. "Everything you've ever said to me. The way your lips moved saying it. Everything about you is written in stone—" He broke off, chest heaving. "Written in stone somewhere I didn't think existed. In me. On me. All over me. You wrote yourself there."

Grace reeled from the joy and the relief that tried to follow, but she forced them to wait. *Wait.* She'd known that she and Aaron were bonded, but that didn't mean he would accept it. Accept her. Forever. Because she wasn't taking any less.

When panic flared in Aaron's eyes, Grace knew she'd been silent too long after his speech, but couldn't speak what he'd written on her stone yet. So soon after he'd driven away, the risk was too glaring.

Aaron gave a brisk nod, his eyes never leaving Grace, as he came forward slowly and reached out, asking without words for her hand. "Do you trust me enough to follow me? Please say yes."

Her response was immediate and honest. She joined their hands, sucking in a gulp of frigid air when electricity zapped straight to her elbow. "Yes."

"Okay," he breathed. "That's something, at least."

Grace watched Aaron's profile as they walked, a burn igniting in her belly every time he glanced over, his expression anxious. All Grace could hear was her own breathing, rushing in her ears like a waterfall. They moved in slow motion—or so it seemed—flakes coasting down from above, falling at their feet. She was so distracted, they stopped at the cabin site without her taking notice. Not right away, at least. But Aaron's subtle head incline at what lay before them forced Grace's attention outward.

The world seemed to crystallize around them, the air stopping to regard the sight along with Grace. Her pulse eased up then, like a roller coaster, shooting into an upside-down loop. Wedged into the ground were five sanded pieces of lumber. They rose out of the ground, standing approximately two feet high. Without a conscious command from her brain, Grace released Aaron's hand and drifted closer. Was it a...sun? Yes, the five smooth portions of lumber were arranged in the shape of a sun. One component was round, stuck right in the center, with four longer, leaner strips extending outward like sunshine rays. Each ray had a name carved into its surface, and when Grace recognized those names as belonging to her friends, her vision blurred. Blurred so much, she could barely read her own name, carved right there on the center piece.

"I know, if you'd been given a choice, you wouldn't have wanted your name in the center," Aaron said behind her, his voice low, gruff. "But you're the center, whether you like it or not. You're the center of me. The center of everything, Grace."

Tears mixed with snowflakes on her cheeks as she remembered Aaron's absence yesterday, into the evening. "You did this for me."

"I had help. It turns out...turns out help isn't so hard to come by if you ask." She heard his feet scuff the forest floor. "It's only half finished. The plans I drew up had a moat."

"A moat?" Grace wondered in that moment if a human being could take flight, if they just wanted it bad enough. Or if two people could hold tightly to each other's hands and accomplish the impossible feat together. She turned to find Aaron mere inches away, his raging storm gaze trained on her. "This...it's all I ever needed. Just this quiet, perfect thing."

"Good replacing bad," Aaron whispered.

Grace's laugh came out sounding watery. "You really were listening." She sniffed and swiped at her cheeks. "Do you honestly think, Aaron, that a man capable of this doesn't have a heart that could capsize the world?"

"Only because it's full of you." Vehemently, he shook his head. "That's it, Grace. That's all I know anymore. You're in there and you're never coming out. And I don't have a plan, baby. There's no plan, except *Grace*." He loomed closer, grasping the sides of her face, sliding his thumbs over her cheekbones. "So I'm begging here. I'm begging you to let me be a part of your plan. Could you do that? You want to go where help is needed and brighten the whole damn world like you've brightened mine? I'm coming, too." His breath wheezed in and out. "If you'll let me, I'll stand beside you and watch you fucking shine. Will you. Will you let me?"

"Yes. Yes. Oh my God, yes." She leapt into Aaron's arms, holding tighter when he grated her name, over and over, his mouth frantic in her hair.

"I love you." He sank to the ground, cradling Grace on his lap, rocking them back and forth. "I love you, Grace. I'm sorry. I love you. I'm sorry."

Battling the urge to shout her happiness was paining Grace's throat so badly, she gave up the fight and let it rip, sending a falcon winging into the sky. "I love you, too."

EPILOGUE

Aaron growled into Grace's neck when the Suburban revved its engine outside the cabin door—for the fifth time. Responsibility urged him to do the right thing, climb off Grace's giving, siren's body and say good-bye to his siblings who, in fairness, had given him and Grace hours of privacy since they'd come off the mountain. Without so much as a nod in Belmont, Peggy, and Sage's direction, Aaron had carried Grace through the door, slammed it, positioned her on the rickety twin bed, and fucked her rotten, a hand stamped over her mouth.

The *first* time anyway. After the residual panic and elation had been bucked from his body into the love of his life, they'd slowed down. Or they'd *tried* to slow down, every single time, with little success. With Grace's legs wrapped around his hips, as they were now, his ability to savor dwindled quickly.

"There will be time," she moaned now, twisting her

slight body beneath him, asking for it. Always asking for it hard. "We have so much time. All of it."

Knowing she was right—thank God—but physically incapable of denying himself the tight stroke of her entrance, Aaron gripped the iron headboard bars and gloried in several rough pumps. "I'm afraid you've signed on with a selfish man, Grace. I'm so selfish for you," he gritted out, reveling in the purposeful constriction of her walls. "Rubbing off on you already, am I?"

He felt a shudder pass through her sweating body, watched it roll on a writhe he knew wasn't voluntary. So goddamn incredible, this woman. *His* woman. "Yes...you are rubbing..."

Something in Aaron—something in addition to the love, light and heavy at the same time—cut loose, allowing him to laugh. He laughed against Grace's swollen lips, but it turned into a sound of remorse when the Suburban honked outside. "All right, we go outside and say good-bye." He dragged his forehead down between her cleavage, nipping the sensitive skin. "And then we come back for more."

When Aaron rolled off Grace with a curse of regret, she turned over and snuggled into the sheets, green eyes smiling as she watched him dress. But the smile faded a few degrees. "Aaron, you're going to miss them. Are you sure you don't want us to go along?"

Us. Knowing she would now and always speak of them as one entity, Aaron felt cool comfort ease through his middle. "We'll see them in New York on New Year's Day. But we're going to see this place through first. It's important." He bent down and kissed the small of her back. "To *us*."

Over the last handful of hours, more than lovemaking

had taken place, although it *had* filled the majority of time. Pendleton had called Aaron, obviously knowing Grace would be with him. To the surprise of both of them—and Aaron's incredible relief—he'd apologized to his daughter for pushing her into a probable media circus to boost his campaign. He'd also acknowledged her ability to decide whom she dated and thanked Aaron for preventing him from making a mistake that morning. After that, Aaron had been asked to remain on staff. There'd been a moment of hesitation on Aaron's end, mainly because he'd been heartened by the additional contentment in Grace's eyes over the father-daughter reconciliation, but in the end, he'd given his resignation.

While Aaron would have done his damnedest to move heaven and earth to make Grace happy...he'd resigned for *both* of them. He genuinely didn't want to shovel bullshit anymore. Didn't matter how effectively he could do it, or if his methods achieved victory; those victories had been hollow for a long time. He'd been chasing one with substance. This love for Grace, *this* was substance. And now that he knew the definition of fulfillment, he wasn't going to bother searching for it in the wrong places.

Looking around the cabin and all its improvements, Aaron recognized what was possible. He and Grace could make a mark together. And he couldn't fucking wait to get started. As soon as they got YouthAspire up and running, he would sit back and let Grace decide where she wanted to light up the globe, and he'd bust his ass to get them there. *Them.* Always, forever, them.

Grace caught his eye, pausing in the act of buttoning her shirt. "Are you over there coming up with ideas for our next mission again?"

God, she sounded drowsy and well satisfied. Best sound imaginable. "Not unless they involve how I'm going to work you into a lather later."

"Oh." Her cheeks flushed. "Carry on."

With a laughing groan, Aaron stooped down, wrapped an arm around the back of Grace's legs, and hefted her over his shoulder. When he walked them into the courtyard, Aaron was thankful the day's snow had kept the volunteers from coming to work because, based on Sage's scandalized look and Peggy's snort, there was no doubt as to what they'd been doing on the cabin's twin bed. For Belmont's part, he leaned up against the side of the Suburban, watching them approach with a mixture of approval and…curiosity. It brought Aaron back to the conversation they'd had in the cafeteria—his brother's restlessness over the little wedding planner—and if Aaron had one regret about bailing on the road trip's second half, it was missing what was to come between Belmont and Sage.

Aaron set Grace down, but kept her up against his side. "You think you assholes can manage to find New York without me there to map the most efficient routes?"

With an exaggerated sigh, Sage floated forward to kiss their cheeks. "We'll manage," she said, before dropping her voice for their ears alone. "It's really unfair of you to leave when I'm still feeling guilty about slapping you."

"I deserved it," Aaron said, tugging Sage close for a three-way hug. "Feel guilty you didn't do it sooner."

Sage stepped back with wet eyes before climbing into the Suburban, laying a hand on Belmont's neck as she went, visibly draining some of his tension.

Grace ducked out from beneath Aaron's arm, giving each of his siblings an unrestrained hug and a few whispered words, fervent promises to catch up in New York. Then she winked back at Aaron. "Go," she mouthed, before dancing back toward the cabin. Watching her pause on the threshold, Aaron could barely catch a breath. Maybe he never would. He didn't know. And that was more than okay.

Not bothering to hide the absolute contentment in his eyes, Aaron swept Peggy off her feet in a bear hug, tickling her ribs for good measure. "I hear there's a man you need to give hell." Grace had spilled the beans over the course of their hours together, mostly because she wished they could be there for Aaron's sister in Cincinnati. "He's not going to know what hit him."

"Yeah, well. Then I'll be returning the favor." Peggy lifted her shoulders and let them fall, before taking Aaron by the sides of his face. "You did good, bro. Real good. I'm so stupid happy for you, I could spit."

Shit. How much could he take in one day? Someone above kept pouring and pouring into his cup, overflowing it and drowning everything in the vicinity. "Thanks, Peggy." He encompassed his sister and brother with a steady look. "Listen, I... you didn't have to stick around. You could have dropped me off and kept going, met me in New York." He swallowed. "I'm really fucking glad you didn't, all right? I wouldn't have figured this out without both of you."

Belmont laid a hand on his shoulder. "Yes. You would have."

Aaron couldn't respond, didn't have the ability, so he only nodded, gripping his brother's forearm tight as he could.

"I wish Rita were here to see all this. The camp. To

meet Grace." Peggy's nose pinkened at the tip. "I wish Mom could be here, too."

They were all quiet a moment, before Aaron spoke up. "Rita will be in New York." He smirked. "If Jasper can convince her to fly."

When their laughter cooled, Belmont turned, opening the groaning driver's side door. But he stopped before climbing in, his stillness demanding both Peggy and Aaron's attention. "I think Mom will be in New York, too." He tapped the keys against his thigh. Just once. "I think maybe she's been here the whole time."

Aaron was still staring after the Suburban a minute later when it rolled beneath the hanging wooden sign, out of camp. But the pull toward Grace was so vast, so huge, he could only smile as the vehicle got smaller, his siblings moving on to their next adventure—and God knew it would be. They were Clarksons, after all.

Sage, too. She just didn't know it yet.

When Aaron turned, Grace was waiting. She opened her arms and he walked into them, the only place he would ever call home again.

Peggy Clarkson had one goal: to stop in Cincinnati and remind football coach Elliott Brooks *exactly* what he'd missed out on. But Temptation has a cruel sense of humor, and Peggy might have just enough time to make one more deliciously hot mistake...

Please see the next page for a preview of *Too Hard to Forget*.

PROLOGUE

Elliott had just blown the whistle to end practice when he felt Peggy approach at his back. Or rather, his players started shoving one another, throwing their chins in his direction, when they thought he didn't see. Had he not put the fear of God into these men yet? Tomorrow's practice was going to be hell.

The hell of right now concerned him more, however. In a matter of seconds, he'd be in her presence again. Her. And there was a good reason for his team and fellow coaches to be staring with their mouths open while Peggy probably swayed up like a runway model. Not only was she a bombshell that always seemed poised to go off any second, but no one ever approached him. If someone got up the nerve to wave or shout his name from the stands, it was a rarity. They just stared at him, as if he were the statue they'd erected in his honor outside the stadium.

Peggy had no such problem, apparently. In fact, before

Elliott even turned around, he could sense her reveling in not giving a fuck, and panic slid into his blood like a sea monster. She'd gotten even braver. Brave enough to divert his path again?

No. Not after all the work he'd done to build it.

During those months of madness her senior year, she'd come to him at night. Or vice versa. When no one else was around. They'd be on each other before the sound of the knock even faded. Christ, he'd taken Peggy in a way he'd never allowed himself before she'd made a home in his head. Without restraint. No boundaries. Zero patience.

Too much of a danger to a man whose entire life was made up of rules. Rules that kept him from looking right or left. Straight ahead only.

"Head to the showers," Elliott boomed, pleased when everyone moved at once, without hesitating, like he'd conditioned them to do. "We'll be back here tomorrow, bright and early. Scrimmage against the B squad."

"Yes, Coach."

"Yes, Coach," came the amused feminine echo behind him. He thought the hour since Peggy arrived had given him time to prepare, but he was wrong. When he turned around, his gut screwed up like a fist. Fuck. Still the most beautiful woman he'd ever seen. It was more than just her blond pinup looks, though, wasn't it? Always had been. There was enough sharp wit in those dark gold eyes for a man to get lost. Like he'd almost done once.

"Peggy," Elliott said, transferring his clipboard to the crook of his arm, so they could shake hands. A reflexive move. That was how he operated. Handshakes. Giving hugs and kissing cheeks weren't part of his day. But even the muscle memory couldn't make it feel natural, though. Not with her.

One of Peggy's eyebrows arched at his outstretched hand, but she recovered, twining their fingers together slowly. At the zing of static, the corner of her mouth jumped, like they'd traded a secret, and God help him, his cock thickened in his jeans. "Elliott," she murmured. "You look exactly the same."

He took his hand back out of necessity. "Three years isn't all that long."

"No. I guess not." For just a second, he thought her flirtatious smile turned forced, but it came back with such a glow, he figured it was his imagination. "It was long enough for them to put a giant statue of you at the entrance." Her teeth sank into that full lower lip and held, long enough to drive him a little insane. "I bet you hate it, don't you?"

"Yes." Damn. It didn't seem possible so much time had passed since they'd stood across from each other. Not when she could still call his bullshit a mile away, the way no one else ever had. "They could have waited until I was dead or retired."

"When it comes to you, I don't think those things are mutually exclusive." She hummed in her throat, her gaze tripping over his chest, lower. "Anyway, they already think you're God, so your immortality is a reasonable assumption." When she took a step closer, he almost dropped the clipboard. In favor of staving her off or yanking her closer? He had no idea. But she only lifted a finger, trailing the smooth pad across the seam of his lips. "The sculptor didn't get your mouth right, though. It's much more generous, isn't it?" Elliott snagged her wrist and her eyes lit with challenge. "Or maybe the sculptor just hasn't experienced it the way I have."

Lust and irritation joined forces in his blood, making it boil. "What the hell do you think you're doing here, Peggy?"

The seduction in her expression lost steam. "That's the first thing you ever said to me." She visibly shook herself, tugging her hand from his grip. "I'm here for alumni weekend. Obviously."

Still stuck on the former statement she'd made, it took him a moment to catch up. "You've never come before."

He counted three breaths from her mouth. "Noticed, did you?"

Time-out. He would have called one if they were in the middle of a game and both sides were firing too hot, swinging on the unpredictable vines of momentum. In many ways, this confrontation so far had been a game. A testing of each other's strengths. Well, they were standing on his field. And on his field, he didn't deal well with surprises and unknowns. Time to put everything out in the open, even though he could feel acid rising in his throat. "Are you here with your husband?"

She froze so long, he wondered if she would answer him at all. "Um. No, he—he's back in California." A wrinkle appeared between her eyebrows. "I wasn't sure...I— I didn't know if you received the wedding invitation. You were moving houses when I left Cincinnati and—"

"My mail was forwarded," Elliot said, his voice low. "I got it."

Peggy backed away with an uneven nod. The currents running between them had changed so abruptly, but he couldn't decide on a reason. He'd admit to mentioning her husband as a way to throw up a necessary wall between them, but—

Elliott's phone rang.

He cursed, digging the device from his back pocket, frowning down at his daughter's name where it flashed on the screen. "Alice," he said to Peggy without thinking. "She should be in theater rehearsal."

"You should answer it," Peggy said, still backing away from him. Way too quickly. "Maybe I'll see you around—"

"Hold on." He should have let her go. God knew he should have. But Elliott didn't walk away from an interaction without a final score on the board. And he swore the stadium lights had shorted out somewhere in the middle of the game. "Just stay right there."

She tilted her head. "I'm not one of your players."

"Please," he growled.

When Peggy shrugged—and stayed put—Elliott answered the phone, teen angst meeting his ear in full stereo. "Dad, I have to change schools. My fucking life is over. You don't understand—"

"Watch your language. And you haven't given me a chance to understand."

A closemouthed shriek scraped down the line. One with which he was well acquainted. "Kim Steinberg broke her leg skiing this weekend and I'm the understudy for her character in *The Music Man* and I don't have the lines memorized. I faked my way through it, because she's never even missed a day of school. Like, ever. Why would she want to stay home when she looks like that? Oh God, oh God. The fucking performance is in five days and I—I don't even know why I'm telling you this. You don't give a shit about my life."

Elliott watched Peggy's expression melt into soft sympathy, whether for him or Alice, he didn't know, but it was too reminiscent of those times he'd confided in her. A rarity for him, to say the least, and something he had no right to miss. "Five days seems more than sufficient to memorize the lines." He pressed the heel of his hand into his eye socket. "I have a few more hours here watching game film, but when I get home—"

"I never ask you for anything, Dad." Her breath snagged on the final word. "I just need help with this. Please. You don't understand."

Guilt battled against the never-ending pressure to win, win at all costs. "Alice," he said tightly. "We're playing Temple on Saturday—"

Peggy laid a land on his arm. "I can go," she whispered, looking a little surprised at herself for making the offer. That made two of them.

"Hold on a second, Alice." Elliott covered the phone with his hand. Trying not to be obvious, he sucked in the scent of Peggy. She'd swept it forward on her second approach, and it brought forth flashes of her head thrown back on his pillow, her mouth laughing into his neck. "That's not necessary."

"It sounds pretty necessary." She took back her touch, fingers curling into her palm. "Maybe just tell her I'm from the school...a fellow faculty member."

Elliott couldn't hide his skepticism. "You still look more like a student."

She wet her lips in slow motion. "Noticed, did you?" Her low, seductive laugh made his boxer briefs feel two sizes too small. "Come on, I'm not meeting with my assigned alumni committee until tomorrow morning. My evening is free." No longer meeting his eyes, she shrugged. "And I know what it's like to lose your mother before you're ready, so I have that in common with Alice. She probably doesn't even know she needs the girl time."

"I'm sorry. I didn't know about your mother." He itched to reach out, run a thumb over the curve of her cheekbone. "I appreciate your offer, but I think we both know any kind of involvement with one another is a bad idea."

"*Involvement* is a pretty strong word." A smile teased her lips, but it didn't reach her eyes. "You're worried for nothing."

"It's never nothing with you."

She held his gaze a long moment, before turning away. "Text me your address, Elliott. My number hasn't changed."

© Nisha Ver Helen

New York Times bestselling author **Tessa Bailey** can solve all problems except for her own, so she focuses those efforts on stubborn, fictional blue-collar men and loyal, lovable heroines. She lives on Long Island avoiding the sun and social interactions, then wonders why no one has called. Dubbed the "Michelangelo of dirty talk" by *Entertainment Weekly*, Tessa writes with spice, spirit, swoon, and a guaranteed happily ever after. Catch her on TikTok at @authortessabailey or check out tessabailey.com for a complete list of books.

You can learn more at:
TessaBailey.com
Facebook.com/TessaBaileyAuthor
Instagram @TessaBaileyIsanAuthor
TikTok @AuthorTessaBailey